FATEFUL

DESTINY

An Epic Struggle to Change the Course of
American History

D1359958

MARSHALL ANDERS

DEDICATION

This book is dedicated to my parents who have always encouraged my writing and my son who represents hope for the future.

CONTENTS

CONTENTS

1

THE END

Darkness is enveloping. It consumes all without boundaries. It dulls the senses and distorts the perception of space and time. After the Great Transformation, darkness had descended, and the country would never be the same.

It wasn't always this way. America was once the envy of the world. A global military and industrial superpower, the United States was a land of opportunity and a magnet for ambitious strivers from around the world. But something changed. Not all at once, but little by little the fabric of American greatness began to unravel like a child pulling on a loose thread. It's hard to say exactly how it began, but once it was in motion no one seemed to have the power or will to reverse its course. Without drastic intervention, America would soon cease to bear any resemblance to its former self.

Axel Berg was once a successful investment manager at a thriving financial institution. He was a responsible member of his community who paid his taxes and followed the law. Aside from one citation for jaywalking in his youth, Axel had lived his life on the straight and narrow. For years, Axel worked hard and contributed to society in exchange for a chance at the American Dream. He had set upon a path to a fulfilling life with his beautiful fiancée, imbued by his love for America and optimism for the future. That was all before the Great Transformation. It was then that everything changed.

Over many decades, the groundwork for drastic foundational change had been systematically put in place. It began slowly and often went without notice. Little by little, people began to observe that something was different about America, but the origins of the evolution were obscured.

1

The values and culture of America gradually became muddled. Core beliefs and fundamental principles began to be eroded. Soon, the movement to fundamentally transform America was so entrenched throughout government and society that it appeared inevitable. The Great Transformation had arrived, and Americans throughout the country felt powerless to stop it.

The powerful have always known that division and isolation are the most effective way of neutralizing your enemies, and Axel had now been completely isolated from the outside world for years. There was no trial, no judge, and no jury. Once the uprising began, courts existed only as an extension of the militarized police and acted as a rubber stamp for the authority of the State. Perhaps the collision course between Axel and the government had been inevitable, but Axel's promising future wasn't disrupted until the fundamental deterioration of America set him on a new path. It was then that his life became clear, and he knew that he had no choice but to fight.

Axel never expected that his journey would lead to this. He had set out on a crusade to rebuild America and restore the prosperity of its people. It was a positive and optimistic mission full of hope. It all ended, however, when government agents whisked Axel away in the dead of night while his fiancée screamed in panic and confusion. He was brutally kidnapped by a squad of heavily armed black-clad police who detained him without identification or a warrant for his arrest. Axel still recalls the look of horror and despair on her face, the final memory of his life left behind, as the agents slipped a black hood over his head and threw him in the back of their armored vehicle.

The squad of officers surrounded Axel as the vehicle bounced over rough roads for what seemed like hours. It was dark in the back of the heavily armored van which, when combined with the black hood obscuring his vision, made it impossible to assess his surroundings. They rode in silence while Axel pondered what fate awaited him. He was terrified. Sweat dripped from his head as he breathed laboriously under the stifling hood. Axel was trying to keep it together, but the sheer powerlessness in the face of authoritarian police power was all-consuming.

Hot, battered, and emotionally drained, Axel felt the truck come to an idle as they finally arrived at their destination. An officer grabbed his arm and jerked him to his feet. As they stood in the back of the vehicle listening to the diesel engine rumble, Axel nervously awaited their next move. After a minute or two, the silence was interrupted by the sound of a heavy latch clanking and an armored door creaking as it opened. Axel could sense the sun from outside the van as stray rays of light streamed through his hood. Abruptly, Axel was jolted forward when an officer shoved him from behind. They were on the move. Someone grabbed his arm and helped him from the back of the truck while the sun enveloped him with intense and unbearable heat. He wondered where they had gone because they certainly weren't in California anymore.

The officers dragged Axel to the facility without a word. Their silence was punctuated by the intensely audible sounds of sand and rocks crunching under their feet. After a couple of hundred yards, they stopped.

A faceless officer blurted out, "We're here."

Axel stood supported by two officers, oblivious to his surroundings and his fate. A loud buzzer rang incessantly before a gust of cool air swept over Axel as the officers guided him forward. The sand and gravel gave way to a smooth polished floor as the door closed behind them. Axel was guided into the facility and ultimately was seated in an uncomfortable metal chair in the center of an empty room. An officer removed his hood before leaving Axel alone in the cold dark room.

After five minutes of darkness and silence, bright floodlights suddenly illuminated Axel as a voice over a loudspeaker authoritatively announced his fate. "Inmate 03041949. By the authority of the President and the power of the State, you have been sentenced to indefinite detention for subversion and violations of the Insurrection Act. There is zero tolerance for speech that incites dissension and acts against the administration. Your sentence shall begin immediately."

Wincing and shielding his eyes from the blinding light, Axel sat silently in disbelief. Just as his eyes began to adjust, the floodlights turned off and a door in front of Axel opened. Light from the hallway illuminated the exit. Axel stood up and walked toward the door, puzzled by the lack of supervision. As he exited the room he saw an elevator at the end of a sterile white hallway. He walked gingerly alone toward the steel elevator doors, glancing around nervously waiting for someone to intervene. There were no controls or buttons for the elevator, but the doors opened when Axel approached as if to beckon him inside. Given the lack of alternatives, he entered the elevator and watched as the doors slowly closed.

The elevator rapidly descended and whisked Axel away into the depths of the facility. It moved both vertically and horizontally, honing in on its ultimate destination with expeditious precision. As abruptly as the unexpected relocation began, the elevator's journey came to a halting end. The doors slowly opened, exposing Axel to his new reality.

Axel was never quite sure how many people were confined in the subterranean catacombs. He often wondered if others shared his dismal fate or if he had been buried alive, pondering his predicament in complete solitude. Dim blue LED lighting exposed the cold steel walls of a cell that contained nothing but a metal toilet and sink unit in the far corner of the room and a ceiling-mounted showerhead centered above a small drain. Food consisting of cold sandwiches and packaged fruit or vegetables was delivered twice daily through a pneumatic tube. This tube was the only physical confirmation that life existed outside of his cell and acted as an umbilical cord that supplied the bare necessities required to sustain Axel with impersonal efficiency. His continued existence depended on the benevolence of an unknown master whose magnanimous gestures of humanity conflicted with the injustice of his imprisonment.

Even as the days came and went, Axel's traumatic introduction to the facility remained vividly etched in his mind. Days became months. Months became years. In the darkness, who can tell? The deprivation and isolation of subterranean imprisonment had drained Axel of the energy of life. Ostracized from the world above, Axel initially was consumed by anxiety, restlessly pacing around his small sterile cell. Anxiety had long since surrendered to despondence as the heavy reality of his predicament weighed on his mind. Will this be the totality of his existence? Is this what the world has become?

2

AND SO IT BEGINS

Axel Berg grew up living the American Dream. His grandfather was a no-nonsense descendent of German immigrants who believed strongly in hard work and pride in one's labor. He had escaped life on the family farm, securing a job at a local oil refinery. It was tough work, but it provided a comfortable middle-class lifestyle for his traditional postwar family. Axel's grandfather worked hard to provide a better life for his family.

Axel's father, Henry, quickly learned the value of a dollar and the meaning of work. There was no gardener to mow the lawn or maid to clean the house. Henry and his sisters were expected to help with chores and support the family. Axel's grandmother, traditional in her values, raised her kids to be independent and maintained order in her household. She could be sharp-tongued and was quick to discipline her children.

These values shaped Henry and led him to a successful career in education. He believed in instilling strong values of thrift, hard work, perseverance, and patriotism in his students. They lived in a small Central California town that was predominantly inhabited by White working-class residents. Crystal Springs was founded by European immigrants that had come to farm the land and build a better future. They shared common values and principles despite disparate backgrounds and economic success. Everyone wanted what was best for the community and their families.

Henry was well known in the community. His family had been there for generations and had always been active in building for the future. Henry's father had built at least a dozen houses in the town and was committed to providing opportunities for others to work and support their families. After observing his father's commitment to the community, Henry developed strong beliefs in the value of patronizing local businesses and supporting the community at large. He would always say, "If our neighbors do better, we do better."

When Axel was born, Crystal Springs began to change. Farming was hard grueling work that wasn't glamorous and was financially risky. Hispanic families started migrating to the community to work on the farms, and the demographic mix of the Crystal Springs schools began to rapidly change. By the time Axel entered kindergarten, more than one in four students was Hispanic. When he graduated from high school, it was evenly split. The farmers became addicted to cheap compliant labor and turned a blind eye to the legal status of their workers. They were reaping the rewards of an abundant low-wage workforce.

As Crystal Springs changed, the sense of community and shared interest began to fade. The original farming families, enabled by more accommodative policies toward immigrants, began to favor their economic self-interest over that of the town. They reaped the financial rewards bequeathed by cheap immigrant labor and quickly abandoned their neighbors. In the process, the profitability of their farms soared and their land rapidly appreciated in value. Meanwhile, the working class Whites that had previously served as the backbone of the town became disenfranchised. Their businesses struggled to survive since most of the immigrants were unable to speak English and tended to support retailers that catered to the Hispanic population. Employment opportunities evaporated, as the sense of community disintegrated and economic opportunism reigned supreme.

Henry observed these changes first hand. As the demographics of his classes changed, he could see the emergence of tribalization first hand. When the Hispanic population was smaller, they were more likely to assimilate into the community and socialize with everyone in the town. It is hard to be an outsider and to be accepted in a foreign land, but they were dedicated to securing a better future for their families. As the pace of demographic change accelerated, there was less impetus for assimilation. The immigrant community began to self-segregate from the indigenous population while simultaneously retaining their historical values and cultural norms.

The White students, steeped in the Protestant values that had been the foundation of the nation, conscientiously approached their studies with discipline and determination. They worked hard to achieve their potential because that was expected of them. They respected Henry and appreciated his commitment to the community. The immigrant population, in contrast, presented new challenges in the classroom. The percentage of students that were non-English speakers began to explode. It was no longer possible to teach math, science, and other disciplines without considering the language and comprehension challenges of these students. The tectonic shift in the community had begun.

Tribalization had emerged in small-town Crystal Springs. Many businesses and farms began to exclusively employ Hispanic workers and operate the job site entirely in Spanish. Locals were effectively shut out of these opportunities as they were unable to communicate with their co-workers or managers. The immigrant community recruited family and friends from their native countries to fill any job openings, and thus an immigrant pipeline was created.

Resentment and frustration grew in the community. Henry watched the animosity intensify as his classroom became more diverse and less integrated. He knew that something must be done, but it became a struggle just to teach the basics let alone inspire values of community and patriotism. Ethnonationalism had become more pronounced in Crystal Springs. The various factions of the diverse student body became increasingly aware that they held different values and allegiances. Henry decided his ability to restore unity and solidarity in the community could no longer be accomplished from the classroom. Something more had to be done.

It was on that day that Henry decided to run for mayor. He was well-liked in the community and was confident in his ability to be a unifying figure. Henry had strong name recognition since most families in the town knew him from his years at Crystal Springs High School. He had deep roots in the community going back many generations. Henry knew that he may be the last hope to prevent the community from devolving into a plantation town, but he was certain to meet fierce opposition. The vested interests benefitting from this demographic and economic transition would oppose his election at all costs.

Henry was hopeful for the future, but he also maintained a pragmatic realism. He wanted the best for his family and hoped that his son would be able to achieve his full potential. Axel had recently graduated from college, and Henry wanted more for his son than what Crystal Springs had to offer. Henry had encouraged his son to pursue opportunities in the coastal cities rather than return to their small Central Valley town. It was a painful decision for him because he missed his son dearly. Henry had dreamed that Axel would start a family and contribute to their legacy in the community, but there had been an undeniable deterioration in the prognosis for Crystal Springs that made Henry less optimistic of the future.

When Henry entered the race for mayor, he was opposed by Pedro Guerrero who was the leader of the local farmworkers union and the son of illegal immigrants from Mexico. Pedro had grown up in Crystal Springs and was well known in the community. Following his graduation from Crystal Springs High School, he founded an employment agency dedicated to placing migrant workers with local farmers. Since he was bilingual, he was well-positioned to bridge the communications barrier between the workers and the landowners. The immigrant community admired his stature among the farmers and his commitment to their well-being. With his strong support in the Hispanic community, Pedro was going to be a formidable opponent.

Henry, true to his character, ran on a platform of industriousness, community, and opportunity. He promised to focus on developing job prospects for all and enticing employers to return to Crystal Springs. The angst and despair among many voters were palpable, and they were clamoring for any shred of hope that their future could be more prosperous. Crystal Springs had been in decline for quite some time, leading to a drastic dichotomy between a few wealthy farming families and the struggling working class. To make matters worse, there was a vast segment of the population that was excluded from opportunities due to demographic changes. These established Crystal Springs residents were cast aside when the community spirit that supported small businesses for generations disintegrated. Henry was determined to restore the success and comradery that the community once enjoyed.

Pedro campaigned vigorously among the immigrant community. He knew that his base of support resided with the wealthy farmers that appreciated his pipeline of cheap labor and the immigrant workers, many of whom he helped migrate to Crystal Springs through farmworker visa programs. Pedro thrived and prospered due to the dichotomy that had developed in the town. He had mastered the art of playing both sides for his own benefit.

"We are building a future of equality and justice for all workers", he would proclaim. "It is time for labor to get their fair share."

It was all a ruse, of course. Pedro received substantial financial backing from the wealthy farmers who were dependent on cheap labor. They wanted desperately to perpetuate and expand the current system. Pedro's ability to maintain the delicate balance between the workers and the farmers enabled him to grow quite wealthy. He campaigned for the interests of farm laborers, but his financial backers knew that he was ultimately on their team.

The campaign for mayor, like most elections, was bitterly disputed. Henry concluded his initial campaign event on a hopeful note. "We will work tirelessly to rebuild our community and return to prosperity. Our campaign is committed to Restoring Opportunity for all Americans!"

Almost immediately, Pedro's campaign manager made a statement to local reporters in response. "Henry Berg's statements are emblematic of a culture of racism and discrimination that plagues our community. It demonstrably proves he is unfit to govern. We must end the institutionalized racism in our town."

Henry was aghast. How could anyone accuse him of such a despicable thing? He just wanted Crystal Springs to prosper, grow, and provide economic opportunities for all. Henry responded to media inquiries by emphatically stressing his commitment to all of Crystal Springs.

"My opponent's accusations are a despicable slander on my character. I want to create opportunities for all and to rebuild our community. We must be united and collaborative in our mission to restore prosperity in Crystal Springs."

This was the high point of the campaign. It was all downhill from there. After months of a bitter and combative campaign, it came down to the vote of the people. Turnout was high since both sides realized the importance of this election in determining the future of Crystal Springs. They were at a crossroads that would determine if the town would become a modern plantation or a thriving vibrant community once again.

When the votes were finally tallied, Henry had defeated Pedro by fifty-five votes in one of the closest elections in Crystal Springs' history. It was clear that the town was deeply divided and in dire need of a sense of community and direction.

Henry gave a triumphant victory speech outside of City Hall. "As your mayor, I will work tirelessly to restore opportunity in this once great town," he proclaimed. "My entire administration will be focused on attracting good-paying jobs and improving the prospects for all. And most importantly, we will reinvigorate a sense of community and shared purpose that will unite Crystal Springs once again."

Henry had many challenges in front of him. It was time to get to work.

3

A FRESH START

Axel had done well at Crystal Springs High School. His father had always encouraged Axel to attend a top university that still emphasized fundamentals rather than cultural indoctrination. It had been a difficult decision for Axel. He had only lived in Crystal Springs and wanted to stay close to home, so he enrolled at a leading state university in the San Francisco Bay Area. Upon stepping foot on campus, Axel knew that he would never return to Crystal Springs. While there certainly were drawbacks to urban living, he embraced the liveliness and activity that was in complete contrast with his sleepy hometown.

At his father's pleading, Axel enrolled in the engineering program with a minor in economics. While he enjoyed the economics classes more than engineering, he could see the utility of each and excelled in his studies. It quickly became obvious, however, that his future would not be in engineering given the current trends in immigration. Axel's engineering classes were dominated by international students. Many of his classmates were friendly, but it became obvious that a White kid from the Central Valley, no matter how qualified, would face an uphill battle at technology firms dominated by Chinese and Indians. Finance and investment management offered better opportunities and higher salaries that were less impacted by foreign students desperate to stay in the United States.

Following nearly four years in Northern California, Axel was hopeful that he could secure a position in the Los Angeles area and enjoy the Southern California beach life for a while. In the spring of his senior year, Axel secured an analyst position at Schwaben Summit Capital. It was a leading fixed income investment manager located in Santa Monica, California. The founder, Dominic Albrecht, was world-renowned as a pioneer in the industry. He had built Schwaben from a small regional player into a global financial powerhouse. While it had grown into a relatively large institution, Dominic still treated it like a family enterprise. He was demanding and relentless in his pursuits and expected the same from his team. Ultimately everyone felt like part of a high-performing team, and each was rewarded for their loyalty and commitment.

As a young man from Central California, Axel was mesmerized by Schwaben. Their offices had sweeping views of the Santa Monica Pier and the Pacific Ocean. Axel sat on the trade floor just fifty feet from Dominic amidst all of the action. For a new analyst, this seemed like an incredible opportunity, but there were also challenges ahead. There was no organized training or mentorship program for new analysts at Schwaben. Instead, new hires were thrown into the deep end and would either sink or swim.

Axel rose to the occasion and thrived at Schwaben. He was quickly recognized for his technical skills and the precision with which he approached his analyses. Flashy self-aggrandizing types usually crashed and burned at Schwaben because they seldom lived up to the lofty image they projected. Axel was quiet and determined at work, but he was recognized as someone that his team could rely on despite his unassuming attitude.

After almost three years at Schwaben, Axel felt that he had gone unnoticed by senior management despite his strong performance. It came as a pleasant surprise, therefore, when he received an invitation from Dominic to attend a party on his yacht in Newport Beach. Axel was just a senior analyst and had yet to have any direct interaction with Dominic, so this would be a great opportunity to network. His team had been very successful since he arrived. In just a few short years, they had tripled assets under management and experienced strong demand for their strategies, but Axel was surprised that Dominic even knew who he was. An opportunity like this for someone in his position seemed like a great honor.

On Saturday, Axel drove south to Newport Beach in his extended cab pickup truck anxious for a day on Dominic's yacht. He wasn't quite sure what to expect, so he was mentally preparing for any number of scenarios. When he arrived, his truck was a little out of place among the multitude of exotic European luxury automobiles. There were three large yachts anchored along the harbor wall, but it was quickly obvious that the largest was his destination. Some of his co-workers had already arrived and were quite boisterous as they guzzled champagne on the back deck. The yacht was at least 100 feet long with a large sun-deck on the bow and two massive party decks on the first and second level of the stern.

"Welcome aboard," Dominic bellowed when he saw Axel approach.

"Thank you, sir," Axel replied. "Quite the yacht you have."

Much like his yacht, Dominic had an imposing presence. Tall, broad-shouldered, and possessing a sharp jawline, Dominic commanded respect merely due to his authoritative posture and intimidating form. He had an intense presence when he spoke as if his words are commands that you cannot help but follow. "Come aboard. I will show you around."

The yacht was truly majestic, adorned with luxurious wood and leather throughout. "This is my third yacht," Dominic said casually. "It was a custom order from Italy. You can't beat the European styling and design."

Axel was speechless. He never would have imagined such an experience would be possible for him.

"Join me on the sun deck, Axel," Dominic said as he led Axel toward the bow.

Axel followed while wondering what Dominic could have planned for a lowly analyst like him. Dominic took a seat on one of the plush sofas and motioned for Axel to sit on another.

"Axel, I have heard good things. Your team has done well these last few years, and they have a lot of positive things to say about you."

Axel smiled. "That's great to hear."

"Yes, Axel. We are looking to build out a values-based investing business, and we want you to spearhead that effort. We have many clients wishing to take a more socially conscious approach to their investment selection. I am hoping that you can help to lead that effort."

Axel was in disbelief. This was a great opportunity. He didn't have a strong vested interest in values-based investing but was anxious to grow professionally and take on more responsibility.

"That sounds like a great opportunity," Axel exclaimed. "I would love to help."

"Great. That's great. Let's discuss more next week, but it is incumbent on you to lead a successful launch of this strategy and contribute to growth in assets under management. The rest of the team will be there to support you, but you will be the lead." Dominic stood and clapped his hands once before turning toward the bar inside the cabin. "Now let's go grab a drink!"

Axel followed, still in shock following the revelation. This was a huge opportunity, and he was eager to make the most of it.

As they approached the bar, Axel could not help but notice a beautiful young blonde woman who was rather short in stature but thin and athletic. She smiled as they came closer. "Hi, Dominic. It is a great day to go out on the yacht!"

Dominic was excited to introduce Axel to the sales side of the business. "Elise, just who I was looking for. This is Axel Berg. He is going to lead our values-based investing initiative."

"Oh, nice to meet you," Elise responded coyly. "It seems like we will be working closely together."

"Elise is the account manager responsible for the values-based investing strategy," Dominic said attempting to clarify the ambiguity. "Together, you will be responsible for getting this strategy off the ground."

Dominic's attention drifted off toward the bar. "Bartender, a Manhattan please! Axel and Elise, what would you like?"

Axel was still digesting the news and marveling at his good fortune. He would be spearheading a promising new product line with limitless growth potential. It could be very financially rewarding for both himself and Schwaben. While working on this exciting new opportunity, he would also be working closely with a stunning young woman who exuded a lively and positive presence. It was difficult to process the life-changing developments that were unfolding.

Once he snapped back to reality, Axel responded, "I'll just have a beer, thanks."

Elise, holding a glass of champagne in her right hand, turned and gestured toward the deck. "Axel, will you join me?"

"Go, please go," Dominic commanded. "You have much to discuss."

Elise led Axel to the port side rail and peered toward the shoreline. While they had been at the bar, the yacht started slowly sailing out of the harbor. When he approached, she turned and asked curiously, "So what do you think of your new assignment?"

Axel tried to play it cool and suppress his excitement. "It seems like a great opportunity. I think we will make a great team."

Elise smiled. "It is a great opportunity. The growth in low-fee exchange-traded funds has put a lot of pressure on fees in our traditional business. Clients are demanding more for less and questioning why they shouldn't just index in an exchange-traded fund. Providing additional customized approaches such as this will help differentiate our offerings."

Axel listened intently while trying to convey his interest. "Have you always worked on this at Schwaben? How long have you worked here?"

"Yes," she replied. "I have been working on developing client interest in this strategy for the past two years. Before my current role, I was an associate working on product development initiatives from which this emerged.

"At this stage, clients want to be able to direct their capital to socially or environmentally favored industries by restricting investments in those sectors that they deem inappropriate. Coal companies, for example, are a major target of environmentally conscious investors. Religious investors may want to limit investments in defense manufacturers or pharmaceutical companies that make contraceptives. Individually, these investment limitations may have a trivial impact but collectively they can influence policy and priorities at companies around the world."

After a brief pause for a sip of champagne, she continued. "As institutional investors with large pools of capital begin to embrace these restrictions, it will have a profound impact. We are able to charge clients higher fees and steer them into a more profitable product for the firm by providing value-added analysis of the social and environmental policies of issuers and their corporate governance standards. We differentiate ourselves through our analysis and ability to implement their prescribed values-driven objectives. This gives us a leg up on generic index-based investing."

"I see," Axel said in acknowledgment. He remained unconvinced. While it seemed like a profitable product for the firm, Axel feared that there were many avenues for abuse. "Who sets the values by which we must operate? Most of our clients are institutional investors where a board or investment consultant must ensure that all actions are in the best financial interests of beneficiaries. It seems that the people setting the policies could use client assets to advance their own political or social agenda."

Elise looked puzzled by the fact that Axel challenged her perception of the inherent morality of values-based investing. After a brief pause to process his question, she attempted to rationalize her position. "Well, the plans select an investment committee that sets policy consistent with the goals and objectives of the beneficiaries. They must determine what is best for their plan."

Axel was unconvinced. It seemed like these investment committees could pursue their own social agenda using the resources of a retirement plan as leverage. Specifically, Axel recalled conversations with his father about Crystal Springs. When his father was younger, people believed in buying American made products and hiring American workers. Crystal Springs had a vibrant small business community with no overwhelming base of power or dominant political force. They all worked together and supported each other so they would all succeed.

As immigration increased and the sense of community faded, some companies adopted diversity and inclusion policies to pander to the new customer base. Companies gradually abandoned American workers in an attempt to cut their costs. They shunned locally made products in favor of cheaper imports or products manufactured using lower-cost immigrant labor. It became fashionable among the wealthy elite, therefore, to favor immigrants over Americans, so policies promoting diversity and inclusion expanded rapidly.

In Crystal Springs, it was the large corporate farms that were the first to vigorously embrace greater diversity because the low-cost immigrant labor enhanced their profits. As the immigrant community grew larger and gained more clout, they sought to further establish policies that legitimized their status in Crystal Springs and encouraged additional waves of migration. Large companies and multinationals observed the changing dynamics and were quick to join the crusade. Soon they all promoted policies supporting diversity and inclusion, but their true motives were simply to gain market share and obtain access to cheap labor.

Now wasn't the time to be arguing his position. He had just been offered a great career opportunity and must embrace it enthusiastically. "You seem to be out of champagne," Axel observed in an attempt to change the subject. "Let me get you another."

"A toast," Axel exclaimed after he returned from the bar with two flutes of champagne. "To a bright and beautiful future!"

"Partners in crime," Elise responded while lifting her glass.

"Partners in crime, indeed," Axel concurred with a smile.

4

COMMUNITY RELATIONS

Once Henry was inaugurated as Mayor of Crystal Springs, he dove into the job with a singular focus on restoring opportunity and prosperity in his hometown. He had retired from his job at the high school after 30 years of teaching and was now committed to restoring a sense of community in Crystal Springs. Pedro congratulated Henry on his victory, but his concession speech primarily reiterated his determination to advocate for the immigrant community with no mention of disaffected Americans or ending divisions in the ethnically segregated town. To Henry, it was obvious that Pedro would not be an ally in his mission to unify the community and imbue a sense of shared purpose and interests.

The Crystal Spring Farm Bureau, a lobbying and advocacy group for local farmers, had requested a meeting with Henry to discuss the agenda of his administration. When the community was comprised primarily of small family farms, this group had acted as a collective to achieve higher prices on their crops and negotiate better terms for the equipment and materials needed to sustain their operations. Attrition and consolidation had reduced its membership over time, and now it acted almost exclusively to advance the cheap labor agenda of the large corporate farms. Henry knew that the Farm Bureau was unlikely to support the goals of his administration, but he hoped to find some common ground. In order to jumpstart the rebuilding and unification of Crystal Spring, Henry scheduled a meeting with the leader of the Farm Bureau as his first order of business.

George McLennan was a large man with a round belly and strong thick hands from years of farming. He was known around town for wearing brightly colored dress shirts with suspenders to hold up his oversized pants that covered half his belly. He arrived at the mayor's office at 7 A.M. sharp on the Monday following the inauguration. George greeted Henry with a loud and jolly voice.

"Mr. Mayor, congratulations on your victory! I am anxious to work with you on your agenda."

Henry had grown up with George and knew him well. Both of their families had lived in Crystal Springs for generations and the McLennan's were the largest landowners in the region. George's jolly sociable demeanor had enabled him to persuade many struggling farmers to sell their farms to his family. In the process, McLennan had amassed an expansive operation that required a steady supply of cheap immigrant workers to harvest the strawberries, grapes, and other crops that he grew.

"Good morning, George," Henry replied from behind the large antique wooden desk that was the foundational artifact of the mayor's office. "Please come in and have a seat. We have much to discuss, I am sure, and I have a busy schedule ahead of me."

George sat down on one of the two wooden chairs facing the desk. He sat tall and straight while his belly stretched his yellow shirt and suspenders. He started the conversation in an attempt to establish common ground. "We are all excited by your election, Henry. Your agenda to unify the community is ambitious but well received. The Farm Bureau is with you and is ready to help in any way possible."

Henry sat silently reflecting on the fact that George had been one of his opponent's largest contributors.

George continued his pitch to curry favor with the new mayor. "You and I grew up together here in Crystal Springs, and I want nothing more than to reinvigorate the community spirit that made this a great town to grow up in and to raise a family. What can the Farm Bureau do to help?"

Henry paused for a moment, contemplating his response. "George, I am heartened to hear that the Farm Bureau is a willing partner and is eager to invest in the community. Your support can go a long way in restoring opportunity and unity in Crystal Springs. First, the Farm Bureau needs to buy more supplies and equipment locally. Too many small businesses have failed when your members abandoned local suppliers in favor of large conglomerates."

George seemed a little shocked by the initial request, but Henry continued with his demands. "Second, we need your commitment to hire from the local population and provide opportunities for people to get ahead. The Farm Bureau needs to stop exclusively relying on cheap immigrant farmworkers and instead provide opportunities for the unemployed and youth of Crystal Springs."

George was visibly flustered and tried to interject, "Henry, you can't expect–"

Henry continued talking, raising his voice to speak over George.

"Finally, we need your public support for our agenda. If you undermine our message and initiatives to restore prosperity in Crystal Springs, the community will remain fractured and continue to act entirely out of self-interest. Do you think the Farm Bureau can be a partner in the community and support these initiatives?"

George was astonished. He had expected some blowback from his support of Pedro in the election but didn't expect such a forceful list of ultimatums from Henry. He had to diffuse the situation while attempting to indicate support for Henry's agenda. "Henry, we fully support your mission to unite the community, but you are asking for a lot. Crystal Springs is incapable of supporting large complex farms. Local businesses do not have the market clout or inventory to sustain our operations, and the immigrant laborers work harder and do jobs that Crystal Spring's residents refuse to do."

"George, let's be frank," Henry interrupted. "You hire immigrants because they are beholden to you for the opportunity to work in the United States, which means you can pay them much less and work them long hours. There are plenty of hard-working young people with an interest in farming and underemployed locals that would be willing to work for a fair wage.

"Additionally, local businesses need a steady and reliable customer base to sustain the breadth and depth of inventory that you demand. When the Farm Bureau stops purchasing from local suppliers, they must cut back on inventory and production, which makes them even less able to support your needs. Inevitably, this leads to an economic death spiral. The Bureau is now dominated by a few large farms whose interests are no longer aligned with those of Crystal Springs. Without your participation in the local economy, this situation will continue to deteriorate."

George realized that he was not going to change Henry's mind. He needed to regroup and reevaluate his approach. George politely sought to defer the resolution of their differences. "Well, Henry, you are asking for quite a lot. I am not in a position to make such a commitment at this time. I will have to relay this message to the Bureau at our next meeting. I would just like to add that there is a large immigrant community that also now lives in Crystal Springs, and you should consider their needs as well."

George stood and reached out his hand. "Thanks, Henry. I look forward to our next chat."

Henry reflected on the totality of their conversation. He was committed to restoring prosperity and opportunity in Crystal Springs, but he was disconcerted by something George had said. The Farm Bureau had supported many immigrant farmworkers over the years, some of which had entered California on temporary farmworker visas while others crossed the border illegally, enticed by the prospects for work. Henry was not in a position as mayor to remove illegal aliens, and there was a lack of political will at the Federal level since the corporations were strongly in favor of a steady pipeline of low-wage workers. He would have to figure out how to unite a diverse community with highly divergent interests.

Crystal Springs had always been a community with strong values and deeply held beliefs. Faith, family, and freedom were foundational principles that anchored the community. Generation after generation, people from Crystal Springs had fought for their families, their country, and the liberties that all Americans enjoyed. It was their blood, sweat, and tears that fostered the unity and community spirit that embodied the town. The sense of shared sacrifice and collective contributions had been eroded at an ever-increasing pace with the influx of immigrant workers. The rapid transformation left many resentful that the bucolic farming community, rich in history and spirit, now resembled an industrial farm plantation serviced by a compliant immigrant workforce.

Henry knew he would have to figure out how to bridge the divide between an immigrant population largely motivated by economic interests and a native population that felt like they were being pushed off their farms, out of their homes, and into bankruptcy by those that put profits before people. These forgotten men and women felt expendable. In a sense, they were. They had invested their fortune and committed their lives to the betterment of the community only to see it all unravel as soulless corporations cast them aside in exchange for lower-cost immigrant workers. Henry would face immense challenges in his quest to end the disenfranchisement and replacement of American workers. As long as the economic incentives were aligned in favor of the immigrant workforce, his quest to rebuild and unify the town would remain a dream.

Henry realized his approach to revitalizing the community must be multifaceted. Most critically, he must address the pro-immigrant policies and corporate greed that encourage both legal and illegal immigration. Pressure must be exerted on the Farm Bureau and other employers that offered below-market wages to immigrants in exchange for explicit or implicit residency privileges. The farmworkers union had evolved into a human trafficking organization that enabled a steady stream of migrant workers to find employment. These immigrant workers were exploited by their employers and subjected to harsh working conditions. The farmers and the union leadership grew wealthy off the backs of desperate immigrant laborers, and the long-time residents of Crystal Springs saw economic and employment opportunities fade away.

Next, he must increase zoning enforcement to address the multifamily occupation of houses and apartments intended for single-family use. Many farmworkers were offered housing on-site and were charged exorbitant rent by their employers for deplorable living conditions. The immigrant farmworkers that didn't have company-provided housing often cohabitated in large groups that far exceeded the intended occupancy of the dwelling. Not only was this dangerous, but it led to the rapid deterioration of neighborhoods and undermined property values. Henry correctly observed that the people who were most invested in the community are the permanent residents with a financial and civic interest in the success of Crystal Springs.

Finally, he would organize events featuring the best of what Crystal Springs has to offer and promote engagement with local businesses and small family farmers. Amidst all the strife among the various factions in the community, Henry knew that he must be the unifying force to restore a sense of common interest and purpose. He must remind everyone of the commonalities that bound them together and the economic potential that existed if they would work toward common goals.

Henry knew that it would be a tough road ahead. Now that the plan was set, however, it was time for action.

5

SHARED VALUES

After months of intense collaboration, Axel and Elise began to attract some big new clients with their values-based investing strategy. Some of the initial clients were charitable foundations and religious organizations that had a relatively narrow exclusion list to reflect their values and philosophy. Elise began receiving interest, however, from some large multinational corporations that wanted to bolster their public image. Additionally, pension funds that sought to advance an environmental and social agenda began to inquire about how their objectives could be achieved. It became clear that, if properly marketed, the potential universe of clients was much larger than initially expected.

Almost all of the clients that expressed interest in the values-based investing approach were interested in socially progressive restrictions that would signal their compliance with and support for the agenda of liberal activists. The global multinational corporations and public pension plans found this especially advantageous. In some cases, the companies legitimately embraced progressive values and wanted to invest in their version of a socially responsible manner. Many, however, were using the investment strategy to greenwash or distract from social, environmental, or governance abuses inherent in their own operations. Either way, Elise was having great success in attracting new assets.

From Axel's standpoint, it was all a matter of implementation. He was relatively agnostic about the actual limitations imposed, as his job was simply to optimize the portfolios subject to the client's guidelines. At times, the constraints became excessively limiting and impacted Axel's ability to construct a diversified portfolio, but in most cases, creating a customized portfolio subject to the client's values was straightforward.

Axel was preparing for a big presentation to Dominic and the Schwaben Investment Committee on Friday. The values-based strategies had just surpassed ten billion dollars in assets, and Dominic had requested an update from Axel and Elise on their outlook for continued growth. This was a huge opportunity for them. It provided high-level recognition of their accomplishments and a venue for them to communicate their vision for the future of the strategy. The pressure was on, and they were both feeling it.

With just a few days before their critical presentation, Axel wanted to convene with Elise to ensure they were on the same page. The trading day was over, and he finally had time to gather his thoughts. Axel felt comfortable discussing portfolio construction and account performance, but he wanted to coordinate talking points with Elise to make sure he wasn't caught off guard. Axel decided to see if Elise was in her office.

Elise had an office on the perimeter of the trade floor. It was ideal for conducting private conversations with clients and staff. Her office door was open, and she was intensely focused on her computer when Axel approached.

Axel knocked softly on her door to get her attention. When she looked up from her computer, he asked, "Elise, would you like to grab a drink after work and discuss our presentation?"

"Sure," Elise responded. She was eager to hash out the details and identify their talking points as well. "How about four o'clock at the Pinnacle?"

Axel was impressed with her recommendation and replied affirmatively, "Perfect, see you there."

They had been working closely for months and had developed quite a rapport. Axel was very fond of her, but an awkward tension existed between maintaining professionalism and fostering a more intimate relationship. He could tell that Elise was interested, but she was naturally waiting for Axel to act. Axel wasn't quite sure how to broach the topic, so the impasse persisted.

The Pinnacle was a swanky bar on the roof of their building. It was a popular spot for happy hour gatherings and after-work meetings due to the great views and ocean breezes. Axel arrived early and waited for Elise at the reception desk. After a few minutes, the elevator door opened like a great unveiling with Elise as the magnificent surprise. She looked stunning even after a long day at work. When she saw Axel at the other side of the reception area, she smiled and walked gracefully with a presence befitting a senior account manager at Schwaben. She put her arm through Axel's and they followed the maître d' to their patio table facing the ocean.

Axel pulled out the chair closest to the heat lamp for Elise. The breeze was brisk yet refreshing. As Axel settled in, he turned to her and asked, "What would you like to drink?"

"Chardonnay is good," she replied.

Axel flagged the waiter and said, "A chardonnay and a Boulevardier please." Long gone were the days when Axel would simply have a beer. He was a portfolio manager now, and he had developed some sophisticated tastes.

He turned his attention to Elise and was filled with a sense of contentment. They had successfully launched the values-based investing strategy and fostered a deep friendship in less than a year. His emotions must have been transparent because she smiled in response.

"You seem quite happy. Are you excited about the presentation?"

"I think I needed a break from the pressure of the presentation, but I have a newfound sense of clarity now that I am here with you," Axel replied.

"Oh yeah, what did your clarity reveal?" She inquired coyly.

"That we are quite the team! We have had great success since we started working together, and I see great things for us in the future." Axel's focus had drifted from work pursuits to other interests.

She smiled and said, "Do tell!"

"I can't reveal all of my secrets!" Axel said with a sense of playful indignation. "But it involves fame, riches, and eternal happiness. Simple things like that."

Their attention had shifted from the initial intent of their rendezvous. Axel's concerns about the presentation had faded and other interests occupied his mind. After an hour of engaging banter and a couple more cocktails, Axel surrendered all of his concerns about Friday and focused on the opportunities in front of him.

"Well, here is to the simple things in life," Elise responded as she raised her glass.

"Indeed," Axel said with a smile.

***

Friday had arrived and it was showtime. Axel and Elise hadn't been very productive when preparing for the presentation, but they had broken the log jam in their relationship. To Axel, that was well worth any additional anxiety about delivering an effective presentation. It was a welcome distraction from the pressures of work and a source of new optimism for their fledgling romance. Axel felt as if a weight had been lifted from his shoulders, and he had newfound anticipation for the future. He would have to channel this energy to deliver an epic performance in his first presentation to the investment committee.

When Axel approached the executive conference room, Elise was waiting outside. She looked stunning in a beautiful black dress that landed just above the knees, classic black pumps, and diamond drop earrings. Her smile glistened as she saw Axel approach.

"Are you ready?" she asked.

"Yes, let's do this," Axel responded.

With that, she turned and led Axel into the conference room where the investment committee was already assembled. Axel stood to the side as Elise took center stage.

"Good afternoon," she began. "Axel and I are here to update you on the fantastic growth of the values-based investing product that we officially launched less than a year ago. Our initial clients are all very pleased with the way Axel has managed their accounts. Given the strong performance of the strategy, we have received increasing interest from potential clients that desire greater customization and even more restrictive guidelines. We have recently funded additional accounts and now have over ten billion dollars in assets under management dedicated to values-based strategies. Prospectively, we see additional demand coming from companies and pension plans with a strong desire to virtue signal and demonstrate their social awareness. Whereas initial clients were motivated primarily by deeply held religious or philosophical beliefs, the acceleration of the culture wars has driven additional demand for values-based or environmental social governance – ESG for short – investment guidelines. The recent inflows have been driven more by optics and social posturing rather than deep-seated principles. That said, we continue to see acceleration in the demand for ESG investing, which is driving issuance geared toward these investors. Axel will now discuss corporate issuance and portfolio construction in more detail."

Axel was impressed. Elise proved to be a pragmatist on the values-based investing product. It was a lucrative strategy for Schwaben that was currently in vogue with prospective clients, but Elise was a realist about the motivations of many clients. There are a few true believers, but many clients are opportunists that are attempting to appease the passionate progressive activists and shape social policy in their favor. Axel was surprised that she was not a dogmatic true believer but instead a skillful marketer that knew how to target the needs and demands of her clients.

Instilled with greater awareness and appreciation for his partner, Axel stepped up to deliver his remarks. "Thanks, Elise. As previously mentioned, the initial values-based investing accounts were relatively straight forward to implement, as they primarily excluded broad swaths of industries based on social or environmental restrictions. In these cases, we would often scale up our other preferred issuers to compensate for the lack of flexibility. Our more recent clients have requested minimum ESG issuer ratings and minimum average ESG scores. These guidelines change the dynamics of values-based investing. When a religious organization restricts pharmaceutical companies that sell contraceptives or provide abortion services, there is little that these companies could do outside of discontinuing those product lines. Therefore, these types of restrictions are primarily to satisfy the principles and morals of the client without explicitly aspiring to social change."

Axel paused briefly to assess the room and then continued. "The new ESG clients have entirely different objectives. Many are seeking to affect social change by using their investment capital as a carrot and a stick. Their assets act as a carrot by enticing issuers to come to market with green or social bonds that are ostensibly used for altruistic purposes. For example, a green bond may finance solar installations or energy-efficient factory enhancements. Conversely, a social bond may be dedicated to financing low-income housing or investments in distressed communities. These clients seek to induce companies to behave in a prescribed manner in order to secure higher ESG scores, access larger pools of capital, and ultimately reduce their funding costs. At the same time, they are punishing companies that don't conform to their environmental, social, and governance demands. We find that many global multinational corporations are quick to comply because there is no countervailing force or dissenting voice to resist the aspirations of the activist community. Companies perceive only positive benefits from compliance with ESG standards, so the issuance of social and green bonds is likely to grow over time. There is serious institutional momentum behind this movement."

Dominic had been listening intently and inquired, "Do you see any emerging threats or headwinds for value-based investing?"

Axel responded with conviction. "No, this movement has legs. As Elise can attest, we are experiencing exponential growth in inquiries about our offerings, and there has been very limited opposition to the values-based investment strategies."

Elise concurred with Axel's assessment but offered further elaboration. "We are projecting rapid growth with some cannibalization of existing credit strategies. Approximately one-fourth of projected ESG asset growth will be migrating from existing credit assets and the rest will be new assets."

"This sounds very promising," Dominic responded. "You two have done a great job launching this product and attracting new assets. We have a bit more to discuss here, but I would like to meet with both of you at 3 P.M. Please come by my office."

"We will be there, thanks," Elise responded.

After gathering his notes and following Elise out of the conference room, he turned to her to gauge her reaction. "That seemed to go well, right? You did a great job."

Elise smiled in appreciation of the acknowledgment. "Yes, Dominic seemed pleased. I hope he has some good news for us later."

"Me too. I am going to get a little work done, but I will meet you there at three?"

"Sounds good," she said before heading back to her office.

After their casual debriefing, Axel returned to his desk and reflected on the presentation. It seemed to have gone well, but he hoped that he hadn't been too blunt about his perception of their clients' motivations. In some ways, Axel felt that the ESG movement attempted to mandate conformity and impose authoritarian rule on the corporate community. Additionally, the trend toward industry consolidation and larger multinational corporations had decreased patriotism and nationalistic impulses. Companies had been mutating into amorphous transnational organizations that were loyal to no nation and took their cues from the demands of the aggrieved masses. They held no individual principles or values except those that they felt would appease the outraged social activist mob and least offend important authoritarian markets such as China. Axel felt that this could be a threat to the values and principles that Americans held dear.

Axel was becoming increasingly uncomfortable with the trends in values-based investing and his role in the process. His actions had negative ramifications for people throughout the industrial heartland of America and his friends in rural communities like Crystal Springs. The ESG movement would favor large multinational corporations and further concentrate wealth and influence on the coasts. Capital would migrate toward those that conform to the demands of activists, and the powerful would use this as leverage to enforce their demands and suppress opposition. If the ESG movement continued unabated, Axel projected that the corporate oligarchy and "Davos class" of millionaire and billionaire executives would have enough power to suppress all dissent and block any competition from startups and entrepreneurs. It was undoubtedly a movement designed to fundamentally transform America and consolidate power among the transnational elite.

Despite his concerns, Axel knew that he had to continue. He was achieving great success and had to persevere unless he wanted to return to Crystal Springs with his tail between his legs. Axel kept telling himself that it was better to be a part of the machine where he could influence the direction of ESG investing in a more constructive direction. If he withdrew in surrender, he would relinquish that power to someone entirely committed to the fundamental transformation of America, the ascendance of immigrants, and the decline of the American people.

The afternoon went by in a flash, and it was now almost 3 P.M. Axel hadn't accomplished anything since their presentation, but it was helpful to reflect on the state of play. Now it was time to learn what Dominic had in store for them and the future of ESG investing. When Axel arrived at Dominic's large corner office, he was working intently behind an array of computer monitors. Dominic saw Axel approach and motioned for him to enter the office.

"Axel, come in and have a seat," Dominic said without looking up from the computer. As Axel sat down, Dominic continued. "Axel I am very pleased with your management of the ESG portfolios and the values-based investing strategies. You and Elise have exceeded my expectations."

"What did I miss?" Elise asked as she entered the office.

"Nothing," Dominic replied. "I was just telling Axel how impressed I am with your performance. I just had a meeting with the executive committee, and they have decided to make values-based investing a major priority for the upcoming year. We will be providing you with additional resources to facilitate the growth of the strategy."

"Wow, that's great news," Elise replied with excitement.

Dominic continued. "Well, there will be additional benchmarks and targets established for growth, but that comes with perks as well. Both of you will be promoted and receive an equity stake in the business. That stake will be benchmarked to asset growth milestones to be established by the executive committee. Your future compensation will be, in part, driven by your ability to achieve the benchmarks they set."

Axel was speechless. What an incredible development! His potential growth and compensation were now limited only by his own success.

Elise maintained her composure and responded, "We are deeply honored by this recognition and assure you that we will deliver."

Dominic smiled as he replied. "I knew that you two would make a great team. Keep up the good work, and we will discuss the details soon."

Axel and Elise took the cue and left the room after thanking him again. As they walked away from the office, Elise turned to Axel beaming with excitement.

"We have to go celebrate," she said.

"Absolutely," Axel responded. Everything seemed to be falling into place for them. Axel knew that tonight was the night to bring it all together. "Our future looks bright, and we have much to celebrate."

"Indeed," Elise said with her signature playful smile. "Indeed!"

6

A REUNION

Axel had not seen his father in some time. They spoke occasionally on the phone, but he had been so busy with work and with Elise that he hadn't been able to travel to Crystal Springs recently. As the holiday weekend approached, Axel decided to visit his father and introduce him to Elise. He had yet to tell his father about the budding relationship that had developed and was sure that it would come as a pleasant surprise.

When they spoke on the phone, it was clear that Henry was quite proud of the success that Axel had achieved in such a short time. Axel knew that it brought Henry great joy to hear of the strong demand for the values-based investing strategy and how that success had advanced his career. Axel appreciated the recognition, but he could sense a note of despair in his father's voice. Henry was struggling to unify the town and implement many of the policy objectives that he had promised during his campaign. He had become demoralized by his inability to get the Farm Bureau to commit to hiring local workers and invest in the community. As a result of his failures, Crystal Springs continued its downward economic spiral, and the resentment of the locals grew.

It was going to be a big weekend for the three of them. Elise had never experienced life in a farming community and was unsure what to expect. She was an Angelino, born and raised, and her only experience in the California Central Valley was passing by on the freeway. To her, the entire region seemed like another world. Elise expressed her apprehension and nervousness to Axel, but he reassured her that his father would love her, and it would be a great experience.

Axel arrived at Elise's condo at 8 A.M. sharp on Saturday morning. They had a lengthy drive in front of them, and he wanted to beat the traffic.

He threw her bags in the back of his truck and helped Elise into her seat. Axel couldn't help but smile because she was clearly overdressed for Crystal Springs. It was obvious that she was looking to make a good impression.

A puzzled Elise asked, "What are you smiling about?"

"Nothing," Axel replied. "You look beautiful and are going to make quite the statement in Crystal Springs."

Sensing that she might have overdressed, her anxiety grew. Then again, this is how she normally dressed and felt most comfortable when she looked her best. "I dress to impress," she responded with a smile.

As they pulled away, she turned to Axel with a look of apprehension. "Tell me again all that I need to know about Crystal Springs and your father. I don't want to say or do the wrong thing."

"Well, you know that my father is the mayor of Crystal Springs and our family has lived there for generations," Axel began. "It is predominantly a farming community with a handful of farming families that have been fixtures of the town since its founding."

"Yes, of course, I know that much," she interjected. "I mean tell me about the culture and the people."

"Well, you must understand that they live a much simpler life compared to Los Angeles. There once was a vibrant small business community that served the farm industry, but that has slowly been replaced by the big box stores in the surrounding larger cities." Axel paused, reflecting on how much detail to divulge before continuing.

"The people that live in Crystal Springs have a slower pace and simpler expectations. A cup of coffee is simply that. They don't seek out fair-trade sustainably-grown organic beans from a special farm in Columbia. They just go to the store and buy some standard ground coffee. Do you understand what I am trying to say?"

"I think so," she replied. "They are poor, lead simple lives, and buy what they can."

"Umm, not exactly," Axel said in an attempt to correct her. "You are correct that most of the people in Crystal Springs have no concept of the life that wealthier people in Los Angeles live except for what is dramatized on TV. Just as we have no concept of the opulent lifestyle and substantial influence of someone like Dominic or the Silicon Valley tech billionaires, most people of Crystal Springs only understand and appreciate what exists in their community. There is one grocery store in town with everything that you could need, but none of the frills of specialty shops in Los Angeles. Similarly, there are some local cafes and restaurants, but they cater to those that don't have sophisticated culinary tastes. Does that make more sense?"

"Yes, of course," she said as she looked at Axel with an engaging gaze. "This is fascinating. Tell me more."

"Well, most of the people are happy with the simple things in life and don't feel like they are missing out due to the lack of luxury goods. It's not that they aren't ambitious and don't want more for themselves and their families, but they are satisfied with a commercial mass-produced beer and don't need a special microbrew IPA to be happy. 'A beer is a beer,' my father would always say."

"I don't think I have ever had a mass-market beer in my life," Elise responded with a chuckle.

"Well you just might this weekend," Axel said with a smile. "To boil it all down, the people of Crystal Springs are generally happy with a simple lifestyle that is centered on family and community. With that said, the standard of living has been steadily declining in the town for decades due to an influx of low-wage immigrant labor and a decline in employment opportunities. Some farmers have been forced to retire, and there has been a lot of consolidation that has concentrated wealth and power in the hands of a few while leaving many with little hope and struggling to maintain their already austere lifestyle. This is why my father ran for mayor."

"I see," Elise responded with genuine concern. "That sounds very sad."

"Yes, it is. When you contrast it with the wealth and privilege at Schwaben, you realize that these people that were once part of the agricultural, industrial, and manufacturing base of the country have been cast aside to further enrich the most powerful. These wealthy elite are operating on a completely different scale and under a different set of rules. It is very sad indeed, but even more so when you realize the forces behind this devastating trend."

"Alright, now you are sounding quite dire," she said. "What are these ominous forces that you speak of?"

"My father's election is an elucidating example," Axel responded. "His opponent ostensibly was an advocate for the immigrant farmworker community. In reality, he was heavily backed by the local Farm Bureau which is controlled by the largest and most powerful farming conglomerates of the region. So where exactly did his true loyalties reside? Many politicians express support for the working man while embracing crony capitalism and aligning themselves with the corporate oligarchs. They manipulate the poor with identity politics and promises of free stuff in order to placate the masses and distract from their large scale exploitation. The donor class demands competition-crushing regulations, access to cheap labor, and approval of mergers and acquisitions that protect their market power. In exchange, the corporate oligarchs support the cultural agenda of the left and offer tokens of goodwill for environmental or social projects favored by activists."

"Wait a second," Elise interjected. "It sounds like you harbor a dim view of ESG investing. Do you oppose the basis of our strategy?"

Axel paused, concerned that he had exposed his inner conflicts over the investing strategy that had been so fruitful for them both. After briefly reflecting on his position, Axel decided that he must come clean with his views on the matter. "I believe that ESG investing promotes an agenda of conformity and adherence to a doctrine that is used to enrich the powerful and suppress dissent. Entrenched interests benefit from increased regulations that make innovation and entrepreneurship more onerous and expensive. This protects their profits and power, enabling them to exert more control and dominance over smaller companies. Multinational companies also fund environmental activist groups that resist development and promote regulations that benefit their corporate benefactors while impeding innovative entrepreneurial companies. When you cut to the chase, ESG investing is aligned with the interests of the corporate oligarchs and politicians who seek to create a modern-day plantation to secure wealth and power."

"Wow, that's a lot to digest," Elise said as she stared blankly ahead. She was stunned at Axel's perspective and was still processing all that he had said. "First we were talking about Crystal Springs, and now you are telling me you don't believe at all in what we do. I had no idea!"

Sensing that he had possibly said too much, Axel decided to leave it alone. They had yet to discuss politics or philosophy, but it should have been clear to him that her cosmopolitan upbringing would have engendered more of a "coastal elite" perspective. She probably had accepted the altruistic posture of ESG investing without considering the darker side of rewarding large multinational corporations with favorable financing in exchange for embracing the agenda of social and environmental activists.

They drove for a while in silence as Elise looked out the window pondering what they had discussed. After a few minutes, Axel turned on the radio to break the silence. They still had over an hour to go.

Before long, Elise turned to Axel and reinitiated the conversation. "I still can't believe you feel that way about ESG investing. Why did you ever accept the assignment?"

"It's all just portfolio construction to me," Axel responded bluntly. "I am simply implementing the directives of the client and seeking to maximize their returns within those constraints."

That response appeared to resonate with Elise to some degree. Her angst seemed to diminish as she considered the cold practicality of Axel's perspective. After a moment of contemplation, she acknowledged Axel's dispassionate approach. "OK, I can see that. I am still surprised, but I can understand your views on portfolio construction."

"I appreciate that," a relieved Axel replied. "How about you take in Crystal Springs with an open mind and let me know if your views have changed by the end of the weekend. We are almost there."

"Sounds fair," she said as they exited the highway. "I am excited and ready to see your hometown and meet your father."

As they drove down a small two-lane road, they had unquestionably entered farm country. The smell of cows and a vista of expansive flat farmland surrounded them. Elise seemed uncomfortable with the smell, perhaps afraid it would permanently permeate her expensive clothes. She was clearly out of her element.

They passed through a couple of small towns identifiable only by a cluster of a few houses and a slightly reduced speed limit. They were on the final stretch to Crystal Springs. The endless farmland began to give way to a small town on the horizon.

"Is that it?" Elise asked.

"Yep, we are almost there," Axel responded.

The main highway passed right through downtown Crystal Springs. As they slowly drove through the heart of the town, the scale of the economic devastation became apparent. Most of the storefronts were empty aside from a lonely "For Sale or Lease" sign in the window. Everything seemed run down and in disrepair with one building suffering from a collapsed roof. The only structure that seemed well maintained was City Hall which had a well-kept lawn adorned with a flagpole bearing the stars and stripes. Elise observed in silence, but she was taking it all in.

The entirety of the downtown area was no more than ten city blocks. As they approached the end, Axel turned and pulled into one of the many open parking spots on the street. They had agreed to meet Henry at one of the few remaining restaurants in town. It was a no-frills diner that served traditional American favorites at a reasonable price.

As one of the few remaining businesses downtown, the diner was a social gathering spot in Crystal Springs, and Henry was a frequent patron. As mayor, he felt it was his duty to engage with the public, and the diner served as a casual environment for residents to broach their concerns or express their support. He was alone in his regular booth sipping on a cup of coffee when Axel and Elise arrived.

"You must be Elise!" Henry said as he stood, beaming with excitement. "It's very nice to meet you."

"Likewise," Elise said politely with a smile.

After a quick hug between Axel and his father, they took a seat in the booth across the table from where his father had been waiting. In an attempt to be friendly, Elise sought to initiate a conversation.

"Congratulations on your electoral victory! How is life as mayor?"

"To be honest, it's been a struggle," Henry replied. "I never appreciated the intransigence of the powerful business interests and the degree of division engendered by the employment biases of these farm conglomerates. Crystal Springs once had a diverse and robust business community where everyone played a small part and could see that they all benefitted from each other's success. Nowadays, the large farms reap a disproportionate share of the financial rewards while everyone else perceives the success of their neighbor as a threat to their own economic survival. It is quite a sad state of affairs."

"I am sorry to hear that," Elise responded. "What will you do to reverse the course?"

"The only hope to save Crystal Springs is to get people to once again believe that we are one community with shared goals, interests, and values," Henry said. "That, however, is easier said than done. There are strong cultural differences between a relatively evenly balanced population of immigrants and local residents. These differences have resulted in ethnic tribalism and resentment. The old-timers feel like the blood and sweat of their families built this town, and now opportunistic newcomers are freeloading off of their selfless contributions. Conversely, the immigrant community has its own values and feels justified in seeking employment where it is offered. They lack a strong attachment to Crystal Springs and share few cultural or economic interests with the people of the town. So we have a stalemate of sorts. Reversing course on the current trend of economic decline seems less likely by the day."

"That's unfortunate," Elise said with genuine dismay. "Now I can see why you wanted Axel to leave Crystal Springs and pursue employment elsewhere."

"I love Axel and never wanted to see him go, but we had to face reality," Henry responded with disappointment. "Crystal Springs may soon become a ghost town. There will be nothing left except large industrial-sized farms run by wealthy landowners and low-wage immigrant laborers that work long hours in the fields. Everyone else will be forgotten and left behind. There is just no avenue for industrious and ambitious people to find success here."

The dire gravity of Henry's assessment was impactful for Elise. She could only imagine the despair and hopelessness that would overcome people living in such an environment. Watching something you loved and devoted your life to wither and disintegrate slowly would truly be devastating. She looked around the diner observing the mostly older White patrons who exhibited the effects of years of hard manual labor with a solemn acceptance that they are the last generation of their once-proud town. The native White population was nearing extinction following the introduction of immigrant workers and the industrialization of the farming sector.

"Good morning Mayor," one of the aged patrons said to Henry upon approaching their table. "Who are these distinguished guests of our small town?"

"You know my son Axel, and this is his girlfriend Elise," Henry responded proudly. "They just arrived from Los Angeles for the weekend."

"Welcome," the patron responded as he focused on Elise. "I hope you have a good time in Crystal Springs. Make sure you get some of their peach cobbler. It is a treat."

As he left, Elise reflected on how life for many of these people was truly about finding small nuggets of joy in a seemingly endless pit of despair. The highlight of their day was some moments with friends, a trip to the store, or a piece of their favorite cobbler. She marveled at their ability to persevere while confronted with the harsh reality around them. This town, like many of the inhabitants, was in a slow march toward death.

Elise gazed out of the window to assess the afternoon activities on Main Street. There was a small carnicería that doubled as a taco shop across the street, but most of the other storefronts seemed empty. A couple of young Latino men were sitting outside the carnicería enjoying a drink. They appeared to be workers at the shop who were taking a break as they waited for customers. Aside from a few cars passing through, there wasn't much activity in sleepy Crystal Springs.

"Where is everyone?" Elise asked inquisitively. "It seems rather quiet for a weekend."

Henry expressed a look of disappointment and responded, "Yes, unfortunately, many of the residents of Crystal Springs struggle financially. Aside from the farmworkers, the town is now predominantly elderly residents that have lived here their entire lives. Some of their children still live here and help care for their parents while struggling to find consistent work. Much like Axel, most of the younger generation leaves to find better opportunities."

"That seems sad," Elise responded.

"Quite sad," Henry agreed. "I am not sure if Axel told you, but I worked at the high school for many years. We have seen a decline in enrollment for at least the past two decades with current enrollment less than half of what it used to be."

"Why is that?" Elise inquired.

"Well, many of the farmworkers are not permanent residents of Crystal Springs. They are either single young men or they have left their families behind while they work here to send money back home. Any immigrant children that do live in Crystal Springs often require additional educational services since they are non-native English speakers. Conversely, much of Axel's generation has left Crystal Springs. Those who remain struggle financially and are unable to afford a family. The few that do have kids usually are living in poverty, and the schools need to provide nutritional support and other services. Most of the children in Crystal Springs receive free meals, so the schools play a vital role in ensuring the safety and development of the kids. Overall, though, many of the kids live in dire poverty with parents suffering from depression, alcoholism, or worse. A lack of opportunity combined with financial destitution quickly erodes an individual's self-worth and leads to feelings of hopelessness. That's why I so desperately wanted Axel to move on from Crystal Springs."

Axel had remained silent during much of this conversation. He appreciated that Elise was engaging with his father and showing genuine interest in his hometown, but he began to feel that the conversation was growing quite dark. His father seemed different. He was always a very optimistic and encouraging person, but something had changed. Perhaps it was his role as mayor or a bout of loneliness, but it was clear to Axel that he must be more engaged with his father and visit more often. Axel assumed that the positive activities that Henry had planned for Crystal Springs would bring some satisfaction and fulfillment for his father and everyone in the town, but the situation in Crystal Springs seemed hopeless.

"Tell us about the Harvest Festival, dad," Axel said in an attempt to refocus the conversation. "How is that coming along?"

Henry's face immediately lit up with pride and excitement. "It's coming along nicely. Did I tell you that the Farm Bureau has signed on to be a sponsor? We will have many participating farms showcasing local produce and products along with a massive barbecue and games for the children. You should come, Axel. Bring Elise!"

"That sounds great," Elise said with a smile. She appreciated that Henry had shown a degree of approval by inviting her to return already, but she also was curious to see the people of Crystal Springs gathered together to get a better sense of the farm community. Much like an observer at a zoo, Elise had a curiosity about how these people lived and their idea of entertainment.

"OK, dad, we will be there," Axel responded. "First, however, let's get through the weekend."

"Yes, of course," Henry said with a smile. "Are you ready to leave and head to the house?"

"Sounds like a plan," Axel confirmed.

"OK then," Henry said as he beckoned to the waitress. "Check please!"

7

REGIME CHANGE

Axel and Elise enjoyed their visit with Henry, but both were glad to return to the Los Angeles Westside. They had grown accustomed to the amenities of urban living and longed for the comforts that they typically enjoy. As they prepared to return to work, Axel reflected on the weekend and how rapidly his life was changing. He knew that his father needed him, but Axel also knew that Henry wanted him to focus on his life and all the good things that had come his way. It was quite obvious during the weekend that things were getting serious with Elise. She was a great partner and companion, but more importantly, she had a compassionate side that Axel appreciated.

It had been a few months since their promotion, and assets under management continued to grow. They knew that their progress was being monitored closely, but Dominic was pleased thus far with the results. Elise cultivated a substantial pipeline of potential clients, and Axel continued to deliver high performing customized portfolios for their existing client base. Axel found it reassuring that they were able to work effectively together at Schwaben without letting their personal lives interfere with their professionalism. Some coworkers might have suspected a romantic relationship, but Axel and Elise were discrete and never discussed their personal lives at work.

When Axel arrived at work on Tuesday, he noticed an e-mail calling for a firm-wide meeting at nine in the morning. It wasn't all that unusual for the executive team to provide periodic updates on performance and asset growth, but it was surprising that such a meeting was called on short notice. He wondered if perhaps there was going to be some major organizational changes or perhaps notable retirements. The executive committee frequently would reevaluate underperforming divisions for potential elimination or restructuring. It was crucial at a firm like Schwaben that capital be optimized and that returns justified expenses. Many senior managers were paid more than one million dollars a year so they must be supporting over five billion dollars in assets to profitably cover the necessary overhead.

After rebalancing a handful of portfolios and hedging some inflows, Axel tied up a few outstanding items and prepared for the meeting. The trading day was well underway at this hour, so it was important to ensure that all time-sensitive trades had been executed and any outstanding programs were being addressed by the appropriate trading desk. It was unusual to have a meeting like this in the middle of the trading day, especially the first day back from a holiday weekend. Axel walked toward the executive conference room and observed many solemn faces. It seemed like something big was about to happen, and everyone had their suspicions.

As they all gathered in the conference room, people were relatively quiet and refraining from the small talk that is common around the office. Many people were staring down at their phones, checking emails, or reading the news. At about five past nine, Dominic arrived with the rest of the executive committee and five men in suits that Axel had never seen before. They all proceeded to the center of the room and lined up behind Dominic.

Dominic stepped forward and stated loudly, "Today is a great day for Schwaben."

The mood in the room noticeably lightened as the potential for mass layoffs or other bad news had been eliminated. After assessing the room, Dominic continued. "I am proud to announce that Schwaben Summit Capital is being acquired by Perennial Life, the largest insurance company in the world with global headquarters in Switzerland. We will continue to operate independently as a premier fixed income asset management company under the Perennial umbrella, benefiting from their expansive client base around the world and significant investable insurance assets. Schwaben will take over the management of a substantial portion of Perennial's fixed income assets over the next five years. These assets alone will nearly double our current assets under management."

"This is a great result for Schwaben that was derived from months of negotiations with Perennial," Dominic declared in an attempt to assuage some of the obvious apprehension in the room. "I would like to hand it over to Etienne of Perennial Life to further discuss what this means personally for all of you."

Dominic stepped back and gestured toward one of the unknown men in suits. He was a slight fellow compared to Dominic and looked distinguished in his gray suit and glasses. There was complete silence as he stepped forward to address the room.

"Good morning, and congratulations to the Schwaben team," Etienne said with a noticeable accent. "We greatly respect the work that you do here at Schwaben and are anxious to welcome you to the Perennial team. I realize that many people may be concerned by an announcement like this, but I want to personally assure you that we intend to retain all Schwaben personnel and are committed to a robust and prosperous future for Schwaben. To that end, you will all be receiving a packet detailing the retention bonuses that will be granted to each Schwaben employee. These bonuses will be payable one year from the closing of the merger and will at a minimum be twenty-five percent of your prior year's compensation. Furthermore, everyone with an equity stake in Schwaben will immediately benefit upon closing through both cash remuneration for the surrendered shares and a new equity grant in Perennial. We are confident that you will be pleased with the equitable arrangement that we have struck with the Schwaben Executive Committee and are excited to welcome you to the Perennial Life team. Thank you."

Dominic once again stepped forward and took command of the meeting. "Thank you, Etienne. We are very excited about this opportunity and look forward to being part of the Perennial team. Now as we adjourn, I want to tell everyone how proud I am to work with such a dedicated and professional team. The executive committee worked very hard to ensure that every Schwaben employee would benefit from this transaction. You will receive your retention packet later today, which will detail the commitment that Perennial Life has made to every one of us. Now it's time to double down and prepare for the explosion in assets yet to come. Thanks, everyone."

With that, people began to silently exit the room. It seemed that most people were in shock due to the unexpected news and were trying to maintain a cautious optimism that the acquisition of Schwaben would lead to additional opportunities for growth. Common knowledge was that such mergers often greatly rewarded the partners and executives while leading to dramatically reduced future opportunities for everyone else. Schwaben would cease to be an entrepreneurial asset manager that treated its employees like family and was nimble enough to capitalize on niche market opportunities. Henceforth, it would be a subsidiary of a massive financial conglomerate. All future corporate strategy and capital allocation decisions would undoubtedly be influenced by Perennial.

Axel wondered if the values-based investing strategy would have been launched under the Perennial umbrella. Worse yet, would he have received the opportunity to manage the portfolios as a relatively young and inexperienced employee? Dominic had recognized his potential, but such opportunities may be more limited under large corporate rule. Nonetheless, this transaction could potentially be a huge financial windfall for him. As part of their recent promotion, both he and Elise had received an equity grant and an increase in their compensation. He was curious to receive the packet and determine the personal impact of this agreement.

No one left work early that day. Everyone was working, some more diligently than others, while awaiting delivery of the packets. At 3 P.M. sharp, a clerk from the mailroom with a cart full of envelopes stamped "Personal and Confidential" began to make the rounds and distribute the packets. Some people opened theirs immediately, intrigued by the contents. Others quietly packed up their belongings and left for the day. It was a very personal event that was uniquely experienced by all. The lives and careers of everyone at Schwaben materially changed that day, and the verdict on the developments had yet to be rendered.

Axel received his packet and decided to wrap up for the day. He was eager to get home and discuss the unexpected developments with Elise. A busy post-holiday trading day had consumed him, and he had yet to chat with her. Axel remarked to himself how quickly life can change. A few days ago he was back in Crystal Springs and feeling good about the turn of events in his personal and professional life, and now he felt a bit unnerved by the magnitude of the recent developments. It added a degree of uncertainty that hadn't previously existed. His lack of familiarity with Perennial made the ambiguity more difficult to quantify. Axel had been confident in the trajectory of Schwaben and the values-based investing strategy that they had launched, but now all of that is in flux.

He was the first to arrive home to the condo that he and Elise now share. After they were promoted, their previously ambiguous relationship became more concrete. They quickly decided that living together would be the next step. Elise had been living in a two-bedroom condo that she rented close to work so Axel agreed to move in with her. The adjustment had been relatively uneventful, and he was happy with the decision.

Axel decided to wait for Elise to return home to open his packet. Perhaps she had already reviewed hers, but they were a team, and he wanted to share the experience with her. Almost two hours passed before Elise arrived home, all the while Axel's packet sat on the table incessantly beckoning him to open it.

"Welcome home, babe," Axel said as she closed the door behind her. "What a day!"

She put her bag on the table and sat next to Axel on the couch without saying a word. She cuddled up next to him and asked, "So, what do you think about all of this?"

"It's not exactly how I thought we would start the week, that is for sure," Axel replied. "It seems like we are in a good position, and we are involved in a growing segment of the business. As for the packet, I haven't looked at mine yet. I was waiting for you to get home."

"Me either," Elise replied. "Should we look now? It is kind of like opening a Christmas present where you have high expectations but at the same time feel you may be setting yourself up for disappointment."

"For sure," Axel said with a smile. "We might as well pull the bandage off and see how it looks. Shall we do it together?"

"Let's do it," Elise said with enthusiasm. "On the count of three. One. Two. Three."

Axel opened his envelope and pulled out a single sheet of paper. Following some initial legal disclosures, which he promptly skipped, was a set of numbers. The most surprising number, however, was the number of zeros in the total. Speechless, Axel could only quietly mutter, "Wow!"

He looked at Elise who had a similar look of disbelief and hadn't said a word. Acknowledging her lack of reaction, Axel prodded. "So? Is it good?"

"Axel," she said before stopping to catch her breath. "I don't even know what to say."

"Me too," Axel replied. "How about we just put our cards on the table, so to speak, and let the numbers speak for themselves?"

"Agreed," Elise replied as they both slowly placed the paper on the table. They briefly examined the other's details before turning to each other with big smiles. Without saying a word, they spontaneously embraced, and neither would let go.

"This is a cause for celebration!" Axel said. "I am dating a millionaire!"

"My mother always told me that I should marry for love and not money, but maybe with you I will get both!" Elise said laughing.

As they composed themselves, it all began to sink in. Between the value of his shares and the retention bonus, Axel would receive an even million dollars. Elise, on the other hand, would receive $1.2 million. They were rewarded substantially for the success of their strategy, and it was clear that Perennial was committed to values-based investing as a growth engine.

Realizing their lives had just changed once again for the better, Axel couldn't contain his emotion. "I love you, Elise."

"I love you too, Axel." She smiled with pleasure before continuing, "Now weren't you taking me to dinner?"

8

LAND OF RICHES

After the acquisition announcement, everyone at Schwaben seemed quite pleased with their retention packages. There was a positive buzz around the office, and the initial trepidation had given way to an optimistic outlook for the future of the enterprise. A euphoric atmosphere persisted for quite some time as people pondered how to spend their unexpected windfall. It only took a few months, however, for warning signs to emerge indicating that it would no longer be business as usual.

While many were blinded by their newfound riches, Axel could sense signs of stress, especially with Dominic. He was quicker to reprimand traders and portfolio managers who weren't performing up to expectations yet he seemed more disengaged overall. Given that Dominic, of all people, must have made a fortune off the merger, Axel wondered if there wasn't some tension between the Schwaben Executive Committee and Perennial.

The tension was confirmed the following Monday. Half a dozen men in suits, led by Etienne himself, appeared on the trade floor early in the morning and proceeded directly to Dominic's office. Axel couldn't help being curious, so he peered over the top of his monitors to see what might be transpiring. After nearly fifteen minutes, they all emerged from the office with Dominic in tow. They assembled in the center of the trade floor where Etienne stepped forward and got on the public address system.

"Good morning," Etienne announced attempting to secure the attention of a bustling trade floor. After a brief pause, he continued. "Most of you remember me from our last meeting, but my name is Etienne, and I am the Director of Investment Management at Perennial. I oversee all of the investment management companies like Schwaben that are subsidiaries of Perennial Life. I am here today with Dominic and my team to introduce

Stefan Klinsmann who has been part of the investment management team at Perennial for two decades. He will be joining Schwaben as co-CIO alongside Dominic and will be the chairman of the executive committee. I wanted to introduce Stefan personally to the trade floor before his formal announcement in a town hall meeting later this week. There, Stefan will communicate some exciting developments at Schwaben in conjunction with Perennial Life. We have a lot of new initiatives planned to accelerate growth and ensure the future success of Schwaben. Thanks and have a great week."

A hushed silence blanketed the trade floor as everyone absorbed what they just heard. This was a dramatic change, as Dominic was the founder of Schwaben and a dominant fixture in the industry. Bringing in another chief investment officer and installing a new chairman could lead clients to question the direction of the firm under Perennial's ownership. It would be crucial that they convey a sense of continuity and stability to the investment community, or there could be a mass exodus of assets.

As Axel pondered the power struggle at the top, the trade floor slowly began to buzz again. There was work to be done and money to be made. Axel marveled at how quickly his coworkers could brush off such a significant development and get back to business. In the end, they had a job to do and were compensated based on their performance not the power struggles at the top. Besides, they were all going to be handsomely rewarded as a result of the merger. There never had been much job security in the investment management industry, and everyone generally looked out for themselves.

News quickly spread about the development. Axel received an email from Elise within an hour asking for details. For some, the change reignited fears of a traumatic transition. The terms of Perennial's retention agreement did not guarantee employment, but it did commit to the payout if you remained with the company for the next year or were terminated. Continued employment remained at their discretion.

The timing of the move also seemed suspicious. Perennial must have been planning this from the start, but chose to reassure Schwaben employees that nothing would change under their leadership. To Axel, this seemed like a poor way to develop credibility and trust. He wondered what could be so important that they would jeopardize the steady growth in assets and high client returns that Schwaben had historically achieved. It must be something big.

On Friday morning, Axel received an email announcing that the town hall meeting was scheduled for two in the afternoon, which was immediately after the close of trading. He and Elise planned to attend together. She was quite concerned about the move, as she had already received many inquiries from clients. They were afraid that a change in leadership would negatively impact the investment process and that politics at the top would be a distraction that would negatively affect returns. Elise was insistent that there would be no changes to the investment process and that Perennial was committed to Schwaben, but she had scant evidence to back up her claims. She needed answers, or clients might start heading for the exits.

As everyone began to gather in the executive conference room, Axel and Elise found seats near the back of the room where they would be strategically secluded from direct observation. They were there to listen, not to engage. In the center of the room were Dominic and Stefan, side by side. It was difficult to read the mood, but there was no friendly banter or conversation between the two leaders. Dominic stood stoically like a military general about to brief the troops. Stefan, on the other hand, surveyed the room in an attempt to ascertain when everyone had gathered and he could start the meeting. He appeared more like a politician preparing to deliver a campaign speech that would be full of platitudes and empty promises.

The conference room was nearly at capacity, so Stefan stepped forward to address the firm. "Good afternoon. As you may have heard, my name is Stefan Klinsmann, and I have joined Schwaben as the new chairman of the executive committee and co-CIO. I am very excited to join such a distinguished team. As a result of this transition, Dominic will continue to set the direction for the trade floor in coordination with myself and the Investment Committee. I will primarily be collaborating with Perennial Life's executive management team to establish the strategic direction of the firm. While there will be limited changes to the portfolio management side of the business, I have some very exciting announcements to make about some new initiatives here at Schwaben.

"To maintain consistent values and principles across the Perennial Life portfolio of companies, we will be establishing a Council on Diversity and Inclusion. The CDI will be responsible for developing policies that encourage greater diversity within Schwaben and creating opportunities for additional engagement and understanding. Employees across the firm can volunteer to be part of the CDI if they are excited by the prospect of fostering a more inclusive environment that recognizes all of our unique strengths, backgrounds, and experiences.

"Another exciting endeavor is what we call Project Green. Schwaben has partnered with leading global environmental groups to fund and promote sustainable energy development, conservation efforts, and other green initiatives. Going forward, Schwaben will contribute two percent of profits to these organizations to encourage good environmental stewardship. To further our commitment to Project Green, we will strategically prioritize our ESG based investment strategies. For those who aren't aware, ESG stands for environmental, social, and corporate governance and is meant to encourage good corporate policies. All account managers will actively promote these strategies and encourage client adoption. As an additional inducement, we will contribute an additional one percent of profits derived from ESG accounts to our global environmental partner organizations.

"Both of these new groups will report directly to the executive committee and will be considered top strategic priorities going forward. Perennial Life believes strongly in these initiatives and considers the principles that they represent to be core corporate values.

"I would like to conclude by recognizing that all of you make Schwaben the exceptional organization that it has become. With your commitment to these new initiatives, we will celebrate what makes us unique and build an even brighter future. I look forward to working with you all. Thank you."

As Stefan concluded his presentation, isolated episodes of clapping ostensibly signaled approval for his remarks, but it was far from a standing ovation. Axel sat next to Elise silently and noticed that Dominic had barely moved. He remained as he began, standing tall with a dominant presence that exuded confidence and authority. One couldn't help but observe a slight hint of defeat on his face, much like a general dispirited by the reality that far too many of his men had fallen in battle. At that moment, Axel felt sorry for him. Sure he was rich beyond comprehension and free from the necessity of labor, but Dominic surely now realized that the firm that he founded and nurtured for decades was embarking upon a much different course than he had envisioned. The awareness that Schwaben was forever changed had become definitively apparent to Dominic, but many in the room seemed to lack a full appreciation of the developments.

Axel turned to Elise to see if she was ready to leave. She nodded in agreement before standing to leave the room. It had been a long week, and this was a lot to digest. They left the building together in silence, but Axel was anxious to discuss the proceedings. In some ways, it was good for them. ESG investing was gaining additional prominence and focus within the firm, yet there was an ominous feeling that Axel could not shake. The entire presentation felt like an indoctrination of sorts, where compliance and agreement were expected. Dominic's silence and lack of participation suggested that all employees, even those at the highest level, were expected to acquiesce. Dissent and alternative viewpoints would not be tolerated. This was authoritarian rule.

On their way back to the condo, Axel was eager to hear Elise's thoughts. "What did you think about all of that? I have a lot of thoughts but am curious about your take."

Elise, in a more cheerful and optimistic tone, replied to Axel's inquiry. "I thought it was quite interesting. It seems very positive for our ESG and values-based investing strategies and could lead to a lot more business."

"Yes, but what about the rest?" Axel interjected impatiently. "Sure, we may get more business, but Stefan seemed to chart an entirely different strategic course for the firm. Particularly one in which the primary objectives of the firm are almost entirely uncorrelated with financial returns."

"It's more about the values of the firm and what you want to represent," Elise said. "If we are good corporate citizens and demonstrate our values through quantifiable actions, then clients will reward us with additional business. I am kind of surprised, Axel, that you don't recognize this since it is the core of our ESG strategy."

This remark stung Axel, and he became defensive. As with many pernicious policies, the negative implications of pervasive adoption of ESG investing were easy to dismiss until they hit close to home.

"I am quite aware," Axel responded. "I do not, however, believe that stating a set of principles and expecting compliance is consistent with policies promoting diversity of thought and inclusion of different views."

"Come on, Axel!" Elise exclaimed in a disapproving tone. "You know what they mean. They want gender and ethnic diversity along with an inclusive environment where people of all types can feel comfortable and respected. That seems like a universally accepted policy and an admirable objective."

"Elise, your statement that it is 'universally accepted' proves my point. You are suggesting that the policies are moral imperatives that are beyond reproach. Dissent is not allowed and perhaps is even considered morally reprehensible. Employment is conditioned upon acquiescence. That seems like a rather fascist system to me." Axel's frustration was beginning to surface.

"Oh, Axel. You are getting a little carried away now, aren't you?"

"This has always been the inevitable outcome of the institutionalization of policies such as these," Axel responded in disagreement. "The large multinational corporations are wedded to a globalist system that is by definition multicultural and supranational. To protect their profits and market power, they must perpetuate that system. They use such policies to ensure that the rules of the game are in their favor."

"Axel, you sound like a zealot now," Elise said laughing.

"Mark my words," Axel said with complete seriousness. "This is just the beginning."

"Of what exactly?"

"A complete reordering of society," Axel answered. "What happened in Crystal Springs is now unfolding on a global scale. We are quickly moving from a system of local control based on common values and interests to a global system dominated by multinational corporations and bureaucratic bodies. Take the European Union, for example. The Europeans gave up national control and governance to a supranational body of bureaucrats that are supposed to represent the collective interests of highly divergent people. When that occurs, you lose accountability and responsiveness. It is much easier to marginalize the disenfranchised by characterizing them as fringe actors and excluding them from civil society. Playing their game and acquiescing to their demands is the only avenue to individual success. Therefore, their game becomes the only one in town."

"I still don't see how the European Union is related to Crystal Springs," Elise countered.

"I will explain," Axel replied. "Crystal Springs was the epitome of local control and shared values. There was a strong sense of civic pride because everyone was invested in each other's success. If the small family farmers did well, they would spend more on equipment and supplies. Those vendors could buy a new delivery vehicle or hire more workers. Everyone did well and no one reaped disproportionate rewards. As the farms consolidated under corporate control, the balance of power shifted. Now, these industrial-sized farms can influence politicians and establish the terms of trade in ways that are not always beneficial to the local economy. Consolidation in the farming sector has eviscerated the small businesses community and destroyed the sense of pride and unity that Crystal Springs once enjoyed."

Elise tried in vain to piece together Axel's logic. "I see some parallels, Axel, but am still not drawing the connection. Are you suggesting that the loss of local control and the erosion of common bonds are similar?"

"The member countries of the European Union previously were relatively monolithic countries with unique cultures, histories, and traditions. Like Crystal Springs, their size enabled the government to be more responsive to the specific needs of the people. The relative commonality among the population led to greater alignment of interests and more social cohesion. In Crystal Springs, this social cohesion emerged from a sense of shared history and values. On a larger scale, you would call it patriotism and nationalism.

"When the European Union established a common currency and the member states ceded local control, everything changed. It was no longer beneficial to serve local interests or priorities. Instead, corporations began to consolidate across countries, and political bodies centralized power at the supranational level. Patriotism and nationalism, similar to the community spirit in Crystal Springs, became the enemy of the system. Instead of unifying around common values and interests, the transnational elite now dictate that diversity is a strength and globalism is a virtue.

"When the farms in Crystal Springs began to consolidate, they became more aligned with national or global markets and their success was more detached from local concerns. Rather than being partners in a community, the farming conglomerates began to view people as inputs in an economic system where profit maximization and market dominance was preeminent. They sought to minimize labor costs by hiring immigrant laborers which incited division in the community and diminished the clout of locals. It ultimately is the goal of the globalist system to fractionalize and marginalize populations so that none has sufficient influence to challenge the authority and legitimacy of the system. Diversity, you see, is a mechanism to dilute the power of demographic groups that share common values and interests. When you reduce their clout, they become dependent on large corporate conglomerates and subject to the whims of the bureaucratic state."

Elise smiled and responded. "That's a lot to process, Axel. Clearly, you have strong views on the matter, but that all seems far removed from the policies at Schwaben."

"Only when you take a more narrow view," Axel countered. "Individually, the policies may seem well-intended and innocuous until you see how they are part of a more pernicious attempt to enforce conformity with a globalist multicultural system. This system concentrates power among a few billionaire oligarchs, multinational corporations, and bureaucratic regulatory bodies. These policies are tools of oppression used to undermine existing social structures, squash competition, and stifle dissent."

"I don't know about all that, Axel. You seem to take a relatively dim view of policies meant to enhance equality, opportunity, and environmental conservation." Elise was beginning to think Axel was going off the rails a bit.

"Enhancing equality and opportunity for whom? Any effort to enhance the prospects for one group necessitates actively disadvantaging another group. It consequently leads to tribalism and division that weaken social bonds and shared interests. On the environmental side, large companies frequently use biased data to support a narrative that is most beneficial to their interests. The corporate establishment seeks to weaponize regulations so they can squash competition, halt development, and reward favored market participants. Often they use activists as their foot soldiers to advance their anti-competitive policies without suffering any negative publicity or culpability for unseemly activities. All of this is to secure and perpetuate their power."

"I prefer to ascribe more positive intentions when considering the motives of others," Elise countered. "I think the policies come from good intentions and a desire to increase equality. I don't believe there are diabolical motives at play."

"We will see," Axel replied. "Instead of idealistic equality in Crystal Springs, you have a demoralized American working-class population that descended collectively into poverty while a few powerful farming conglomerates grew extremely wealthy. That doesn't seem like a moral or just society to me."

9

HARVEST FESTIVAL

Stefan's appointment as chairman of the executive committee fulfilled the fears of many and marked a dramatic shift in culture for Schwaben. In the ensuing months, there was an endless array of announcements and proclamations from the Council on Diversity and Inclusion. The not so subtle reminders about the new social order and the principles of the firm were grating. From Axel's perspective, discrimination and bias had become institutionalized. The Council took every opportunity to propagandize the firm, attempting to convince employees that sexism was pervasive and systemic racism was a well-established reality that was corroborated by abundant evidence. The racialization of the firm and frequent sermonizing about pervasive bias was leading to resentment among the staff and paranoia about the motives and intentions of their coworkers. Social cohesion was cracking, and this was affecting morale.

Axel was becoming more and more disillusioned. He once was proud and passionate about his work at Schwaben, but he now felt like he was working for the enemy. The implied animosity toward White males at Schwaben made Axel feel complicit in his own persecution. Despite his growing frustration, Axel needed a job. Payment of the retention bonus was still months away, and he could never leave that much money on the table. He wondered, however, if many others were feeling the same way. It wasn't exactly a topic you could discuss because dissenting views weren't tolerated, and speaking to the wrong person could cost you your job. Axel remained mum, bottling up his emotions while trying to persevere.

Given the bleak outlook at work, Axel needed some stability and positivity in his private life. The inaugural Crystal Springs Harvest Festival was this weekend, and he and Elise were going to make the trip to support his father and his hometown. Henry made it a priority to encourage everyone from the community to attend, and expectations were high. It would be a nice weekend away from the drama at work and an opportunity to spend some quality time with his father.

On Saturday morning, Axel and Elise set off for Crystal Springs. Their return visit together would be a time to celebrate. Elise turned to Axel and said, "I am so excited about the Harvest Festival!"

"We will have a busy weekend. Are you nervous?" Axel had been looking forward to this weekend for quite some time. He was anxious to arrive, but heavy traffic was slowing their progress.

"No," she said with a smile, "are you?"

"I am just happy to have another long weekend with you in Crystal Springs. I know it means a lot to my father, and he appreciates us coming to support the Harvest Festival. He is waiting for us, and I wish this traffic would clear up."

Elise knew that it was futile to grow frustrated with Los Angeles traffic and concluded Axel must be a little nervous. It was a big weekend for them all. "What is on the agenda for today?" Elise asked in an attempt to keep Axel's mind occupied and calm his nerves.

"We are meeting him at the house to get unpacked, and then we will join him in a parade through Main Street."

"We will be in a parade?" Elise exclaimed. "How exciting!"

"It is Crystal Springs, so don't expect the Thanksgiving Day Parade or anything," Axel replied with a chuckle. "After the parade, I think we will get to check out a few of the vendors and survey the scene before my father gives a speech to kick off the festival. Then we can enjoy the rest of the evening together."

Elise couldn't help but tease Axel. "We will be dignitaries at the inaugural Harvest Festival! They will probably want to do a profile on us in the paper. Honored guests travel from Los Angeles to attend the Harvest Festival!"

"That's probably not far from the truth," Axel said with a smile. "I am sure the people from the local paper will be milling around to get some quotes."

As they approached Henry's home, Axel couldn't help but get a little excited. He was proud of his dad and how hard he had worked to rebuild the town. The task had been arduous and quite thankless, perhaps even more than they had expected. It often seemed like half the town hated Henry and the other half was dissatisfied with the pace of progress. Corralling these opposition parties together to participate in the Harvest Festival was a monumental achievement in diplomacy.

Axel pulled into the driveway and Henry immediately came out to greet them. He met them at the car and gave Axel a rather uncharacteristically warm embrace. "Axel. Elise. Thank you so much for coming to Crystal Springs for the Harvest Festival. It means a lot to have you both here. Your presence is symbolic in that the Harvest Festival is all about bringing people together. I have high hopes that a lot of positive developments will emerge from this festival."

Elise came around to the driver's side of the car and hugged Henry. "Congratulations, Henry on pulling this off. We are honored to be a part of the Harvest Festival celebration. In fact, we have a little news to celebrate as well."

Axel turned and gave her the evil eye. She wasn't supposed to broach the topic so casually, but now the ball had been set in motion.

Henry perked up with a bright smile. "Oh yeah, what's that?"

"Well, dad, I was planning to tell you at a more opportune time, but it seems the news is too big to keep quiet," Axel said with a sharp gaze directed at a smiling Elise. "We wanted to tell you that we are engaged to be married. The wedding – "

"Congratulations to both of you," Henry interjected. "This is such wonderful news! Your mother would be so proud and happy that you found such a beautiful and intelligent woman. I am so happy for both of you."

"Thank you, Henry," Elise replied while blushing slightly. "Axel is a good man, and we are very happy together. I can't wait to officially be part of the family."

"Come," Henry blurted excitedly. "Come inside. Let's celebrate before we leave for the parade. There are a lot of good things on the horizon."

As Elise gushed about her ring and the proposal to Henry, Axel couldn't help but reflect on his good fortune with a tinge of guilt. He had left an economically depressed Crystal Springs behind and found both career success and the love of his life in Los Angeles. Things truly were looking up for him, but he also saw his father and the people of Crystal Springs continuing to struggle in what seemed like a losing battle. Today, however, was about celebrating progress and cherishing little victories. Axel resolved to focus on the positive and be there fully in support of his dad.

After about an hour of chatting, they left the house to convene at the parade gathering site. The plan was to start from the south end of town at the grocery store parking lot and proceed down Main Street before culminating in the park on the north end of town. All told, the parade route would cover approximately one mile, and the procession would lead everyone directly to the Harvest Festival. Henry had volunteer organizers setting up in the park and working with the vendors and farmers to ensure things would proceed smoothly.

When they arrived at the grocery store, a large crowd of parade participants had already gathered. The high school marching band was slated to lead the parade while the color guard carried banners announcing the first annual Harvest Festival. They were to be followed by the fire department in their antique fire engine and by a handful of farmers who volunteered to exhibit their old tractors. Following them would be a float prepared by the Farm Bureau and a group from the local farmworkers union. Finally, a police motorcycle duo was scheduled to escort the brand new convertible that would transport Henry, Axel, and Elise along the parade route.

Henry spotted his driver and motioned for Axel and Elise to come along. As they approached, the thin middle-aged man with a mustache was finishing up a cigarette next to a white convertible.

"Jim, this is my son Axel and his fiancée Elise," Henry said when they were all together.

"Well hello! I am Jim, the manager of Crystal Springs Auto. It will be my pleasure to drive you today in this beautiful automobile. I think we are getting set up here, so let me help get you situated." Jim took Elise's hand and helped her into the backseat of the car. "Let's have the mayor sitting in the center here if you don't mind, and then Axel you sit here on the other side."

When they were all comfortably seated, Henry grabbed both of their hands and said, "Thank you guys for being here."

This was Henry's big day. While it was a great political opportunity for him to be seen as the leader that brought this great community event together, it also celebrated his efforts to build more unity and spirit within the community. To Henry, a community was much more than random people that lived as neighbors during their struggle through life. A good community was like an extended family that would always be there to celebrate successes and provide neighborly support when someone was struggling.

Jim got behind the wheel and turned on the convertible just in time for the drum major and color guard to lead the marching band onto Main Street. With that, the parade had commenced. The street was lined with people, many of whom must have come from the surrounding farm towns to enjoy the festivities. The music of the band comingled with the purr of diesel motors and the siren of the fire engine to create a symphony of sounds. Axel turned and saw his father beaming with pride while acknowledging the crowds. Elise occasionally waved to the enthusiastic spectators much like a local beauty queen would do in recognition of her fans. She seemed to be enjoying her moment of fame in small-town California, far removed from her hectic life in Los Angeles. A parade was pure Americana, and it was a refreshingly simple way to celebrate the history of Crystal Springs.

The crowds gathered behind the convertible and followed it to the park as if they were being escorted to the Harvest Festival by the mayor himself. Jim pulled into the parking lot and drove directly toward the stage where Henry would address the festival attendees. After they parked, Jim jumped out of the car to assist his distinguished guests from the vehicle. Once everyone was out of the convertible, Henry grabbed his jacket and straightened his tie in preparation for his big speech.

Jim turned to Axel and Elise and asked, "Can I escort you to your seats while the mayor makes his final preparations?"

"Of course," Elise replied. She was enjoying the attention and glamor of the proceedings. She took Axel's arm and followed Jim toward the rows of folding chairs arranged for the crowd. It wasn't the Oscars, but it was quite exciting given the rustic setting in Crystal Springs.

As they were leaving, Axel turned to his father and said, "You'll do great, dad."

Henry smiled and waved before following his assistant to the back of the stage where a set of stairs provided access to the platform. George McLennan, the President of the Crystal Springs Farm Bureau, was going to introduce Henry before the grand opening speech at the inaugural Harvest Festival. As Henry waited by the stairs, he listened as George addressed the crowd.

"Thank you, everyone, for coming out tonight to celebrate our community and its rich history. As many of you know, my name is George McLennan, and I am the Farm Bureau President here in Crystal Springs. My family has lived here for generations, and we love this town. When our great mayor proposed the idea of the Harvest Festival, I just knew that the Farm Bureau must be a founding sponsor. We hope you get the chance to visit with many of our local farmers, enjoy some of our local meat and produce, and remember what makes this community special. With that, I would like to introduce the man who made all this possible – our great Mayor Henry Berg."

George stood at the podium clapping as Henry walked up the stairs. When Henry turned to the crowd, he immediately noted how expansive it was. The rows of seats were filled, and there were hundreds of people standing beneath the trees. He smiled and waved as he walked toward the podium with overwhelming satisfaction. When he approached, George reached out and shook his hand before he walked back to the stairs.

Henry settled in behind the podium and raised both hands toward the sky. "Welcome, everyone, to the first annual Crystal Springs Harvest Festival."

He paused to soak in the applause before continuing. "This event was conceived from a desire to celebrate what makes us great – our strong community spirit and rich history. Some of us have lived here for generations and others have moved to Crystal Springs more recently, but all of us want what is best for our town and our community. Many industrious generations have worked hard in the fields, the machine shops, and the stores to build a community that supports each other and aspires to a brighter future. Tonight is the culmination of more than a century of labor and sacrifice that built this town into what it is today. We must now preserve that legacy for the next generation so that they too benefit from everything that makes Crystal Springs special and unique. We are better together. Now let us enjoy the harvest of our labor and celebrate the contributions of our neighbors and friends. Thank you all, and enjoy the Harvest Festival!"

Henry stood at the podium waving to the crowd while he searched for Axel and Elise. He finally spotted them in the first row off to the right where both were leading the standing ovation. Henry smiled and waved to them before turning to leave the stage.

As Henry began to descend from view, Axel turned to Elise and said, "That seemed to go well, don't you think?"

Just as Elise was about to reply, the murmur of the crowd was abruptly interrupted by a loud pop succeeded by another pop. Axel was startled but assumed it was nothing until he heard a woman scream in terror from behind the stage. "Stay here!" he blurted out before rushing toward the back of the stage.

As Axel rounded the corner, he could see Henry's hysterical assistant standing next to his father who was awkwardly splayed at the bottom of the stairs. Henry's head slumped to one side, and he was motionless as Axel approached. "Call the ambulance!" Axel commanded the assistant.

It wasn't entirely apparent what had happened until Axel knelt beside his father. When he put his hand on the side of Henry's head to turn it toward him, he immediately felt the sticky warm blood that streamed down his father's face. Henry remained limp and motionless, as Axel stared at his blood-soaked hand in panic. Elise had defied his orders and stood behind him gasping in horror with her hands over her mouth.

Desperate for a glimmer of life, Axel shook his father by the lapels and tried to get him to wake up. Instinctively, Axel knew that his father was dead but he couldn't relinquish hope and surrender to grief. As Axel struggled to revive his father, the paramedics arrived and took over the futile efforts. By this time, the motorcycle officers from the Sheriff's department that had escorted them along the parade route no more than an hour before were establishing a perimeter around the scene while they waited for reinforcements.

Axel stepped away from the body as the paramedics worked diligently to revive Henry. Elise put her arms around Axel's neck and buried her head in his shoulder crying while Axel stood in disbelief. This was supposed to be a celebratory weekend in Crystal Springs. Things like this don't happen here.

One of the paramedics turned to Axel and shook his head. Henry was unresponsive, and they had been unable to revive him. As the paramedics stayed with the body, reality set in for Axel. His father had been killed, murdered in fact, by an unknown assailant with over a thousand people gathered on the other side of the stage. There was no way to maintain containment or ensure that the perpetrator didn't disappear into the crowd and leave the scene entirely. Axel wanted answers.

Henry's assistant was still hysterically crying as she sat on a chair while being interviewed by an officer. Axel was sure that she must have intimate knowledge of the crime given her proximity to his father. His disbelief was giving way to anger. Axel wanted vengeance. There must be justice for his father and severe repercussions for his killer. "My father is dead," he stated bluntly as he approached one of the officers. "What leads do you have?"

"Sir, I am sorry for your loss," the officer responded. "We are still interviewing witnesses and processing the scene so we don't have any information for you at this time. Perhaps you would like to have a seat, and we can collect your information –"

"My information is not going to help you identify who murdered my father," Axel interrupted. "I am happy to give a statement, but shouldn't you be chasing down more pressing leads?"

"We are doing everything we can," replied the officer. "May I suggest that you and your fiancée give a brief statement to that officer and go home to try to get some rest. We can take your full statement tomorrow after we have gathered additional forensic evidence from the scene."

Axel escorted a distraught Elise to the investigative officer as instructed. They provided basic information to the officer before walking in somber silence toward the parking lot. Jim was waiting patiently by the convertible, decidedly less ebullient after what had occurred. He offered his condolences and suggested that he drive them to Henry's house. They rode in silence, and their mood was melancholic following the biggest tragedy to beset Crystal Springs in its history. This was rural California, not a narco-state where political assassinations were commonplace.

When they arrived at Henry's house, Axel slumped on the couch without a word. Elise snuggled next to him trying to provide some comfort. After thirty minutes of silent contemplation, Axel reached for the television remote. He could no longer wait patiently for answers. Axel flipped through the channels until he found a local news broadcast and sat in silence waiting for some word. The exhaustion of grief had overcome Elise as she slept clinging to Axel's arm. He watched patiently, segment after segment, yet no coverage was forthcoming. Frustrated and despondent, Axel helped Elise get more comfortable before he fell asleep on the other sofa.

Hours later, Axel was abruptly awakened by a knock on the door. A sheriff's deputy was standing on the porch in the bright morning sun. Axel invited the deputy inside and took a seat on the sofa next to Elise. "Do you have anyone in custody?" Axel asked impatiently.

"I am sorry for your loss," the deputy began. "We don't have anyone in custody, but we have some good leads. I wanted to ask you if you have any additional information that could help our investigation. I understand that you were in the audience and couldn't see behind the stage is that correct?"

"Yes, all we heard were two pops that sounded like firecrackers," Axel responded. "Only when we heard the scream did I know something was definitely wrong."

"OK," the deputy continued, "do you know if your father had any enemies or people that were unhappy with him?"

"My father was the mayor, so of course some people weren't happy with his policies. He was adamant about rebuilding the community and restoring the sense of unity that once existed in Crystal Springs. At the same time, he was opposed to the discrimination against local businesses and workers by the corporate farm industry that hired illegal immigrant farmworkers, undercutting local laborers and suppressing wages. He defeated Pedro in the mayoral race, and so there could be some animosity there or within his farmworkers union."

"I see," the deputy replied while scribbling information in his notepad. "Had your father received any direct threats or had he been the victim of harassment since becoming mayor?"

Axel paused before answering. His father had seemed off for months, but Henry had never revealed any reasons for his mood. "No direct threats to my knowledge, but I had the sense that my father was perhaps depressed. He never told me anything directly, and I just assumed he was a bit demoralized by the lack of progress on his agenda and the pushback he was receiving from the pro-immigrant constituencies in town."

As the deputy was busily taking notes, Axel turned his focus to the TV where a breaking news accouchement flashed on the screen. He quickly unmuted the TV so that he could listen to the report.

"Tragedy in Crystal Springs," the reporter begins. "Henry Berg, Mayor of Crystal Springs, was gunned down by an unknown assailant at the first annual Harvest Festival organized by the mayor himself. A crowd of over a thousand people had gathered to enjoy the festivities, but immediately following the mayor's speech, a gunman fired two shots killing the mayor instantly."

The camera panned out to show Pedro Guerrero standing next to the reporter. "I am here with Pedro Guerrero, President of the local farmworkers union and Mayor Berg's opponent in the last mayoral race. Mr. Guerrero, I understand you were at the Harvest Festival when Mayor

Berg was murdered?"

"Yes, it is quite a tragedy," Pedro responded. "Crystal Springs is a quiet and peaceful town. You would never expect a thing like this to happen."

The reporter probed further. "I understand the mayor had organized the Harvest Festival to foster a sense of unity and community spirit in Crystal Springs. Why do you think the gunman targeted the mayor at such a public event?"

"The mayor would often speak of community," Pedro replied. "Even in his speech yesterday, he mentioned the legacy of industrious generations that built the town. What Henry never grasped is that this rhetoric fails to acknowledge the transformation that has occurred and marginalizes the immigrant community. It is not surprising that a man who sought to demonize the immigrant community and scapegoat them for the decline of the native population might have some opposition."

"Have you interviewed Pedro yet?" Axel asked the deputy. "He certainly seems to harbor animosity toward my father, and he probably is aware of many others who do as well."

"We have someone on their way to speak with him now," the deputy replied. "All I can say for now is that we have some valuable eyewitness accounts that have helped immensely. We have some leads."

"OK, well don't let me keep you from your work," Axel responded as he stood to escort the deputy to the door. "Please keep us informed of any developments."

Axel returned to the living room where he had left Elise on the sofa. "I don't even know what I should be doing. I feel like we are stuck here waiting for something that will never happen. My father is gone, and there is nothing that can bring him back. Closure is impossible, and there is no punishment severe enough. He was so excited for us and had so much to look forward to. He didn't need this job, but he cared about the town and the people."

He sat down next to Elise and broke down. The finality of all that had happened overwhelmed Axel. His father would never be there to share in his joys, celebrations, or successes. Anger and grief consumed him. Axel's father had worked so hard to bring the town together, only to be destroyed by it. Crystal Springs would never be the same.

10

A LEAD

Despite suffering from incredible grief over the loss of his father, Axel returned to work the next week. He had to keep his mind off of the tragedy and wanted to get as far away from Crystal Springs as possible. Unfortunately, the prominence of Henry's murder meant that many of Axel's coworkers had heard the news which made it difficult to put the experience out of his mind. It had been over a week without any word from the investigators regarding suspects or additional leads. Axel was beginning to expect that something or someone was preventing them from making an arrest. With all those people around, someone must know the identity of the perpetrator.

Axel tried desperately to focus on work and sought solace at home with Elise. She had been very supportive and was quite traumatized by the whole ordeal as well. That evening when they finished dinner, a report from Crystal Springs popped up on the evening news. Axel quickly unmuted the TV to see if it was about his father.

"Breaking news in the search for the killer of the mayor of Crystal Springs," the reporter began in a dramatic tone. "Investigators have identified a single male suspect who is believed to be the gunman. The suspect occasionally lived in the Crystal Springs area and was known to have worked on various farms in the region. It is believed by investigators that the suspect fled the area following the incident and could be trying to escape to Mexico. If anyone has additional information on the suspect's whereabouts, please contact the Fresno County Sheriff's Department."

Axel shook his head with frustration. "They purposely neglected to divulge any identifying characteristics for obvious reasons. How will anyone provide tips to the investigators without a clearer picture of the suspect?"

"While I agree that they were vague, I don't understand what you mean," a confused Elise replied. "Are you suggesting a cover-up?"

"Perhaps there is a more nefarious motive, but I was simply implying that it seems obvious that the suspect is a Hispanic male farmworker that probably was here illegally and now is fleeing to Mexico to evade arrest. Why not be more direct in the depiction of the suspect and provide some identifying characteristics? They go so far out of their way to avoid perpetuating stereotypes or fomenting hostility against illegal aliens that they obscure the truth and impede the pursuit of justice. It is despicable!"

"It certainly was a rather vague report," Elise agreed. "I would like to think they didn't deliberately mislead the public, but I see your point."

"I think I need to follow up with the investigator," Axel said in frustration. "The trail will grow cold if they don't act quickly." Axel dug through his wallet to find the business card of the investigator who visited his father's house after the murder. He dialed the number on his cell phone and awaited an answer.

"Fresno County Sheriff's Department," said the investigator at the other end of the line.

"Hello, this is Axel Berg. I am following up on the current investigation into the murder of my father. I just saw a rather vague news report. Do you have an identifiable suspect?"

"Good evening, Axel," the investigator replied. "I am rather limited in what I can disclose, but yes we have narrowed our search to a single suspect. We are pursuing all leads."

"Well if you cannot divulge any details about the suspect, then how do you expect to receive additional information that may lead to his arrest?" Axel replied angrily. "I expect justice to be served, and it seems to me that someone is trying to obscure the truth. You just broadcast on the nightly news that you have identified the suspect, so he clearly will be on the run now. Why not divulge his identity so that additional leads may emerge?"

"I understand your frustration," the investigator said. "I can assure you that we have all hands on deck and are actively pursuing the suspect."

It was clear to Axel that the investigator was being evasive. "This is a high profile case that demands justice. I expect regular updates going forward, or I will be forced to discuss my concerns with the media. We cannot allow what seems to be a politically motivated assassination to occur in the United States. There must be severe repercussions!"

"I appreciate the phone call and will keep you informed of any further developments," the investigator replied in an attempt to placate Axel. "Enjoy the rest of your evening."

Axel was furious. Perhaps he had been too withdrawn from the investigation and needed to get more involved. "That was fruitless," he said to Elise. "Do you think I should speak to the media to generate more focus on the case?"

"I have a friend who works at the Los Angeles Tribune," Elise said in an attempt to be helpful. "Perhaps you could discuss your concerns with her and see if she can uncover more details?"

"That is a great idea, babe," Axel replied enthusiastically. "Could you set that up?"

Elise texted her friend and immediately received a response. "She would love to speak with you. How is tomorrow morning?"

"Perfect," Axel replied. "Maybe now we will get some answers!"

Elise's friend called Axel right on time. "Good morning, Axel. This is Elise's friend Mary Ann from the Los Angles Tribune. She told me that you would like to discuss the murder of your father, is that correct?"

"Yes, it's nice to speak to you. I am frustrated by the media accounts on TV and the level of detail I am receiving from the Fresno County Sheriff's Department. By all accounts, they have identified the suspect and know who they are looking for. At the same time, they refuse to divulge any identifying information. It is almost as if they are covering for someone."

Mary Ann was listening intently. "Axel, before I called you I spoke to my colleague who has been covering the case. He has a very similar perception. The investigators and witnesses have generally stonewalled my colleague, but he has confirmed that the suspect is indeed a Hispanic male in his twenties. Let me work with him, and let's see if we can get additional information."

"Thank you," Axel responded. "I suggest you talk to Pedro Guerrero of the local farmworkers union. He all but blamed my father for his own death on the nightly news and seemed to have specific knowledge that he didn't divulge. Perhaps you can extract information from him."

"Great, I will call you later today with what we find," Mary Ann replied enthusiastically. "Can we count on an official comment from you for an upcoming article?"

"Sure, I look forward to your call," Axel said before hanging up.

It was rather late before he heard from Mary Ann. Axel had taken Elise to dinner and was getting ready for bed when the phone rang.

"Hi, Axel, this is Mary Ann. My colleague and I were able to dig up quite a bit of new information and will be publishing a story in tomorrow's paper. It appears that your suspicions were correct. The suspect is an illegal alien farmworker who has been twice deported. He was working for a large farm in the region when your father was elected, but he was fired about six months ago after your father put pressure on the Farm Bureau to hire American citizens. In the meantime, he was unable to find consistent work despite assistance from Pedro and union officials. He was known for getting violent when intoxicated, and was previously arrested for assault before his last deportation."

"Wow, it is all making sense," Axel exclaimed.

"There is more," Mary Ann continued. "Investigators have known about him for a week, but those in the immigrant community pressured the Sheriff's department to hold back certain information to prevent immigrants from being stigmatized. They were concerned that detailed media reports would foment anti-immigrant animosity."

"Of course, because that is of paramount importance," Axel responded sarcastically. "Justice for my father's murder is of secondary concern."

"While they were playing politics, they allowed him to flee the area and escape to Mexico," Mary Ann declared decisively. "Our contact at Customs and Border Patrol told us that they have him on camera crossing the border by foot into Tijuana at the San Ysidro Port of Entry last week. The most recent leaks to the TV reporters were made strictly to obscure the fact that they screwed up and let him escape. I know this is a lot to take in, but we would appreciate your official comment for inclusion in the article."

Axel was furious. His father was murdered by someone who should never have been in the United States, and now the perpetrator will escape justice entirely. He tried to compose himself before responding. "Mary Ann, you have done great work. I am deeply troubled by what you found, but I appreciate the work you and your colleague have done. I will give you my statement on the matter as you requested."

Axel paused, gathering his thoughts and reflecting on his response before continuing. "My father dedicated his life to Crystal Springs, literally and figuratively. He worked for decades teaching at Crystal Springs High School and could have retired in comfort. Instead, his love of the town and his neighbors inspired him to run for mayor to reverse many troubling trends that exist in Crystal Springs. Ever since I was a child, the town has steadily declined which caused suffering and despair among longtime residents. Their economic and emotional struggles can be directly linked to consolidation in the farm industry. These corporate farms prefer low-wage immigrant laborers that have displaced local workers from the fields. Additionally, the small businesses in Crystal Springs lost contracts to larger institutional suppliers. The town has been bifurcated with the wealthy industrial farms growing in power and stature while the exploited immigrant labor force survives on subsistence wages. What is left is a hollowed-out middle class comprised primarily of longtime residents of Crystal Springs who have been cast aside in their own community. In the end, you have a divided community with a decimated middle class and no hope for economic revival. My father sought to restore a sense of community and reinvigorate economic growth in Crystal Springs. His reward for that ambition was to be murdered by an illegal alien.

"Say what you may about the plight of illegal aliens and immigrant workers, but advocating for the rights of citizens should not be considered objectionable. Requesting that employers put American workers first should not be considered offensive. It should not be controversial to suggest that the wealthy should not be able to exploit immigrant workers to enrich themselves while decimating the middle class. All Americans should be able to stand by these principles in support of their community without fear of violence, intimidation, or assassination. Until there is justice for my father, the forgotten man and woman will rightly believe that opposition is futile and they have been permanently displaced in their own country."

"Wow," Mary Ann replied in recognition of the emotional depth of Axel's statement. "I feel like I have a much better understanding of the passion and sense of obligation that characterized your father's life. I appreciate you sharing that and will incorporate it into our piece. Thank you, Axel, for directing my attention to this case and offering your insights."

"Thank you for getting to the bottom of it," Axel replied. "I look forward to your article. Have a good night."

11

THE RECKONING

Axel arrived early to work the day after speaking to Mary Ann. He was reviewing the primary market activity and developing plans to address flows for the day when he received an email from Elise. The subject of the email simply said, "Read." The body of the email was empty, but there was a file attached. Axel opened the file and found a copy of Mary Ann's article in the Los Angeles Tribune entitled "Mayor's Murder Exposes Deep Divisions in Crystal Springs."

The article was quite well written. It began by describing the gruesome events at the Harvest Festival before offering a relatively flattering overview of Henry's life and his love of Crystal Springs. Then the article savaged the Fresno County Sheriff's Department for covering up key details of the investigation and for allowing the suspect to escape to Mexico. The article concluded with some of Axel's statements about his father's advocacy for the people of Crystal Springs. It read like a skillful amalgamation of a tragic story of economic decline in a small Central California town combined with a crime report and a flattering obituary. Axel felt some degree of relief and justice for his father. At least the article memorialized Henry for the good work he had done for the town and accurately depicted the struggles of the citizens of Crystal Springs.

It wasn't long before other people noticed the article as well. Many coworkers began to drop by to express their condolences, but others evinced pure hate through their piercing gaze. Axel must have struck a nerve with some of his coworkers due to his blunt advocacy for those Americans that had been left behind. In his current state of grief, he didn't care. People needed to come to grips with reality and stop obfuscating the truth. The complete mismanagement of the investigation and the carefully crafted narrative about the murder was an inexcusable attempt to distort reality for political gain. Those with wealth and power in Crystal Springs don't want anything threatening their pipeline of low wage immigrant laborers.

When Axel got home that day, Elise was already there. "What did you think about the article?" he asked. "I thought it seemed quite good."

Elise had a concerned look on her face and didn't echo Axel's enthusiasm. "Axel, some of what you said is rather controversial. Did you tell all of that to Mary Ann?"

"Of course," Axel said with surprise. "I gave her the facts and the truth. Someone needed to provide her with the history of Crystal Springs and the origins of the current divisions."

Elise frowned as she replied. "Many people will not look favorably on what you said. I know you and your father are passionate people who care about the people of Crystal Springs, but the optics of your statements are poor. They make you seem anti-immigrant."

"That is how people frame the debate to prevent dissent," Axel replied. "That is exactly the type of attitude that led the investigators to withhold identifying information enabling the killer to escape. I do not ascribe to that."

"Fair enough," Elise said with an exasperated tone, "but there may be blowback."

"My father was killed, murdered in cold blood, by an illegal immigrant. One must be willing to confront the truth to learn from it." Axel was tired of excuses and obfuscation. The facts were plain to see, but some people considered it taboo to speak them out loud.

The next morning, Axel arrived at work and began his daily routine. In many ways, his job was very repetitive. Some days there may be inflows and other days there were outflows, but regardless it was a very similar process. While he was reviewing the activity for the day and the announcements of new corporate bond issuance, a representative from the human resources department approached his desk.

"Axel, good morning," she began politely. "I am very sorry to hear about your loss."

"Thank you," Axel said politely while wondering what precipitated this unscheduled meeting.

"I was hoping that we could chat further regarding your recent experiences," she continued. "Do you have a moment now?"

"I was just going through a review of the morning activity, but I can join you briefly," Axel said in an attempt to be courteous. The morning was a critical time to get trades lined up for the day, and this was an undesirable interruption, but he felt that he should cooperate.

"Great, let's go grab a room in the HR department," she replied with a smile.

When they arrived, a man that Axel didn't recognize was waiting for them in the room. He greeted them upon arrival. "Welcome, Axel. Please sit down. I am the Director of Human Resources here at Schwaben. I just want to start by expressing our deepest condolences for your loss. It's truly a tragic situation."

"I appreciate that," Axel said in a perfunctory manner. He was not here to be placated and had no interest in empty platitudes.

"We realize that periods of grief can be very stressful and difficult," the Director continued. "The manner in which your father died must make it even more difficult."

"Yes, it's quite difficult to accept that your father was murdered," Axel responded defiantly. Axel was quickly growing tired of everyone's inability to speak directly.

"I can only imagine," the Director replied politely with stoic poise. "It is quite a tragedy."

The Director paused as if preparing to pivot. It was abundantly apparent to Axel that they were not there to discuss his grief or express sincere condolences for his loss. He wished they would get to the point and stop wasting everyone's time.

"Axel, you are aware of the firm's Diversity and Inclusion Policy, correct?" the Director asked.

"I believe so, why?" Axel responded. It was beginning to become clear that, as Elise expected, they are aggrieved by Axel's comments that were published in the article.

The Director elaborated. "The policy details our fundamental belief that all employees should be valued and respected. No one should be the target of harassment, discrimination, or denigration as a result of many protected factors including race, gender, national origin, or immigration status. It is Schwaben's policy to be a welcoming place for all employees where they are safe from hate and violence. Axel, we have become aware that you granted an official interview to a reporter regarding your father's death, is that correct?"

"Yes," Axel acknowledged curtly. It was clear this was becoming a bit of a witch hunt.

"Well, Axel, in addition to the Diversity and Inclusion Policy we have a Media Policy that strictly forbids media interviews that may reflect poorly on Schwaben. All media appearances are required to be pre-approved by our legal team to ensure they comply with the policy. That said, we have reviewed the article from the Los Angeles Tribune and have many concerns about the content."

"What would that be?" Axel interjected coyly. He was quite aware of their probable objections but honestly didn't care. "I provided the reporter with an accurate and detailed account. My information was critical in her discovery of the truth behind my father's murder."

"That may well be," the Director responded. He was growing a little impatient with Axel's implicit defiance. "However, the Media Policy strictly prohibits such contact with the press. Additionally, the content of your comments could be perceived as offensive or even racist by an objective observer."

"Racist!" Axel exclaimed indignantly. "That's a bit of a stretch don't you think? When did it become 'offensive' and 'racist' to discuss the impacts of illegal immigration on the citizens of the United States? When did immigrants become a protected class above and beyond average Americans?"

The Director ignored his questions as if they were rhetorical. "As stated, our Diversity and Inclusion policy prohibits discrimination and targeted harassment based on immigration status. Your statements to the press created a hostile work environment for our Hispanic employees and the immigrant community at large. Additionally, your public stature as a Portfolio Manager makes your statements deeply damaging to Schwaben's reputation. We cannot have clients perceiving your statements to be official viewpoints of the firm."

"Pardon me," Axel interjected, "but the article neither references my affiliation with Schwaben nor does it directly impugn any class of people."

"That is beside the point," the Director rebutted. "Your comments violated policy by expressing bias against immigrants. The executive committee, in conjunction with the Council on Diversity and Inclusion, has established a zero-tolerance policy for acts of bias or discrimination. As a result, the chairman has decided to terminate your employment here at Schwaben Summit Capital. It is with great sorrow that we must part ways, but the executive committee has authorized full payment of your retention bonus along with six months of pay in exchange for signing a non-disclosure agreement and waiving your rights to sue. You will be required to turn in your key card, and the contents of your desk will be mailed to you. We wish you luck in all your future endeavors."

"Right, ok then," Axel said in disgust as he stood up and tossed his key card on the conference room table. "Send the documents to me, and I will have my lawyer review them."

The woman who had brought Axel to the conference room escorted him to the elevator. She was obviously uncomfortable and didn't say a word. As Axel left the building, he reflected on what had just transpired. He had no regrets. It was bad enough to promote investment strategies that were contrary to his beliefs and undermined his principles, but it was even worse to think that he was expected to stand by quietly as investigators and powerful interests covered up his father's murder for the sake of political correctness. Axel had subjugated his values to sustain his lucrative position, but the emotional cost of being at odds with his principles on a daily basis had taken its toll. The death of his father, especially given the circumstances of the crime, had made it impossible to maintain his silence any longer.

When Elise got home that evening, she said nothing and just threw her arms around Axel. After what seemed like an endless embrace, she said, "I am so sorry, Axel."

"It's for the best," he replied. "They said the executive committee established a zero-tolerance policy. So basically they have become the speech and thought police."

"I never thought they would go that far," she continued. "I mean, I knew they wouldn't be pleased, but it seems like an overreaction."

"Well, it should have been obvious once Perennial took over and instituted the Council on Diversity and Inclusion that they were going to have an anti-White and anti-male bias," Axel said bluntly. "At that point it became inevitable. They were on a mission to eliminate anyone like me."

"Oh Axel," Elise said with a sigh. She felt he was being overly dramatic as usual, but she also could acknowledge some truth to his statements. Before Perennial, they would have rallied around Axel in his time of need. Now, he is a pariah and is further victimized by the politically correct mob. "Whatever you plan to do next, I will support you."

"I haven't given that much thought yet," Axel replied. "I do know, however, that going forward I am going to live a purposeful life true to my beliefs. I owe that much to my father and the forgotten men and women of Crystal Springs. I owe that to myself."

12

NEW BEGINNINGS

It was more than a week since Axel was fired, and he was feeling quite liberated. When Dominic was in charge, there was recognition for good performance and dignity in the proficient execution of responsibilities. Everyone collaborated for the benefit of their clients and the firm. Once Perennial took over, individual contributions seemed less important than compliance with the mandates of the Council on Diversity and Inclusion. Job performance was now evaluated in the context of the employee's diversity characteristics.

Working in such an environment took a toll on Axel's psyche and spirit. He struggled philosophically with the implementation of ESG and values-based investing directives that encouraged firms to introduce discriminatory diversity and inclusion policies. Once Perennial bought Schwaben, Axel was confronted by the same authoritarian policies that he helped to promote. Under the edicts of the CDI, alternative viewpoints were forbidden, and advancement depended on where you stood in the social hierarchy. It was a deliberate attempt to upend the existing social and economic structure of the company and, for that matter, of the United States.

Axel agreed to Schwaben's terms and had received a nice payout for his contributions. Now it was time to decide what would be next. He knew that his termination from Schwaben and the existence of the article about his father would very likely blacklist him from virtually all investment management companies. All large financial institutions, much like Perennial, had embraced social and governance policies that would assign a White heterosexual male citizen the lowest priority in hiring. Once Axel's publically expressed views on immigration are considered in combination with his poor ranking on the diversity index, he would immediately be eliminated from consideration.

After some introspection, Axel decided that it was important for his next role to be meaningful and personally fulfilling. He knew that it may take a while to identify that position, so Axel decided to spend a week in Crystal Springs. It was time to finally face the reality of his father's death and begin to organize his affairs. Elise offered to join him, but Axel knew that he needed to do this alone. It would be difficult for Axel to go through decades of accumulated possessions and all the memories associated with them, but he knew that it would be his last chance to remember his father and their life together.

When Axel arrived, the house stood ominously quiet. He entered the front door and looked around, reflecting on the symbolic importance of many of the items in the house. Axel walked slowly through the rooms both assessing the situation and contemplating the significance of the undertaking in front of him. While there was much to be done at the house, he also had to prepare for an afternoon meeting with the executor of his father's estate. He decided that he would make some cursory progress and then get some lunch on Main Street.

Axel barely scraped the surface before the doorbell rang that afternoon. He went to the door and saw a stocky man of average height standing on the porch in a suit.

When Axel opened the door, the man greeted him politely. "Good afternoon. Are you Axel?"

"That's me," Axel replied.

"Hello, Axel. My name is Roger Thompson, your father's lawyer. We spoke on the phone about your father's estate."

"Yes, please come in," Axel said gesturing with his hand toward the living room. Axel cleared off the sofa for Roger before sitting down in the chair across from him.

"Axel, I am very sorry for the loss of your father. He was an irreplaceable force in Crystal Springs, and I fear that the town will never be the same. We were friends for many years, and I will miss him greatly."

Axel smiled and nodded in recognition as Roger continued. "Henry was very organized with his affairs. He had a small life insurance policy that should cover any end of life expenses and leave a little remaining. Additionally, I have details on some investment and retirement accounts that he owned, which we can officially transfer to you. Henry left the house to you as well as all of the contents. He knew that you would be unlikely to return to Crystal Springs, so he asked me to refer you to a few trusted real estate agents when you are ready to sell. There are a few other assets such as his car and a safe deposit box at the bank. I would be happy to transfer ownership to you at your request."

"Thank you," Axel replied. "I would appreciate it if you could just line everything up for me to keep things simple. I can provide you with whatever information you need."

"Very well," Roger responded. "By the way, Axel, we all saw the article from the Los Angeles Tribune and were very proud of the way you handled things and obtained answers for us all. I also heard about the unfortunate reaction of your employer. Have you decided what you plan to do next?"

"I am still sorting that out," Axel replied, "but I appreciate the encouragement."

"Your father deserved justice and at least you exposed the truth regarding his death," Roger continued. "He would be proud of your tenacity. Speaking of that tenacious spirit, a good friend of mine, who was also a friend of your father, is running for Congress in Arizona. He is a philosophical kindred spirit of Henry and is well versed in the politics of Washington, DC. I am sure he could use some help with his campaign, and perhaps he could be a good ally in your search for future opportunities."

Axel paused reflecting on the suggestion. The last thing he had considered was getting into politics, but he did have free time on his hands and would possibly make some valuable connections.

"Perhaps you can make an introduction," Axel replied.

"Of course," Roger said. "It would be my pleasure. I think it would be a great opportunity. Dr. Pete Ambrosia is admired for his patriotic views in his district and beyond. I will tell him that we talked, and I will encourage him to reach out to you."

"Great," Axel said as he stood up and reached out to shake Roger's hand. "I appreciate the recommendation and everything you are doing to settle my father's estate."

"My pleasure," Roger said as he left. "We'll be in touch later to finalize the paperwork."

Over the next week, Axel worked diligently to sort through everything in his father's home. Some things had sentimental value, but primarily he was organizing items for donation or disposal. It was a tedious task to go through everything in detail and verify its importance. By the end of the week, he was physically and emotionally exhausted, but the house was quite well organized and prepared for sale. As Axel was packing the last few boxes into his car, his phone rang.

"Axel?" a man's voice inquired.

"Speaking," Axel responded.

"This is Dr. Pete Ambrosia. Roger called me and said you might be interested in working on my campaign."

"He gave you a glowing endorsement," Axel said, "so I agreed to explore it further with you."

"Great. Axel, I am in the area visiting my mother. How about we meet for lunch at the old diner in Crystal Springs to discuss the possibility? Does noon work for you?"

"Sure, I will see you then," Axel replied. Axel was planning to return to Los Angeles, but he decided that one last hurrah at the diner before leaving town might lead to new opportunities. He sat on the sofa after hanging up the phone and thought about all the years he had spent in this house. Axel enjoyed growing up in Crystal Springs, but the simplicity of a middle-class lifestyle in a small American town was no longer a reality. Everyone remaining in Crystal Springs, except for the few rich farmers, was now struggling just to get by. Unfettered immigration and decades of globalist policies had eviscerated the post-war idyllic middle-class way of life.

As Axel lamented the end of a simple wholesome lifestyle, he stood up and prepared to finally leave his childhood home. His memories of a simple family-focused American existence were fading by the day. In the era of globalism, such a lifestyle was becoming impossible. Axel surveyed the room to take a final mental photograph before locking the front door, perhaps for good. Now it was time for new beginnings and to make a difference for all the people left behind.

Axel arrived at the Crystal Springs Diner just before noon. A tall thin man with a gray mustache and a cowboy hat was standing out front awkwardly as if he was waiting for someone. As Axel approached, he instinctively asked, "Dr. Pete?"

The man responded in a gruff raspy voice. "Axel, it is nice to finally meet you. Let's grab some lunch. I am starving."

Axel followed him into the diner where they were seated by the hostess. "I will have the steak and eggs and a coffee," Dr. Pete immediately instructs the waitress.

"I will have the same," Axel responded to keep it easy. "Dr. Pete, have you been here before?"

"Yes, quite often. I grew up in Crystal Springs and went to school with Henry and Roger. After college, I lived in the suburbs of Phoenix and established a pediatrics practice. That practice enabled me to develop strong connections with many in the community. The community has always been supportive of me because they know that I am a compassionate person and I understand their struggles and frustrations. As I was handing off some of my patient responsibilities to younger physicians in our practice, I decided that I was ready to make a difference for the community by serving them in the U.S. Congress."

"Roger mentioned that you and my dad were 'kindred spirits' philosophically," Axel said. "How so?"

"Well, Axel, you could say that much of my district is very similar to Crystal Springs. It is less agrarian, but it has similar economic and demographic trends. We have a lot of blue-collar hard-working people that are just trying to do better for their family and help their kids succeed. For decades now we have seen the rich and powerful dramatically outpace the working man and woman. Politicians on both sides of the aisle refuse to acknowledge the factors that have caused this dichotomy because they have sold out to powerful business lobbies and special interest groups. They offer platitudes like 'tax breaks for the middle class' or 'increase taxes on millionaires and billionaires' as if that is a solution to greater inequity and reduced opportunity. Such sound bites work well at campaign rallies and on commercials, but they do nothing to address the root cause of the economic disparity. By failing to address the true issue, the problem has metastasized and will now require radical reform to restore the balance of power that once made America the greatest country in the world."

"So what do you propose are the root causes of the problem then?" Axel probed. So far all he had heard was typical political posturing.

"I am glad that you asked," Dr. Pete replied eagerly. "Your question demonstrates that you understand the difference between rhetoric and substance."

"There is no shortage of rhetoric out there," Axel interjected, "but those that talk the most are usually doing the least."

"I will agree with that," Dr. Pete said with a chuckle. "To answer your question, I think we need to consider the multiple dimensions of the problem. First, the rapid expansion of globalization has dramatically enhanced returns on capital while diminishing the returns on labor. Politicians in both parties have encouraged consolidation, growth, and international expansion based on arguments of improved efficiency and enhanced competitiveness. We have witnessed the emergence of corporate oligopolies that work in conjunction with political bodies and international organizations to secure their profits and expand their power. They lobby for regulations that squash competition and solidify their market position. Some companies, such as the large global commercial banks, have been allowed to dominate so many market functions that they have been deemed 'systemically important' intuitions and will never be allowed to fail. Once you have that degree of power and economic importance, you have immense political and social influence over public discourse and policy development. Do you think that any economic policy or regulation is crafted without first consulting these institutions?"

"Of course not," Axel replied.

"Exactly right," Dr. Pete continued. "So we have established that globalization has led to rapid industry consolidation and concentration of power. This is very similar to the dynamic your father spoke about in Crystal Springs with the consolidation of the farm industry. Once consolidation occurs and market power grows, what is almost always the next step in pursuit of even greater profits for capital?"

"Well, continuing your example, in Crystal Springs the farmers squeezed suppliers and sought to reduce the cost of labor," Axel replied.

"Correct," Dr. Pete agreed. "For decades now we have had politicians on both sides embrace a litany of arguments in support of both legal and illegal immigration. They have argued that we need more skilled workers, that we have a shortage of science and engineering grads, that immigrants fill jobs that Americans won't do, that we have an aging population, and that immigration is a net positive for the country. All of these arguments are nothing more than attempts to misdirect public attention from the true motivations for increased immigration. They don't want the public to know that immigration strictly benefits businesses to the detriment of American workers by suppressing wages and increasing competition for jobs. When American workers and graduates see coveted positions being offered to foreigners, they are justifiably angry with their elected leaders. When American workers are fired and forced to train their cheaper immigrant replacements, they should be furious. But in the end, politicians are always seeking to obscure the truth and deflect blame."

"Well they certainly have obfuscated on this issue for years," Axel concurred. "Many seem to be politically benefiting from expanding a compliant voter base, but how have they been so successful in convincing people that immigration is not to blame for stagnant wages?"

"A very good question," Dr. Pete replied. "On the left, the default response is to blame the rich, systemic racism, gender discrimination, and white privilege. They use the politics of division and tribalism to engender animosity toward others and silence opposition to their policies enabling unfettered immigration. The left promotes diversity as a virtue and attempts to attack anyone who opposes their policies by calling them racially biased or discriminatory. They actively seek to undermine the virtues of America and denigrate values that helped this nation achieve unprecedented success.

"On the right, politicians routinely cater to corporate interests and attempt to maintain the status quo. They resist attempts to reign in legal immigration which largely undermines white-collar jobs and college graduates. The right may rhetorically denounce illegal immigration as unlawful, but they never aggressively pursue legislative action to stop it. Whenever a critical vote on restricting immigration comes to the floor, there will always be enough conservatives to end its chances. You can be assured that the business community will convince many on the right that without an abundant immigrant workforce, their business wouldn't be able to survive. They always neglect to mention that their real concern is their inability to maintain current profitability if they had to pay market wages for labor. Thus, an endless pipeline of compliant low wage immigrant labor will always be ensured by the feckless right."

"That seems like an intractable dilemma," Axel observed. "If both sides are playing for the same team, then the outcome seems predetermined."

"Well there remains another confounding impediment to the restoration of the American Dream," Dr. Pete proclaimed. "Globalization has decimated our manufacturing base while compliant politicians have entangled us in one-sided trade agreements that undermine American prosperity. These politicians facilitated the offshoring of intellectual property and manufacturing capabilities which ultimately enriched other nations at the expense of the American middle class. The consolidation that occurred due to globalist policies has resulted in many companies that are nominally American but are frequently run by immigrants with no allegiance to the United States. Some explicitly embrace the interests and values of foreign countries to the detriment of the economic interests and civil liberties of American citizens. They masquerade as American companies while actively conspiring toward our demise. What they value more than anything else is unassailable market power, a servile and compliant workforce, and the ability to silence or muffle all dissent. They embrace policies that try to weaken the collective power of workers by using the same tribalization tactics as the left to demoralize their biggest threat – empowered and educated White American workers – while enflaming animosity within divided minority groups. These global multinational corporations are truly the most powerful barrier to American resurgence and widespread prosperity."

"I will acknowledge," Axel conceded, "that your analysis aligns with my perception of reality, but I cannot conceive of a viable solution to these problems."

"There is no silver bullet," Dr. Pete agreed. "Our current situation has been years in the making, and there will be no quick remedy. We must embolden people to resist at all levels, both overtly and subversively. Those that benefit from increased globalization and immigration vehemently hate us. Some even want us dead. The tragic murder of your father is evidence of their desperate and unwavering commitment to the fundamental transformation of America. They want to erase our history and the legacy of our forefathers to remake the country into a hierarchical authoritarian regime. At the top would be the corporate oligarchs and their political partners who would control a large servile working-class population. At the bottom would be a significant caste of untouchables that possess neither the intellectual abilities nor the social capacity to be of value in their new economic regime. Already, their revolutionary movement has so deeply infiltrated corporate and cultural institutions that their success seems all but inevitable. Our only chance to prevent the wholesale transformation and repopulation of America is to educate as many people as possible about their true intentions. We must infiltrate their corrupt institutions and subvert their ambitions. I am running for Congress so that I may help spread the word and inspire that movement."

"That certainly is a dire prognostication," Axel said with some skepticism. "I am not sure how I could help as I no longer have a job or influence."

"Ah, but you are discounting the inspirational power of your story," Dr. Pete replied. "Your father, desperate to restore unity and prosperity to an economically ravished town, was assassinated for attempting to put Americans first and reverse the tides of globalism. In recognition of the selfless sacrifice of his father, his only son leaves a lucrative position in investment management to pursue his father's dream."

"Quite dramatic," Axel replied while trying not to roll his eyes. He was never one for embellishment.

"Powerful," Dr. Pete replied. "You would certainly be able to garner a lot of attention and disseminate the message. I would love for you to join me on the campaign trail for a bit and give it a shot. If you decide that it is not for you or believe it isn't an effective message, then you can walk away at any time. However, if you are devoted to our cause and want to honor your father, I believe that you have a compelling backstory that will captivate many. Think about it, Axel. I don't need an answer immediately, but I will start campaigning vigorously in a few weeks and would love to have you as part of the team."

Axel contemplated the offer. There was much to consider, and he wouldn't be able to answer immediately. This would be a big change in direction and one that required careful deliberation. "I will give it some thought," he replied.

"Great," Dr. Pete said enthusiastically. "Axel, if you would allow an old man to give you some advice, I would suggest that life delivers unexpected opportunities often disguised by tragedy and difficulty. The difference between successful and unfulfilled people is often their ability to recognize and embrace the opportunities that life presents."

"A poignant observation," Axel said with a smile. "I appreciate the advice and will give your offer serious consideration. It was nice to meet you, Dr. Pete."

"And you, Axel," he replied. "Let's stay in touch."

13

AN HONORABLE LEGACY

Axel was excited to return to Los Angeles after his lunch with Dr. Pete Ambrosia. It had been a long week in Crystal Springs, and he missed Elise greatly. Through all the tragedy and turmoil, she had been a steadying force and a comforting partner. Axel had a lot on his mind following the lunch with Dr. Pete and was eager to discuss the opportunity with Elise.

When he arrived home, Elise had arranged a romantic welcome home dinner paired with a fine Bordeaux wine. It was a refreshing treat compared to what he had been eating the prior week in Crystal Springs. Once they sat down to dinner, Axel was eager to share the developments of the past week. "I had a very interesting lunch today with a congressional candidate from Arizona who grew up with my father."

"What a strange coincidence," Elise said as she sipped her wine. "How did that go?"

"He thinks I have a compelling personal story that would resonate favorably on the campaign trail," Axel replied. "I think he believes that I will bolster his candidacy while also establishing myself as a serious advocate for displaced and forgotten Americans. It could be an interesting opportunity to honor my father and advance his agenda."

"Well is that your agenda as well?" Elise asked. "I mean your father paid a significant price, and Crystal Springs seems to be worse off now than before his election."

Axel paused to consider her claim before responding. "I share my father's ambitions, but I agree with your point that the backlash against my father's agenda seems to have engendered an extreme overreaction and a further deterioration of the community. Crystal Springs, without a doubt, is worse off following my father's administration. One must ask, however, if the decline of Crystal Springs was inevitable and was simply accelerated by the backlash against my father's policies?"

"There certainly was a backlash," Elise responded with a sense of concern. "Henry incited vehement opposition in the immigrant community which ultimately led to his death!"

"Well do you think the appropriate response should have been to surrender Crystal Springs to the corporate farms and immigrant laborers?" Axel inquired assertively. "That is the path that the town was on before the election of my father. While his election incensed the opposition and incited reactions, I believe my father was the final barrier to their complete takeover of the town."

"So is resistance futile then?" Elise responded. "Why would you sacrifice your reputation on a hopeless crusade?"

"That is exactly the problem," Axel argued. "Conservatives try desperately to hold on to a shred of dignity as they retreat from battle after battle. By conceding ground, they have surrendered key strategic positions that now require a herculean effort to reclaim. In states like California, conservatives are nothing more than a clean-up crew searching for glimmers of hope amidst the wake of the destruction created by the left. At that point, you are nothing more than a guerilla force planning strategic attacks to weaken your enemy while waiting for an opening."

"Sounds pretty much like a lost cause to me," Elise retorted. "Why not blow with the winds of change and adapt to the new system?"

"The 'new system,' as you call it, has no room for people like me," Axel argued. "They believe that the White European settlers that founded America were fundamentally racist colonizers that grew rich by exploiting the native population and people of color. Their movement seeks to destroy the Historic American Nation and remake it as a nation of immigrants that openly discriminates against White people and traditional Americans. It is essentially the repopulation of America enabled by complicit White liberals and global multinational corporations with zero loyalty or affinity toward America. It is quite clear that failing to engage in this battle will ensure our destruction."

Elise laughed and said, "Axel, this is a new level of exaggeration even for you."

"That's what all the White people sympathetic to the globalist movement believe," Axel replied. "History is full of examples of what happens when people sell out their friends and neighbors in an attempt to curry favor with an oppressive and bigoted regime. White Americans will never be accepted in the new multicultural globalist regime and will only escape the fate of the condemned as long as they prove useful. I would rather go down fighting than bend a knee to the mob."

"Well it sounds like you have made your decision," Elise said with a smile. "I love your passion, but I worry about your safety. I have waited my entire life to find someone like you, and I don't want to lose you."

Axel sought to reassure Elise. "Don't worry. It's just a political campaign at this point. Let us hope that diplomacy and reason can avert a worst-case scenario."

"Indeed," Elise replied as she raised her glass. "Let me toast to your new adventure! May your crusade to preserve America be successful and without incident."

"Cheers," Axel replied.

***

Over the next few days, Axel had plenty of time to consider his discussion with Elise. He valued her opinion and felt like she had some compelling arguments against his involvement in Dr. Pete's campaign. He had to weigh the reputational ramifications of actively lobbying for America First policies against any future career ambitions. Some companies may excuse his cooperation with the Los Angeles Tribune for an article, but active public campaigning with Dr. Pete would make him a target for permanent cancelation. The left has pioneered intimidation tactics and social ostracism as tools to silence dissent and demoralize their opponents. It was much easier to appease the mob and acquiesce to their demands than to stand on principle and virtue.

Axel was raised to stand up for what he believed in. Some people could sell out for personal gain, but that was not in his nature. With that said, he knew that he needed to be strategic in his actions. Charging up a hill alone into the oncoming fire is not an act of honor on behalf of the cause but rather an exhibition of vainglorious ignorance. Martyrdom has never swayed public opinion and is quickly forgotten as historically insignificant. Axel knew that to have an impact, he must ally himself with other patriots that had clout and prominence while also developing a deep network of like-minded partners throughout industry and society. These would be his conditions for participation.

Axel decided to give Dr. Pete a call to discuss his thoughts. "Dr. Pete, this is Axel."

"Axel, good to hear from you," Dr. Pete responded. "I have been hoping you would call."

"I have given a lot of thought to your proposal and discussed it in detail with my fiancée," Axel replied. "I would like to discuss a few thoughts that I have before committing."

"Fire away," Dr. Pete said. "I am eager to hear your feedback."

"I am not interested in burning my reputation simply to be a flash in the pan," Axel stated emphatically. "If I am to participate, I need to be much more than just an opening speaker for you. I want to build a private network of supporters so that we can organize people in influential or powerful positions to actively undermine the existing orthodoxy. Over many decades, the left has sought to shift corporate and public policy to their advantage. We must counter the erosion of our culture and values while advocating for actionable policy goals that restore American greatness and arrest the trend toward multicultural globalism. For our America First movement to have a lasting impact, we must build an expansive network of dedicated activists who will once again make it acceptable to put yourself, your family, and your neighbor ahead of multinational corporations and economic opportunists that seek to displace Americans. It must be more than just one man on a crusade, and the cause must always come first."

"That is quite an ambitious agenda," Dr. Pete replied after listening patiently. "I am just one man, and my primary goal is to secure election to Congress. My campaign doesn't have the infrastructure to achieve what you have set forth, but if you are willing to coordinate those efforts, then I think it would be a very worthwhile endeavor. Building a network of committed supporters would enable us to have much more influence to pursue our policy agenda."

Axel contemplated the enormity of the task he proposed. It would be all-consuming and would require significant investment. He knew, however, that his father's death would be in vain and the future of the American people would be bleak unless someone stepped up to prevent the fundamental transformation of America. The death of his father stirred deeply held emotions that led him to discover a newfound determination to restore American greatness. He had made up his mind.

"I am in," Axel replied with enthusiasm. "I just need your commitment that the policies and priorities of the American First Network will be solely under my discretion. It will be separate from the campaign except that it will be used to motivate the base and inspire people to vote. Agreed?"

"Fair enough," Dr. Pete agreed. "It should be a symbiotic relationship that benefits us both. I have a campaign stop this weekend outside of Phoenix. Can you make it?"

"Just send me the details," Axel replied. "I will be there."

"It's time to take back the country," Dr. Pete said with conviction. "I will see you there."

Axel hung up the phone. He was excited about the opportunity in front of him. While he made significant amounts of money at Schwaben, he always felt like he was contributing to the subjugation of the American people and the ascendance of global interests and the transnational elite. Heterosexual White men, in particular, were the primary target for displacement. He could no longer tolerate playing a role in his own destruction. Now he felt inspired and full of purpose. There were no riches to be earned or glory to be secured, but there could be immense fulfillment if he was able to help restore American greatness and end the repopulation of America.

Axel knew that this first campaign event would be important to establish the credibility of his fledgling America First Network. He had been giving great thought to the bedrock American institutions and foundational legal principles that have slowly been eroded for years. The leftists and globalists have undermined the pillars of American society to weaken it and prepare for the fundamental transformation of America. They wanted to weaken communities and destroy the nuclear family so that people will be dependent on the government for support. Axel needed to be able to clearly define the stakes and create a sense of urgency to inspire action. It had become too easy to dismiss isolated events as small setbacks while failing to see how collectively they are destroying the country.

If there was one thing that Axel learned during his career in investment management, it was that everything people cherished in life was fleeting. Most financial assets were simply a claim on future cash flows. There was nothing intrinsically valuable or tangible about owning a stock or a bond. At best, bondholders could be assured of some recovery in the event of default by seizing and liquidating the assets of the firm. At worst, an equity investor or bondholder could be entirely wiped out. People who owned financial assets were invested in the continuity of an economic system, one that had been developed over centuries by politicians, industrialists, and financiers in the United States.

With very few exceptions, the American people believed in the permanence and stability of their political and economic system. It had survived a civil war, economic depressions, two world wars, and countless disasters. The founders had created an enduring constitution that proved prescient in its ability to maintain relevance over centuries of development and change. People believed that property rights, civil liberties, and the rule of law would support institutional stability and give credence to contracts and agreements. But over the past few decades, the permanence of this system has become seriously in doubt.

The rapid expansion of immigration combined with a lack of incentives to assimilate has increased tribalism and has fostered the rise of anti-American sentiment among its own residents. Some immigrants, including recently elected Congressional Representatives, openly slander the American people and assail the institutions that form the foundation of modern society. They overtly seek to upend the current system and replace it with one that favors immigrant and minority communities. Without a doubt, they pose a threat to the lives and security of all Americans who have worked hard and played by the rules. Axel knew that they must be stopped.

Most people were completely unaware of how fragile the current system had become. While working hard and taking care of their families, they go about their daily lives with their trust placed in their elected leaders to protect and secure the American political and economic system. Many Americans trust that their money is safe in the bank, their property will not be seized, and the value of the dollars in their wallet will be roughly the same day after day. All of this depends on the smooth functioning of the government and the economy. On the current trajectory, continuity of the economic and political system is increasingly in doubt. It would be up to Axel to convince them that the time for action is now. Axel believed that people were awakening to the new reality. He believed that it was time to change the world.

14

THE CAMPAIGN

Axel arrived in Phoenix on Friday night. He wanted to finalize his speech and mentally prepare for what was expected to be a large crowd. A lot was riding on this event, and he needed to deliver an effective and captivating speech to build momentum for his movement. He had settled on three key themes for his speech. First, he would establish the threat posed by decades of corporate consolidation, globalization, and virtually unlimited immigration. Next, he would discuss how multiculturalism without assimilation is an unstable and destructive environment. Finally, Axel planned to explain how current trends threatened everything that Americans held dear. If he was able to successfully put it all together, it would be an epic speech that would make his father proud.

He was scheduled to meet with Dr. Pete at noon on Saturday to discuss the schedule, review expectations, and make last-minute preparations. When he arrived at the venue, there were already people gathering outside. Axel knew that Dr. Pete was popular, but it was impressive that he had amassed a sizable crowd hours before the event. Most tired old politicians were lucky to draw two dozen people and even more fortunate if none of them fell asleep. Axel found Dr. Pete backstage chatting with some of his campaign staff. For a fleeting moment, it was eerily reminiscent of the horrific night at the Harvest Festival, but Axel snapped back to reality when Dr. Pete called out to him in excitement.

"Axel!" Dr. Pete exclaimed. "We have quite the crowd and are expecting even more. This is going to be a great event."

"I saw that on the way in," Axel replied. "There is nothing like a little pressure for my first speech."

"Oh Axel," Dr. Pete said with a chuckle, "they will eat up everything you have to say."

"What time do I go on?" Axel asked. He wanted to walk the stage and check the microphones to make sure that he was comfortable with all of the equipment.

"You still have two hours," Dr. Pete responded. "Are you ready to inspire the crowd?"

"My speech is ready," Axel replied with confidence. "The rest is up to God and the people."

"You are in good hands, Axel. Let me know if you need anything." Dr. Pete then shifted his attention to his staff to discuss final preparations for the event.

After getting comfortable with the room and the stage, Axel retreated to the speakers' lounge backstage to make final preparations. He had never spoken to such a large crowd and admittedly was a little nervous. Even so, the thought of all that his father had sacrificed in pursuit of an American resurgence was enough to inspire all the passion and confidence that Axel required. He was doing this for all of the forgotten men and women in Crystal Springs and around the country who have seen their American Dream outsourced, downsized, or shuttered completely. They would be without a voice no longer.

Dr. Pete's campaign event planner opened the speakers' lounge door and signaled a five-minute warning. It was time. Axel finally felt like he had realized his purpose. He hadn't set out to do this, but a confluence of events, some of which germinated decades before, brought Axel to this point. It was up to him to honor his father's dream and deliver for the people that built this great country.

The event planner was standing patiently backstage with a clipboard in her hand when she saw Axel approach. A loud country song, which served as the interlude between Axel and the recently completed introductory speaker, was booming from the speakers on the other side of the curtain. When Axel arrived at the staging area, the event planner turned to him and said, "You are up."

"Any last words of wisdom?" Axel asked as he straightened his tie.

"You've got this," she replied, "just speak slowly and remember to breathe."

Axel took two deep breaths as she opened the curtain to expose the path to the podium and the enthusiastic crowd. He smiled and waved to the crowd as he walked at a measured pace directly to the podium. Behind Axel was a large screen where a graphic was being displayed that read Axel Berg – America First Network. His name and reputation were now on the line. It was time to deliver.

"Good afternoon Arizona," Axel said with great enthusiasm and volume. He paused briefly as the crowd focused their attention before continuing. "My name is Axel Berg, and I am a lot like you. I grew up in a small Central California farm town where my family had lived for generations. My father was a teacher and my grandfather worked at an oil refinery and had a small farm. My parents and grandparents believed that family and community came first and that hard work was the path to success. Everyone in my town worked hard and took pride in their work. We once had a close-knit community that looked out for each other and supported local businesses. But that has all changed.

"Change came slowly at first. A small farmer, perhaps unable to continue to operate his farm in his old age, decides to sell. Another farmer, perhaps struggling financially, also decides to sell. Slowly but surely, consolidation concentrated the wealth and power of the town into the hands of a few. The deterioration of the town began to accelerate. The large industrial farms, no longer loyal to the town or the community, found it financially advantageous to contract with national suppliers and to hire low-cost immigrant workers. My hometown was no longer recognizable.

"When politicians encouraged globalization and industry consolidation on a massive scale almost fifty years ago, hardworking families across this country experienced the same suffering and disappointment as those in my hometown. The pain was initially felt through waves of corporate downsizing and layoffs when the combined companies tried to boost profits by cutting workers. As the trend continued, the powerful companies started to outsource production to low-cost countries further eroding the middle class. When additional outsourcing became uneconomical, these global multinational corporations, lusting for profit, forced American workers to train their low-cost immigrant replacements. Politicians, the majority of which are silent partners in the globalist cabal, expanded the many ways in which people could immigrate to the United States legally and turned a blind eye to the millions illegally crossing the southern border. All this time, hardworking Americans saw their hours cut, their wages stagnate, and their dreams crushed. They were now simply inputs in the globalist economic machine, easily replaced by compliant and desperate immigrant workers.

"While the once prideful middle-class workers saw opportunity and hope vanish, the global multinational corporations raked in record profits and saw their stock prices skyrocket. Emboldened by greed, these corporate masters sought to expand their market share and global presence. Their allegiance was no longer with the American people but to the global economy. The families, towns, and communities of the United States were casualties of their quest for global economic domination. In the perspective of the corporate executives, there were billions of compliant workers around the world that could be mobilized into service, so it didn't matter if the workers of Prescott, Yuma, or Flagstaff struggled to provide for their families. It didn't matter to these global corporations if the Americans who had lived here for generations, built this country, and protected it from foreign enemies were left languishing in despair as they were replaced by cheap immigrant labor or had their jobs outsourced to China. None of this matters to the globalists and multinational corporations because they are not American. They do not care about you or our country.

"For years, we have been told by our leaders that America is a melting pot where immigrants from around the world come together and thrive. The first Americans were settlers and pioneers that sought to escape tyranny and build a nation based on liberty and freedom. As the country grew, more people immigrated to the United States out of a desire to become Americans. The common bond that united everyone was a shared national identity and enduring principles that defined what it meant to be an American. Immigrants assimilated and were expected to pledge allegiance to the United States of America. We were one united nation that stood tall and proud.

"Globalization and open borders have changed all of that. Millions of foreigners are allowed to live and work indefinitely on temporary visas. Millions more are unlawfully present, working and hiding in the shadows. On top of that, we have admitted broad swaths of refugees who are not required to assimilate and seek to replace the culture and values of America with those of their homeland. In some major American cities, more than half of the population is foreign-born. They have no incentive to assimilate, no allegiance to America, and no vested interest in the history and sacrifice of the American people. Most are economic opportunists that came to America for jobs and higher wages. The American people are being displaced by the unlimited flow of foreign workers who do not value our history and do not love our country. They hire people from their homeland over Americans and send money to family abroad rather than building a future in America. They salute the flag of other nations, speak foreign languages, and are loyal to their native countries. Cultural genocide is upon us. The melting pot has become a powder keg!

"American Exceptionalism is being cannibalized from within. The exploitive forces of globalism and unlimited immigration are a virus that is ravaging our nation. You can stand by, helplessly incapacitated, while the American Dream disappears and our nation withers, or you can join me and resist the transnational elite's takeover of America. The fight will not be easy, and we have already ceded significant ground, but Americans don't surrender. My father stood up to these forces in my hometown and was murdered by a twice deported illegal immigrant who was angry that he lost his job. I continue my father's fight for the sake of my family, my community, and my fellow Americans. I am asking you to join me and the America First Network as we combat the forces of globalism and the immigrant invasion. Stand with me, and we will restore the American Dream. Fight with me, and America will be exceptional once again.

"Thank you, Arizona, and thank you to the great Dr. Pete Ambrosia who will fight for Arizona and for all Americans as your representative in Congress. Thank you."

Axel left the stage to roaring applause. He turned to wave once more to the crowd, and as he disappeared behind the curtain the crowd broke out in a deafening chant. "U.S.A., U.S.A., U.S.A," they proclaimed proudly in unison.

Dr. Pete was standing backstage making final preparations with his staff when he saw Axel emerge through the curtains. The chants of the crowd continued to bellow from the other room as Axel approached. "I knew your message would resonate, Axel. Great job."

"Thanks, Dr. Pete," Axel replied with a smile. "I hope I set them up nicely for you."

"You have stirred the enthusiasm and passion of the crowd," Dr. Pete responded. "Now we must focus that energy toward electoral victory and changes for the American people. Here we go."

Dr. Pete patted Axel twice on the shoulder, much like a football player who is fired up after a big play, before walking over to his event planner, who was patiently waiting in preparation for his grand entrance. On the cue of the event planner, the classic song God Bless the U.S.A. projected gloriously from the speakers inspiring the crowd to sing joyously in unison. She swept open the curtain, and Dr. Pete emerged to roaring applause. He waved to the crowd while beaming magnificently from the spotlights shining down from above. The crowd loved him. He represented their yearning for a better life at a time when hope seemed to be vanishing at a rapid pace.

As the song ended, Dr. Pete addressed the crowd. "I love you Arizona! Thank you. Thank you all for coming out tonight. How about Axel Berg and the America First Network? He is great, no?" Dr. Pete stepped back from the podium nodding his head yes and gesturing backstage.

"Let me tell you something before we get started here tonight," Dr. Pete said as if he was letting the crowd in on a secret. "Axel is the real deal. I knew his father since we were kids, and he was a great man. It was a real tragedy what happened to him, a tragedy that happens all too often. Axel is committed to helping us restore American Exceptionalism and secure opportunity for all Americans. But this mission of ours, I cannot do it alone. We need more loyal patriots to step forward and join us. It will take people of all kinds throughout industry, the public sector, and our communities to do what they can, either overtly or covertly. That's what the America First Network is all about. I hope you join us on our mission to restore American Exceptionalism."

As Dr. Pete continued, Axel listened from backstage. He thought that his speech had gone well, and the endorsement from Dr. Pete would go a long way to building support. Even so, a sense of concern beset Axel. If people clamored to join the movement, then he must be ready to constructively direct their enthusiasm. Axel needed to prepare to act quickly or their interest may wane. As he thought about the next steps, Axel decided a list of priorities and corresponding tasks was necessary to guide interested parties toward the most impactful activities.

After Dr. Pete's presentation, they gathered backstage to discuss the event. "Axel, your first speech went remarkably well," Dr. Pete said. "Would you like to join us at additional campaign events this week?"

"Absolutely," Axel replied.

"Great," Dr. Pete said approvingly. "Talk to my team to get the schedule. Be prepared to receive a lot of interest following this event."

"Preparing to mobilize supporters is my top priority," Axel agreed. "I will coordinate with your campaign staff on future events. Thanks again for the support."

"Absolutely," Dr. Pete replied. "We are going to achieve great things together."

Dr. Pete's campaign manager interrupted their conversation to discuss statistics on the potential voters who attended the rally, so Axel left the venue for his hotel. He was exhausted. Axel had a newfound optimism that change was possible, but he knew that the heavy lifting was still ahead. The globalists had wealth and power, and the immigration activists had armies of desperate agitators that could be activated at a moment's notice. Combined, they could be an insurmountable force, but Axel refused to be intimidated. It was time to fight!

15

THE DAWN OF A MOVEMENT

Offers of support began to pour in after Axel's speech. He had established a website to gather indications of interest in a manner that would maintain anonymity. After signing up, volunteers were prompted to take action and were guided to appropriate levels of involvement based on the level of obscurity that they wished to maintain. If no anonymity was desired, they were encouraged to actively campaign for Dr. Pete, organize America First events to recruit new members, and openly advocate for their views. At the other end of the spectrum, the website provided instructions for covert actions at places of employment and other venues where they could influence policy and shift the culture in favor of America First.

Axel worked all night to establish the pathways of involvement. He was exhausted, but the level of activity was promising. Every volunteer was encouraged to become engaged, and the website aggregated statistics on the pledges of support. To the outside world, it was all anonymous. Axel wanted the America First Network to maintain a low profile so that the opposition could not dox supporters or disrupt events. Only Axel would have access to the list of volunteers that would be housed in a secure database. It was up to him to grow support and keep people active.

As he continued to travel around Arizona with Dr. Pete, the America First Network grew in number and prominence. Axel started mingling with people at the events in order to engage with those that identified with his speech and wanted to learn more. At an event in Prescott, a middle-aged woman approached Axel and was eager to talk to him.

"Axel, my name is Katy Wilson, and I found your speech to be truly compelling."

"Thank you," Axel said with a smile. "Have you joined the America

First Network?"

"Not yet, but I intend to," she replied. "I have a group of women who are active in politics here in Prescott, and we would like to get more involved. What do you recommend?"

Axel contemplated the answer to her inquiry. The America First Network was conceived as primarily a subversive group that organized and directed individuals to action. He hadn't considered the possibility that groups of people would so openly want to support the cause. "Katy, I appreciate your enthusiasm. I would suggest that your group actively engage in activities that do not drastically impair your public image. Campaign for Dr. Pete, lobby your city council or local school board, and actively recruit for your group. To protect your members from scrutiny, you should advance the America First cause in a way that doesn't make you or any of your members seem like a social pariah. We want to keep this close to the vest so the opposition can't try to marginalize us."

"Doesn't that seem like a slow process with limited impact," Katy countered. She was eager to get involved.

"Let me offer you an anecdote," Axel suggested. "I had a high paying prestigious job at an investment management firm and was fired following my father's murder for daring to express relatively innocuous views about his killer's legal status in America. My reputation has now been tainted among the anti-American and anti-White social activists that control this country, so my prospects for employment at any large firm are virtually nonexistent. You and your members need to avoid a similar fate. Openly, you should appear as wholesome and productive members of your community. The truly ambitious could even try to act sympathetic to the left's causes in order to infiltrate their organizations, learn of their plans, and identify their tactics. It is best, however, to keep actions limited to individuals or very small groups to protect each other's anonymity. If one person gets burned for being America First, then they won't have exposed the entire network. Does that make sense?"

"That actually sounds pretty exciting," she replied. "Like our own spy network!"

"In a way," Axel responded. "Think of it more like a massive sleeper cell of patriotic Americans. We hide in plain sight. We are employees, neighbors, businessmen, and teachers. We go about our lives keeping our true thoughts to ourselves. You let people like me, Dr. Pete, and others advocate publicly for you while you quietly and nimbly exist in the shadows. Some day you may be activated to engage in direct action, but in the meantime, you keep a low profile and support the cause subversively. You raise your kids to be patriots, take care of your friends and neighbors, and build a strong community of support. The time for action will come, and we should all be prepared, but it is best to sit back and build our base of support for now. In the meantime, small subversive actions should be our immediate focus. Death by a thousand cuts."

"Seems like that would lead to a slow death," Katy correctly observed. "It might be hard for people to be patient when they are suffering so much and helplessly watching the nation crumble. My ladies fear for the future of their children. The American Dream is on life support and desperately needs resuscitation."

"I understand," Axel said in an affirming manner. "Our elected leaders and the powerful business interests have been slowly destroying the American Dream for so long that people are tired of losing. They are tired of empty promises and false hope. But burning all your credibility and relinquishing your power in a desperate uncoordinated action will have no lasting impact. It will be a flash in the pan that is soon forgotten."

"No one wants to be a martyr," Katy agreed, "but guerrilla warfare inevitably seems to result in a stalemate at best, don't you think?"

"Our immediate goal should be to weaken their grip on power and divide and frustrate their base of support," Axel argued. "This is what they have done to us for years. They divided the nation into factions that individually have no clout and collectively can be subjugated under their control. Conservatives, especially, have a diverse set of priorities, and their elected representatives offer platitudes to assuage their concerns while working against their interests behind closed doors. We can no longer trust any politician who doesn't demonstrate an unwavering commitment to America First priorities through both words and actions. We must unite under a unified America First banner and focus exclusively on the restoration of the Historic American Nation. To do this, we must weaken the globalists' grip on power through subversive action and by expanding our network of America First patriots. When they are sufficiently weakened and we have a critical mass of supporters, then we can take more direct action to restore American Exceptionalism."

While supportive in principle, Katy still seemed to harbor some reservations. It was obvious that she had hoped for immediate and dramatic action. Axel offered one final argument for restraint.

"The left has slowly diluted and chipped away at the Historic American Nation for over fifty years. America's cultural roots have been disrupted by a transformative influx of immigrants that want to fundamentally alter America. They have no desire to assimilate. Instead, they want to remake America in the image of their native land. Social cohesion and shared values have been corrupted by alien viewpoints that are at odds with America's founding principles. The immigrant masses predominantly despise our history and give no reverence to the incalculable blood, sweat, and sacrifice that built this nation. But these changes did not occur overnight. The decay of American Exceptionalism has occurred gradually over many decades and will only be reversed in a similar timeframe. Our immediate goal must be to prevent the repopulation of America by immigrant invaders and to build a coalition of patriots to restore American greatness. We must reverse the tide before we can advance to victory."

"My ladies and I are with you, Axel," Katy replied with a smile. "We are ready to do whatever we can to help."

"Great," Axel said. "For now, expand your group and increase your influence locally. Support Dr. Pete and avoid anything that draws negative attention to you or your organization. Resist any attempt by the left to implement anti-American policies locally, and be sure to raise your families to respect American values. The time will come for more significant action, so prepare yourselves and your families. We will never bend the knee. We will never surrender."

"God bless you, Axel," Katy said as she gave him a big hug. Years of despair and frustration suddenly surrendered to hope once again. The future was still uncertain, but hope is a powerful force.

Axel had numerous conversations with passionate Americans like Katy at each campaign stop. Dr. Pete had a rabidly loyal group of supporters that recognized his passion and commitment to restoring opportunity and the American Dream. The election was fast approaching and the schedule was heavy, but Axel was having a great time meeting like-minded people across Arizona. Word was spreading rapidly and interest in the America First Network was growing around the country.

Their next stop was Lake Havasu City which is situated on the Colorado River and the border of California. Axel often went there with his father to go fishing and boating on the lake, and he was quite familiar with the town and its people. Dr. Pete was expecting a big crowd that would include not just locals but many Californians that were visiting and wanted to hear them speak. It was a highly anticipated campaign stop, and Axel was excited to return.

On the day of the event, Dr. Pete seemed a little frazzled. Typically he was calm and joyful, but something seemed to be bothering him. Axel saw his event organizer backstage and went to investigate. "Is everything alright with Dr. Pete?" he asked.

She seemed to be bravely hiding some concern when she responded. "Yes, Axel, everything is OK. There have been some rumors about out-of-state agitators attending the event tonight, so additional security has been hired, and the local police are on alert. It's probably nothing, but you never can be too safe."

"Absolutely," Axel replied. "Thanks for letting me know. I will keep my eyes open."

"I know you like to wander the crowds and mingle," she said. "Let me give you a radio tonight in case you need assistance or see anything suspicious."

"I appreciate that," Axel said. He wasn't too concerned, but it was good to be alert and prepared. No one expected his father to be murdered by an illegal alien at the Harvest Festival either.

Later that evening, Axel's speech went off without a hitch. The crowd was boisterous and energetic as he described how they would never stop until they restored American Exceptionalism. As Dr. Pete was preparing to take the stage, Axel secured a radio from the event organizer and set off into the crowd. Almost immediately, a heavyset man and his wife began calling out to Axel.

As Axel approached, the man said, "Axel, we came all the way from Fresno to hear you speak."

"Well thank you," Axel responded. "What did you think?"

"You are an inspiration to us all," the man replied. "I am a truck driver, and I cover the Western United States. The word is out, man. You are famous!"

"Is that so?" Axel replied with humble modesty. "I am glad to hear the word is spreading."

"It sure is," the man responded. "I tell everyone I know. The American people are rising up, my man. People like you and Dr. Pete will lead us to greatness once again."

Axel thanked the trucker and was about to continue mingling when there was some commotion on the other side of the room. A woman screamed as two men knocked her to the floor and climbed on the stage. Dr. Pete was speaking at the podium and turned toward the disruption without any sense of alarm. Axel went for his radio, but before he could speak three muscular men from the security team tackled the protesters to the ground with extreme force. The crowd cheered loudly and started chanting.

"America First. America First. America First..."

After they subdued the protesters and were preparing to remove them from the venue, Dr. Pete calmly returned his focus to the crowd and addressed them with conviction. "Many misguided souls seek to divide our country, displace our people, and debase our values. We will not back down to anyone!"

The crowd erupted in applause louder than at any other event. Axel stood with the people watching Dr. Pete in action. "We will not surrender our nation to the globalists and outsiders that despise our country, our people, and our history!"

Following another round of enthusiastic applause, Dr. Pete continued. "America is our legacy. It is our birthright. It is our destiny!" He paused as the applause amplified into a raucous roar. "Success is inevitable. America First is our destiny!"

Dr. Pete stood at the podium looking to the sky with both arms raised to the heavens. The crowd was deafening as Axel stood proudly in amazement. He turned to see the burly truck driver yelling proudly with a tear rolling down his face. These people, the forgotten men and women, had been ignored and taken for granted for years. Axel knew they would be silent no more. The American people were rising and would not be stopped.

16

ELECTION DAY

Dr. Pete Ambrosia never lost a beat following the Lake Havasu event. He continued on a grueling campaign schedule, unfazed and stronger than ever. Axel was impressed that someone twice his age had the stamina and determination to keep pushing forward. His grit and perseverance endeared Dr. Pete to his loyal supporters. They saw in him their champion who resolutely embraced their cause and would never stop fighting for them. Never before had someone so completely put the interests of average Americans ahead of all others, and they loved him for it.

After a strong closing push, both Axel and Dr. Pete's campaign team were relieved it was Election Day. They had left it all on the field and now it was in the hands of the voters. The campaign had established their Election Day headquarters outside of Phoenix where they would make last-minute calls and try to get out the vote. Axel volunteered to help and hoped that his appearance on the campaign trail would lend more credibility to his pleas for support. Polling was limited, and the race was expected to be close. The future of the movement would depend on having a stalwart like Dr. Pete in Congress, so every vote was important.

This was a general election, so Dr. Pete's congressional race wasn't the only contest that mattered. A new President would also be elected this year, and the candidates were bitterly fighting to the end. The conservatives had nominated an Indian American woman from the South named Nagila Rao. Her parents had immigrated to the United States where her father was a professor at a prominent university, and her mother was an engineer at a global technology company. While she often spoke of her struggles growing up in the South as an Indian American, she actually lived a life of privilege compared to most. She grew up in a wealthy neighborhood and attended private schools before going to an Ivy League university to study law.

Nagila's leftist opponent was a decrepit White man from Delaware who seemed completely detached from reality, not to mention from voters. Jim Banks had been a U.S. Senator for over forty years and often sounded like he was still living in a prior decade. He seemed better suited for a retirement home than the White House, but the polarization of America made it quite a race. Voters undoubtedly were voting more for the party than for the candidate, as Jim was unquestionably not up to the job.

The presidential race shouldn't be close, but a history of false prophets on the conservative side of the aisle left many apprehensive about Nagila's commitment to their values. There were many instances in her past where she disparaged average Americans. She often questioned Americans' ethics and was patronizing in her accounts of their behavior. Contrary to her self-portrayal as a disadvantaged child of immigrant parents, her family was wealthy and privileged as a member of India's Brahmin elite. She carried those attitudes with her and was frequently condescending.

Axel could not in good conscience support either candidate. He vowed to always put the American people first, and neither of the presidential candidates would even remotely do that. The next four years were going to be a battle for the soul of the nation, and Dr. Pete was needed on the front lines to defend what was left of the country. With the polls closing soon, the phone bank began to wind down in preparation for the release of the election results.

When he finished his final call, Axel headed to his hotel room to change for the festivities. As he entered the room, the distinct aroma of a familiar fragrance brought him great comfort. Elise had come to join him for the much-anticipated victory celebration and was already dressed in an elegant black dress and heels. Axel was ecstatic. He had been traveling around Arizona tirelessly and had barely seen her for the past few months. Finally, he could take a break and reconnect with his fiancée.

As they entered the elevator to go down to the ballroom, Elise turned and said, "I am so proud of you Axel."

"For what?" he asked.

"You have embraced what your father started and achieved great success," she replied. "Axel you started a movement that has the power to reshape the country and make a profound difference for the people."

He had been so busy, he seldom thought about what he had achieved. Every day seemed to include a new campaign stop or an event where he was recruiting new volunteers. He had yet to reflect upon the magnitude of the success that he had achieved.

"I love you, babe," he replied. "I really appreciate you joining me here for the election night festivities."

"Are you kidding me?" she asked with a smile. "I am ready to party!"

The ballroom was already packed when they arrived. Axel mingled and introduced all of the campaign staff to Elise. He wasn't generally the most forthcoming with details about his personal life, so it came as a surprise to many that he was engaged. She had a genuine warmth and social grace that made it easy for her to flourish in this type of environment. After about an hour, they were interrupted by the early results. With only ten percent of the precincts reporting, Dr. Pete's congressional race was too close to call. Even more notable, however, was that Nagila Rao had the early lead in Electoral College delegates. Axel thought for sure that the senile old man would prevail over the elitist conservative. There were still many states to report, but she was performing quite well in those that had already reported.

Axel saw Dr. Pete speaking with his campaign manager and wanted to introduce him to Elise. As they approached, Dr. Pete beckoned to Axel as if he had something important to tell him. He put his arm around Axel's shoulders before speaking directly to Elise. "This man has accomplished great things. I couldn't have been this successful without him."

Elise beamed with pride as she replied, "I couldn't agree more."

Axel turned to Dr. Pete to acknowledge his compliment. "Dr. Pete, you exaggerate. It has been my honor to have been a part of this campaign. By the way, I want to introduce you to my fiancée Elise."

"It's so nice to meet you, Elise," he replied with a smile. "Axel is generally all business so I am glad you could join us and lighten him up a bit."

"I will do my best," she replied enthusiastically. "Hopefully we will have a great victory to celebrate."

"It is looking good according to my staff," Dr. Pete said confidently. "If the final votes come through in our favor, then the real work will still be ahead. So be sure to enjoy yourself tonight. This may be the final hurrah before the real battles begin."

"We will," Elise replied as Dr. Pete stepped away. She grabbed Axel by the arm and said, "Let's go get a drink."

As they headed to the bar, an additional update was broadcast to the crowd. With forty percent of the precincts reporting, Dr. Pete was ahead by five percent. Cheers erupted in the room, but the reporter announced that it was still too soon to call the race. It had been almost three hours since the polls closed, and anticipation was growing. The supporters in the room were impatiently waiting for what seemed to be Dr. Pete's inevitable victory. The room was buzzing with energy and tension.

Axel and Elise were chatting and enjoying their drink when Dr. Pete's event organizer began bustling around frantically on stage. The room gradually grew quiet as everyone anticipated a forthcoming announcement.

Meanwhile, some of the media in the back of the ballroom appeared to be preparing their equipment and focusing their cameras on the stage. Five minutes later, all of the lights in the room dimmed except for those highlighting the podium and stage. A live feed from the local news was televised on the two large monitors at either end of the stage. Suddenly, the audio from the broadcast was turned on just as the reporter began delivering the results.

"We have an official announcement to make in the highly contested congressional race in Western Arizona," the reporter announced. "The controversial conservative candidate Dr. Pete Ambrosia has defeated his opponent to become the newest Representative from the State of Arizona. We are about to go live momentarily to hear his victory speech."

The room erupted with cheers. All of Dr. Pete's supporters had desperately fought for his election. Now that it was official, a great wave of relief comforted everyone in the room. The campaign team had expected this outcome, but the patriotic Americans supporting Dr. Pete were accustomed to disappointment. Finally, they had someone truly representing their interests heading to Washington, D.C.

As the cheers began to subside, Dr. Pete walked on stage eliciting even greater applause. He stood boldly at the podium with a giant campaign sign directly behind him announcing his presence to the world. As the media started to broadcast, Dr. Pete addressed the room and the viewers.

"Good evening Arizona! Thank you to all the patriotic Arizonans who enthusiastically elected me to restore American greatness. Your confidence in my leadership is on display for all to see, and I will not disappoint you. I have traveled far and wide speaking to the American people, and they have made their voices loud and clear. You yearn for a return to American Exceptionalism. You long for the days when the American Dream was for every American citizen, not just the wealthy or the connected. You miss the days when American values meant something and when people took pride in their nation and community. Together, we will restore prosperity and opportunity for all Americans and end the degradation of our great nation.

"America is at a crossroads. We can once again put the American people first and build a prosperous nation for all, or we can stand idly by as the globalists and corporate elite plunder the nation and replace the population with compliant immigrants. America is your birthright. America is our legacy. We must put America First once again! The fight has just begun. Thank you, Arizona, and God bless America."

The crowd cheered triumphantly as balloons and confetti rained down from the ceiling. When Dr. Pete left the stage after his victory speech, Elise turned and embraced Axel in a congratulatory hug. While looking at him lovingly, she marveled at the unexpected path that had brought them here.

The tragic death of Axel's father ultimately led to an interview with a reporter that precipitated Axel's termination from Schwaben. Now her fiancée was leading a movement that helped to elect a congressman and was influencing national political discourse. What possibly could come next?

Still locked in an embrace, Elise said, "How about we continue this celebration upstairs, Axel?"

Axel looked at her and smiled. She didn't have to say another word.

***

Axel awoke the next morning with a sense that the world had changed. As he lay in bed next to his beautiful fiancée, he was inspired by the dramatic victory that they had achieved the night before. While this was just one congressional race, Dr. Pete had won in a landslide and demonstrated that principled leaders could restore hope and unity among the American people. Axel had feared that too many people were complacent and wouldn't come to the polls because they failed to grasp the stakes confronting the nation. Dr. Pete's victory gave him a reason to believe that the American people had awakened from their stupor and would rise to fight for their nation.

Elise sensed Axel stirring next to her. She turned to him, still groggy from the night before. "Good morning, babe. I am hungry. Do you want to get some breakfast?"

"Absolutely," Axel replied. "Would you like to go to the restaurant in the lobby?"

"That sounds great," Elise concurred. "Let me freshen up and then we can go."

When they arrived at the hotel restaurant, it was bustling with activity. Most of the patrons were focused on the televisions located around the restaurant that were still covering the election results. Elise and Axel were seated in a comfortable semi-circle booth on the periphery of the room. Once they were settled, Axel couldn't help but look at the nearest TV. When they left the party last night, the presidential race was yet to be determined. Axel wondered if Nagila Rao had held on to her early lead, but when he looked up he couldn't believe his eyes. She had won in relatively convincing fashion and was scheduled to address the nation at any moment.

Axel turned to Elise and gestured to the TV. "Can you believe this? I know the old man was senile, but I never expected such a strong victory."

"Wow," she replied. "I didn't expect that either, but she must have some crossover appeal to be able to win so decisively."

As they waited for their breakfast to arrive, the news network cut away from their anchor's coverage to go live for the President-elect's speech. "Good morning fellow Americans. I am humbled and honored by the faith you have placed in me as the first Indian American President of the United States. As a child of immigrants who came to this country with nothing, I have lived the American Dream and am truly blessed to be born in such a land of opportunity. I am living proof that, in America, anyone can reach great heights through hard work and determination.

"Under my administration, all people will be valued and appreciated in American society. We will lift up those who have fallen, and provide a helping hand to those in need. We will stand with everyone that seeks a better life and a better future for their families. We will strengthen our ties with foreign leaders and expand our trade agreements to bring more nations into the global economic community. Given an equal playing field, our companies and workers can compete with anyone in the world.

"As part of my growth agenda, I will be proposing major investments in infrastructure and technology to ensure that the United States remains on the cutting edge of the modern digital economy. Our technology companies are global leaders and will be critical partners in our quest for a diverse and prosperous America. We will invest in the technology of the future and improve access to broadband in poor and minority communities.

"My administration will cherish the diversity of the American people and will support the pursuit of freedom and liberty around the world. We will fight to end hate and discrimination both at home and abroad. We will be a shining city on a hill that welcomes all to pursue their dreams. Together, we can achieve great things, we can reach new heights, and we can ensure that America remains the land of opportunity. America will reinvent itself once again as we lead the world forward to a prosperous and inclusive future. Thank you, America. God bless you, and God bless the United States."

Axel and Elise silently fixated on the television for the entire speech. When it ended, they just looked at each other. Elise raised her eyebrows without saying a word. She knew what Axel was thinking before he even said it.

"How the hell did she ever get elected?" he asked emphatically. "She subtly undermined everything that is America. She more or less embraced open borders, tech oligarchy, and identity politics. I thought she was supposed to be the conservative candidate!"

Elise could tell that Axel was angry. He had worked so hard to get Dr. Pete elected and to build the America First Network. Now the President-elect proposed a platform that is diametrically opposed to his objectives. She knew he was disappointed. "Sorry, Axel. At least Dr. Pete will be in Congress to continue the fight."

"Without a doubt, the fight will continue," Axel replied. "We will not stand by while she seeks to replace Americans and put corporate and foreign interests first. They may want to marginalize Americans, erase our history, and replace our values and traditions, but I, for one, will not roll over without a fight. America first is our destiny, and we will not yield."

17

A NEW AMERICA

The election was bittersweet for Axel. Dr. Pete's victory had been invigorating and inspired overwhelming hope and optimism for the future. Axel felt like their message had resonated with voters, and the results affirmed their policy prescriptions. On a national level, however, Nagila Rao's victory suggested a thorough embrace of globalization and open borders was imminent. It was quite demoralizing to think that a conservative President seemed likely to implement policies that would accelerate the decline of the middle class.

After the grueling schedule that he and Dr. Pete had maintained, Axel decided to spend some time in Los Angeles with Elise and reformulate his strategy for the America First Network. More and more patriotic Americans were signing up every day as the word spread. Axel was convinced that anonymity was essential in the midst of widespread cancel culture and outright political violence. Except for a select few that were powerful or wealthy enough to survive public exposure as an America First patriot, the network needed to pursue subtle persuasion and subversive actions to protect its members. They would need to promote nationalist principles from within every organization and institution in America to win the hearts and minds of the people. The globalist machine had the upper hand, and it was time to begin eroding that advantage from within.

As Axel reflected on the battles ahead, it became frighteningly clear that they faced a hydra of immense scope and power. The globalists and leftists had created a formidable administrative state which used regulations to protect favored businesses and erect barriers to entry that limited competition. Activists, often funded by the corporate oligarchs, would leverage a compliant court system to extend the reach of the regulations.

Industries that are out of favor or companies that don't comply with the social or environmental agenda of the activists would be targeted for annihilation.

The administrative state was keen to favor certain companies, genders, races, or other interest groups that are deemed to be disadvantaged by social justice warriors. Similar to the extortion rackets of the past, many companies viewed compliance with the whims of the woke mob as a cost of doing business. Layers upon layers of regulations slowed economic growth and concentrated power and wealth among the corporate aristocracy. Just like a mob boss that hands out bribes and kickbacks to grease the wheels, corporations showered politicians, lobbyists, and think tanks with abundant financial support to protect their profits and ensure that globalist propaganda is disseminated.

The transnational elite and corporate oligarchs sought to secure permanent control by importing armies of legal and illegal workers that would compliantly serve their employers. Most could be relied upon to perpetuate the globalist system that helped them escape their home countries and achieve protected status in a multicultural America. If the corporations didn't support mass immigration with jobs and visas, the economic opportunism fueling the invasion would wane and many would return home. Instead of instituting policies that favored American workers, the government lavished impoverished communities with an endless array of welfare and government subsidies that did little to mitigate poverty. As a result, poverty-stricken Americans became economically dependent on the State while immigrants became vassals of their employers.

It wasn't going to be easy for the forgotten men and women of America to disrupt this system of patronage and bureaucratic malfeasance. There were supporters on the left who embraced unfettered immigration and were enamored with the social and environmental policies they could achieve with unlimited administrative power. Conversely, there were supporters on the right that embraced a dogma of free-market capitalism and were willing to accept the regulatory barriers that protect and enrich entrenched interests. With globalists on both sides of the aisle, Axel decided that a political solution was unlikely to prevail. Even if conservatives could achieve complete control of the legislature and the Presidency, the power of the administrative state and the courts would be impossible to overcome. There may be small victories here and there, but they would be symbolic and would do little to stop the momentum of the open borders globalist machine. Every day that the percentage of foreign-born residents of the United States grew, the hope for resurrecting the Historic American Nation diminished. It was time to mobilize the silent and disillusioned masses before it was too late.

Axel concluded that, for now, subversion was the most effective response. He needed a silent army to undermine the actions of the globalists at every turn. Axel realized that this battle would not be won overnight. There would be no glorious battle where patriot heroes would achieve immortal fame for their decisive victory. They needed to inspire the self-interest of the millions of Americans that saw opportunity and prosperity slowly fading away.

President Nagila Rao had just taken power as Axel was finalizing his plans for the America First Network. She moved quickly to leverage the administrative state to enact her agenda. Work visas such as H-1B and H-2A, ostensibly temporary in nature but often permanent in reality, were dramatically expanded to open the floodgates for multinational corporations. Both Immigration and Customs Enforcement and the Border Patrol were ordered to intervene only if drug smuggling or criminality was suspected. The Department of Justice was instructed to expand the use of hate crime legislation to enhance penalties for crimes committed against immigrants or people of color by White Americans. Concurrently, the Department of Labor drafted new regulations that mandated gender and ethnic diversity at companies throughout the country. These regulations compel employers to favor immigrants, people of color, and LGBTQ applicants. Perhaps most appallingly, the Department of Education insisted that critical race theory be taught in all schools that receive federal funding. President Rao enthusiastically embraced the concept that race is a social construct that White Americans had used for generations to disadvantage immigrants and people of color. Under her administration, there would be restorative justice to address the centuries of White hegemony in the United States.

"We are living in a new multicultural America where race, gender, and immigration status will not be determinants of your success," she declared.

President Rao received little pushback from the legislature in response to her radical policies. Most politicians were either secretly or overtly in favor of her actions while the rest realized that resistance to the bureaucratic state was futile. A few lone voices were brave enough to speak against these racist and anti-American policies; among them was Congressman Pete Ambrosia.

"The President hates White Americans," Congressman Ambrosia said in a speech on the House Floor. "She expects White Americans to performativity denounce their race, their heritage, and their culture in an act of submission to a new order. She wants to demoralize patriotic Americans and destroy their sense of national identity. President Rao demands that you disavow your friends, neighbors, and family for being proud of their heritage and supportive of their community. Once you have thoroughly vilified your race and acknowledged the moral superiority of the multicultural mob, you may be accepted as a collaborator but you will never be their equal. You will forever be White vermin that must be exterminated."

The Speaker of the House banged her gavel demonstrably in protest of the Congressman's speech. "The House will be in order," she stated authoritatively. "Sir, you are in clear violation of House rules of decorum and debate. I order the previous remarks stricken."

"The only one lacking decorum, Madam Speaker, is President Rao," Congressman Ambrosia retorted. "Her racist policies seek to emasculate White Americans and consign them as vassals of the State. In her new multicultural America, White citizens must be eradicated to pave the way for the ascendency of others."

"Sir, you are out of order," the Speaker proclaimed with great frustration while continuing to bang the gavel.

Congressman Ambrosia continued. "I will not bend a knee to you or the racist mob. I will not be silenced. I will always stand for the people. You will not replace us!"

"Enough," the Speaker shouted. "Sir you are out of order, and we will stand in recess until tomorrow."

With that, she banged the gavel one last time and left the House Floor. Congressman Ambrosia, satisfied that his point had been made, gathered his belongings and headed to his office. As he left the House Floor, he was mobbed by reporters seeking comment on his speech.

"Congressman Ambrosia, what motivated your racist rant?" a reporter shouted.

"Congressman, are you a White supremacist?" another inquired.

"Sir, why do you hate immigrants?" someone shouted from the outskirts of the crowd of reporters.

"I have hate in my heart for no one," Congressman Ambrosia replied. "Contrary to the multicultural mob, I will not demand that anyone denounce their heritage. I do expect, however, that everyone who immigrates to America should embrace our values and pledge their loyalty to the United States. We are not a country of tribes, factions, or castes; we are one indivisible nation with a distinctly American culture and proud national identity. Those that do not share these values are enemies of the people. They should not be allowed to undermine and dismantle America from within. We have blindly allowed these subversives to infiltrate our great nation. They must be stopped, and I will tirelessly fight for the American people and the country we love. America deserves leaders that refuse to cower before the mob and will not surrender the nation that we built without a fight. America will be great once again."

When finished, he turned and walked directly toward his office. The reporters shouted additional questions that were as inane as the first and fell on deaf ears. Congressman Ambrosia had made his point. At this time, there was nothing pertinent left to be said. He knew that the political forces were stacked against him. He must be strategic and play the long game for the hearts and minds of the people. His voice must be amplified by the forgotten men and women of America who struggled daily to hold on to the American Dream. Congressman Ambrosia knew that this dream is increasingly out of reach for many, and it would take every American patriot to restore the promise of America.

When he entered his office, his secretary told him that Axel had called just moments before. He closed the door to his office and settled in behind his desk before returning Axel's call.

"Axel, this is Dr. Pete. How are things in California?"

"They are coming along," Axel replied. "I just saw your speech and your comments to the reporters. That was very powerful."

"Thank you, Axel," Dr. Pete responded. "We have many challenges before us, and there is much work to be done, but we have now established that any attempts to subjugate ordinary Americans to the globalist revolution will face resistance. We will no longer be shamed into repudiating our heritage or bullied into affirming inaccurate representations of American society. The American people have found their voice, even if they must speak through me."

"Absolutely agree," Axel concurred. "Speaking of the challenges before us, I think it is time for me to get more involved once again. I have been busy organizing and guiding the supporters that we identified during the campaign, but I think it is necessary to expand our reach throughout the country. Many of the mainstream conservative conferences will reject our nationalistic views since they philosophically embrace globalism and corporatism. Instead, I propose that we embark on a national tour that serves to galvanize our supporters and raise funds for your campaign and the movement."

"That sounds like a great idea," Dr. Pete said enthusiastically. "First, I will need a few more months to establish our position here on Capitol Hill. In the meantime, please work with my staff to develop a modest schedule targeting locations where we would have strong support. I will continue to draw more public attention to the movement to engender interest in our events."

"Perfect, I will coordinate with your staff," Axel replied. "I am looking forward to more policy speeches soon."

"You won't have to wait long," Dr. Pete said with a chuckle. "Talk again soon."

Dr. Pete didn't exaggerate. Just a few days later, he publicly announced his first major piece of legislation to an eager press corps. "Today we announce our American Workers First bill, which requires all employers to demonstrably prefer American citizens in all hiring decisions. No immigrant workers can be hired without documenting a complete absence of qualified citizens. We anticipate that a dearth of potential employees should occur only in highly specialized or skilled positions, which comprise a minority of jobs in America. Our legislation will make it illegal to discriminate against Americans in favor of immigrants. Any employer that fails to prioritize American workers will be subject to civil penalties and damages.

"The President's attempt to cast aside talented and motivated American workers in favor of an endless supply of cheap immigrant labor is a betrayal of her oath of office and her obligations to the American people. We will not let President Rao replace Americans with economic migrants who have no loyalty to our country and bleed us dry while they remit most of their wages to their families abroad. We must focus on opportunities for Americans who will invest in their communities and rebuild our great nation. As the people's representatives, we should always be putting the American people first and acting in the best interest of the United States. Sadly, it seems our President and many other elected leaders still maintain loyalty to foreign interests and sell out the American people without hesitation. This ends now. The American Dream will be resurgent once again!"

"Congressman," a reporter shouted, "your bill seems dead in the water given that it is at complete odds with the President's policies that favor immigration."

"I was not elected to serve President Rao," Congressman Ambrosia retorted. "I represent the people of Arizona and all of the forgotten men and women of this country. I will not surrender our nation and our legacy to people that do not believe in American Exceptionalism or the divine destiny of the American people. We will not submit to those that don't share our values and are loyal to foreign powers. The cultural and ethnic genocide in America ends now."

Another reporter from the crowd challenged Congressman Ambrosia in a bitter and emotional tone. "Sir, you denounce immigrants and blame them for the ills of America. It seems like you are swimming against the tide because the future of America is neither White nor native-born. Immigrants are leading America forward and leaving you behind."

"That is what you want people to believe," Congressman Ambrosia said. "You seek to denigrate the American people and demand they repudiate their heritage. People like you want to demoralize Americans, squelch their hope, and diminish their will to resist. You want to convince them that globalism is inevitable and a multicultural America is our destiny. I am here to say, unequivocally, that America First is resurgent. American patriots will not stand idly by as you attempt to replace them. We surrender our legacy to no one. America First is our destiny."

The battle lines were drawn, but the fight was yet to come.

18

RETURN OF THE RALLIES

After his conversation with Dr. Pete, Axel started his search for appropriate rally venues and coordinated his efforts with the congressman's staff. Over the next few weeks, they identified potential sites and ranked them in terms of the concentration of potential supporters, accessibility, and relevant security concerns. It was decided that metropolitan areas in blue states were too great of a security risk, even if there was a large base of potential supporters. They opted for mid-sized cities in states with a conservative majority, where they could draw a large audience without attracting violent opposition.

They decided that their first rally would be held at the Fieldhouse in downtown Indianapolis, Indiana. Its central location in the state and proximity to Chicago, Cincinnati, and Louisville would provide easy access for a broad swath of Middle America. Following Indianapolis, they were planning on rallies in Pittsburg, PA and Birmingham, AL before making a final stop in Houston, TX. Congressman Ambrosia and Axel were taking a big risk embarking on this tour. Dr. Pete was well known throughout Arizona and in some parts of California, but he was new to the national scene. He had certainly made a splash in the opening months of his first term in Congress, but there was a lot of uncertainty about his ability to fill venues and make this a worthwhile campaign.

Axel and Dr. Pete's team were working tirelessly to market the event and drive interest. The Fieldhouse could easily seat more than ten thousand people for the event. Anything less than half of that would suggest that they failed to draw a crowd and would destroy the momentum they hoped to carry forward to future rallies. With just days to go, they had ten percent of the stadium filled with donors and enough ticket requests to imply that the ultimate attendance would be sufficient to fill the remaining seats. They expected that many people wouldn't end up coming, so they decided to over-allocate tickets to ensure a full venue.

On the night before the event, Axel and Elise's flight arrived in Indianapolis. After making their way through the airport, they hailed a taxi for the half-hour drive downtown to their hotel at Monument Circle. They checked into their room and freshened up before heading to the hotel bar to grab a drink with some of Dr. Pete's staff. His event organizer greeted them enthusiastically when they arrived.

"Axel, Elise, come join us," she said. "We have some exciting news to share."

Axel and Elise followed her to a table with a half dozen of the Congressman's staff already enjoying themselves. After Axel helped Elise to her chair, he sat down next to her and replied, "So what is the news?"

"We have secured over sixteen thousand ticket requests and have sold more than two thousand premium donor tickets so far," she said with excitement. "I have made arrangements with the Fieldhouse to be able to accommodate everyone if they show, but we have secured enough interest to make it a successful first rally."

"Great job," Axel said supportively. "Congressman Ambrosia has developed quite a buzz recently, so I am fairly confident that people will come to hear him speak. We will just have to determine if the attendees are simply curious about the novel new Congressman or if they are committed to the movement. This is a critical event to expand our network and build more momentum."

She nodded in agreement and said, "We have lined up campaign staffers and appropriately vetted volunteers who will gather information from each attendee and explain the importance of the America First Network."

"Great idea," Axel said before taking a sip of his cocktail. It seemed like Dr. Pete's staff had things in order, and he was eager to spend some time alone with Elise. She had been looking forward to this weekend away and to seeing Axel back in action. When he finished his drink, he took some cash from his wallet and left it on the table. After wishing everyone a good night, he and Elise retired to their room for the evening.

The next morning, they arrived at the Fieldhouse early to prepare for the rally. Axel was scheduled to speak first to introduce the America First Network and the principles of the movement. Then Congressman Ambrosia would take the stage in front of what would be their biggest crowd yet. Dr. Pete was quite charismatic and continued to perfect his rhetorical style. Axel was confident that the crowd would be engaged and inspired by his speech.

At noon, the team met to discuss logistics and security for the day. People were already gathering outside of the Fieldhouse which was a good sign for attendance. It was determined that everyone would be screened before entry, and both uniformed and undercover security would patrol the arena. They didn't expect any issues, but you never could be too careful. Dr. Pete's team had publicly advertised the rally, so the time and place were well known to both the America First supporters and the opposition. None of the congressman's staff would be cavalier about the risks, and security was a top focus.

Within hours, a line of people stretched down both Pennsylvania and Delaware Streets on either side of the Fieldhouse. It was a hot day, yet people had gathered in the relentless sun hours before the event to secure the best seat possible. Dr. Pete's event organizer, in consultation with the Fieldhouse staff, decided to start admitting people into the venue. There would be a lot of people to screen, and they were interested in developing greater engagement between the America First Network and the thousands of excited supporters.

Axel was in a suite preparing for his speech and relaxing with Elise when the crowds began to assemble inside the Fieldhouse. He watched in pleasant amazement while the arena slowly filled with people. This was going to be a huge event and a great opportunity to expand their movement. Axel was marveling at the crowd size of their first large scale regional rally when Dr. Pete and his adviser arrived in the suite.

"It's going to be a big night," the congressman said with excitement. "You and the team did a great job, Axel."

"Thank you, sir," Axel replied. "I am just amazed by how successful we have been at driving enthusiasm and support. Less than a year ago, I wasn't even dreaming of being involved in such an endeavor."

"We are just scratching the surface," Dr. Pete replied. "Millions of Americans are yearning for someone to affirm their self-worth and tell them that it's OK to be proud of yourself, your heritage, and your country. Americans want someone to tell them that they matter and that they will be put first once again. They have been scared into submission after years of bullying by the left, the media, and multinational corporations. There is safety in numbers and people are waking up to the fact that they are not alone. They are the silent majority that does not agree with the current direction of the country. We have awakened a beast, Axel."

"Amen," Axel replied enthusiastically. "I can't wait for your speech today. Good luck."

"See you backstage," Dr. Pete replied. "It's time to start a revolution."

After spending some time with Elise and watching the crowds assemble, Axel kissed his fiancée and headed backstage. When he arrived, Dr. Pete's event organizer was scurrying about orchestrating what would be the biggest production since they started campaigning. She spotted Axel and beckoned to him impatiently.

"Axel, come get ready," she shouted. "You are on in fifteen minutes."

Axel smiled as he followed her orders. He didn't want to make her job more difficult, but she was obviously overwhelmed with the magnitude of the rally. When he reached the staging area, her assistant started coaching him on the approach and last-minute instructions. He couldn't help but peek out from behind the curtain to check on the crowd. The Fieldhouse was full and there was a buzz of anticipation in the crowd.

While Axel was assessing the situation, the event organizer returned to coach him through his grand entry. "We have a surprise intro tonight," she told Axel giddily. "Are you ready?"

"All set," Axel replied.

She grabbed her radio and signaled to the control room that they were ready to begin. Almost immediately the lights in the Fieldhouse grew dim. The crowd cheered with excitement as an announcer came alive with a deep booming voice on the public address system. His emphasis and enunciation created great drama and suspense as he addressed the frenzied crowd.

"Ladies and gentlemen, welcome! Welcome to the dawn of a new future. Welcome to the resurrection of the American Dream. Welcome to the rebirth of the Historic American Nation. Welcome to the America First Revolution."

Red, white, and blue lasers projected varying patterns on the stage as deep techno beats replaced the voice of the announcer. It was time. The event organizer smiled with pride as she signaled to Axel that the stage was his.

Axel emerged from backstage with a triumphant and confident gait as he clapped and waved to the crowd. When he reached the podium, he pointed up to the suite where he was sure Elise was watching with pride as her fiancé was about to address a raucous and passionate crowd.

"Good evening, Indianapolis," Axel exclaimed with great enthusiasm. When the cheering subsided, he continued. "My name is Axel Berg, founder of the America First Network, and I want to welcome you to the REVOLUTION!

"My father was a patriot just like you. He believed in hard work, perseverance, and always giving your best effort. He cherished the postwar ideals of a prosperous middle class, traditional nuclear families, and robust local communities. He believed that American Exceptionalism derived from the strength of its people and their established norms and values. But when my father, the mayor of a small California farm town, sought to restore opportunity and prosperity to the citizens of Crystal Springs, he was murdered by an illegal alien that believed he was more entitled to the American Dream than you.

"For decades, the American people have elected politicians from both parties that betray them in favor of multinational corporations and open border policies. You have been forced to choose between politicians that pander to corporate oligarchs and those that seek to replace you with low-cost foreign workers. These open border zealots provide work visas to foreign students that deprive your children of coveted employment opportunities. Every year the American Dream slips further from your grasp as you are replaced by a compliant and servile immigrant workforce. The repopulation of America is underway while our leaders greedily profit from our suffering. If we don't act now, our nation and our heritage will be lost.

"I stand here before you, not for my own enrichment or personal gain, but because I believe in American Exceptionalism and the Historic American Nation. Our forefathers dedicated their lives to the betterment of our nation and to secure the American Dream for their families. They sacrificed to build the most powerful and prosperous nation in the world, but now our leaders are surrendering our legacy to immigrants and corporations with no loyalty to America. They are opportunists that seek to expropriate what is rightfully yours for their personal gain. We, the American people, will not stand by as our nation is plundered and our people are replaced. We will not acquiesce to the fundamental transformation of America.

"My fellow patriots, today you have taken the first step toward restoring the Historic American Nation. You stand here proudly with us, united in the conviction that America is comprised of people with a common history, values, and beliefs that differentiate us from the immigrant masses that seek to replace us. You stand here with me to proclaim that we will not be silenced, we will not be subservient, and we will not surrender to the globalist cabal. We are Americans, and we never back down from a fight.

"For years, we have elected leaders that made empty promises and consistently failed to deliver. They told you Americans just weren't qualified for the jobs of the twenty-first century. They said that American manufacturing just couldn't compete. They said that immigrants were needed to fill jobs that Americans just won't do. They sold you out to corporations and the open borders lobby because they knew that you had no power and no voice. This is the case no longer! We have a powerful voice in Washington. We have a leader who puts America First and fights every day to restore the American Dream. Congressman Pete Ambrosia stepped forward and declared that the American people will be silent no longer! Congressman Ambrosia is the tip of the spear and has taken our fight to Washington while the America First Network of patriots seeks to discretely advance our cause throughout the nation. I ask that you, my fellow patriots, please stand and make your voice heard once again. It is time for all America First patriots to rise and support Congressman Pete

Ambrosia!"

Axel raised his fist triumphantly to the sky as the crowd roared in approval. Throughout Axel's speech, the crowd became increasingly engaged. The excitement of the America First movement began to rekindle hope after years of despair.

After basking in the glow of an arena reverberating with energy, Axel turned to walk off the stage. As he exited, the lights once again grew dim except for a spotlight shining on the center of the stage. While the crowd rumbled with anticipation, the Fieldhouse audio began to play clips from Congressman Ambrosia's previous speeches. At first, they were barely audible but slowly they became louder and louder creating an intense feeling of anticipation.

"America First shall prevail," a clip of Congressman Ambrosia said over the audio system. "The American People will be resurgent once again... America is our legacy... America is not an idea, but a nation of exceptional people... The Historic American Nation is the foundation of American Exceptionalism... America First is our Destiny." The audio became louder and louder until it reached a booming crescendo. The introduction concluded by thunderously repeating the phrase "America First."

The crowd began to chant in unison with many pumping their fists in the air expressing their deeply held conviction. Red, white, and blue lights flashed the phrase throughout the arena in rhythmic synchrony with the chanting crowd. Axel was standing backstage with the congressman's event planner as they reveled in the enthusiasm. Her big smile revealed her overwhelming satisfaction and pride in what she had created. While they stood together enjoying her choreography, Congressman Ambrosia arrived to take the stage.

The congressman emerged from behind the curtains and stepped into the spotlight as the crowd cheered. He pumped his fist in unison with the crowd and chanted, "America First." When he reached the podium, the Fieldhouse was electric. This was the moment they had all waited for. Hope for a resurgent America had finally arrived.

"Wow," Congressman Ambrosia said as he surveyed the crowd and pointed at various people in the audience. "How great is Axel? He's great, no?"

Following a pause to allow the audience to react, Congressman Ambrosia continued. "Axel's family, like many of yours, has suffered greatly under the open borders globalist administrations that chose immigrants over Americans, corporate profits over paychecks, and authoritarianism over liberty. These tyrants think that you will silently submit. They think you will dutifully obey. But we gather here tonight to declare that we are Americans, and we will not allow our values to be eroded. We will not stand by as our culture is debased. We will not watch silently as our history is erased. We stand here proudly tonight, united in purpose, and declare once again that Americans will not be intimidated, we will not be silenced, and we will never surrender!"

The Fieldhouse reverberated in deafening applause. Congressman Ambrosia had awakened a sleeping giant. Collectively, the forgotten men and women were a force that previously lacked organization and leadership, but they have finally found both in Congressman Ambrosia and the America First movement. After almost a minute of pure exuberance from the audience, the congressman continued.

"For decades, our leaders have been stupid. They have been weak. They sought compromise with globalists. They tried to appease multinational corporations. They attempted to negotiate with open borders activists. At every turn, they surrendered. Piece by piece, all the things that make America great were relinquished without receiving anything in return. These people cannot be allowed to take over our country. We will not allow them to fundamentally transform America.

"We were once led by brave American patriots. These great men, our great men, were strong and proud. They believed in the inherent exceptionalism of America. Bold people, characterized by grit and ambition, built this nation and left their descendants a great legacy. We cherish this legacy because it is our heritage, our culture, and our divine destiny. Tonight, my fellow America First patriots, we declare our domain once again over this great nation and reclaim our legacy from those that attempt to wipe out our history and destroy this proud country.

"We serve notice tonight that we will protect this nation, this land, and our people from all enemies, foreign and domestic. We will not be displaced. We will not be silenced. We will not be canceled by evil hateful people that do not share our values and have no loyalty to our great nation. Until today, no one in charge has stood up to defend America. No one stood up to defend you, the American people, from an invasion by illegal aliens or from ruthless corporations that eagerly replace American workers and encourage the repopulation of America.

"The forces of globalism and mass immigration have conspired to elect weak leaders who bow to our enemies, kneel before the mob, and disparage the notion of American Exceptionalism. We are ruled by economic mercenaries who don't share our heritage, aren't loyal to our country, and have no common bonds with the people. Almost every institution in the United States is now actively hostile to the American people and consciously engaged in dismantling the social norms and values that form the basis of our great country. The powerful forces backing the globalist revolution tell Americans to get in line or get the hell out of the way. Pride in one's nation, you see, is anathema to a globalist society.

"My fellow patriots, let me be blunt. The people behind the open borders globalist cabal will stop at nothing to achieve the complete transformation of America. Patriotic Americans that fight to preserve our legacy and believe in American Exceptionalism cannot be allowed to subsist. They are coming for you, me, and anyone who clings to what is left of the Historic American Nation. These evil forces despise our virtue, envy our excellence, and covet our legacy. They want us silenced. They want us marginalized. They want us exterminated. But we are righteous. We are proud Americans, and we will not surrender our nation without a fight!

"We need bold strong leaders who exhibit pride in our nation and are unapologetic for our heritage. The people demand that our government and our institutions work for them, not for multinational corporations and economic migrants. We expect strong nationalistic policies that put the interest of Americans before everyone else. No longer will we tolerate weak leaders that are ashamed of our history and apologize for our prosperity. No longer will we appease our enemies or submit to those who wish to destroy us.

"From this day forward, we will hold our heads high and proudly proclaim that we will not allow our enemies to disparage our heroes, erase our history, and destroy our country. We will not compromise with those that want to replace our people. We will not appease those that seek to fundamentally transform America. This is a war for the future of our country. They cannot be allowed to prevail. We will not allow them to destroy America. America First is our divine destiny, and we will not surrender without a fight! Thank you, my fellow patriots. God bless you, and God bless America!"

Congressman Ambrosia basked in the magnificence of a packed Fieldhouse as he waved to the exuberant crowd. This, without a doubt, had been his most powerful and inspiring speech yet. It was a call to action and a definitive declaration of opposition to the current administration. Certainly, his speech would receive a lot of attention nationally for its content and tone. The battle lines had been drawn, and now they would have to see how many people would rally to the cause.

When Congressman Ambrosia exited the stage, Axel immediately went to congratulate him on his epic speech. Before he could say anything more, the congressman's event organizer approached with a worried look on her face. She was flanked by the head of security and a team of Indianapolis police officers.

"Congressman Ambrosia," she said nervously, "these officers report that a crowd has amassed outside of the Fieldhouse that seems to be on the verge of violence."

"Do we have a plan to safely evacuate the attendees?" the congressman asked.

The head of security chimed in. "Yes sir. We have a special exit where we have busses waiting to escort people to their hotels or their vehicles. The Indianapolis police have blocked off a corridor to provide safe and efficient transit for our guests. As for you and your team, we have vehicles waiting that can transport you to the airport."

"Excellent work," Congressman Ambrosia said. "Let's prepare for departure and convene in the suite in fifteen minutes. In the meantime, please announce the exit procedures to our guests so that they will be safe."

After everyone gathered in the suite, they were ushered by the security team to a procession of black SUVs designated for the congressman and his staff. Axel and Elise joined Dr. Pete and the head of security in the middle vehicle. As they left the Fieldhouse staging area, they saw rows of police vehicles blocking off the streets. Police officers in riot gear stood as a barrier to what looked like an angry mob of a thousand people or more. It was dark, but many seemed to be dressed in black and were wearing masks.

Elise looked at Axel with concern. Their procession of black SUVs seemed sure to draw the attention of the mob. As the police escorts led them onto the street, the mob became more agitated and began to throw objects at the vehicles. The riot police were helpless to stop the projectiles as they rocketed randomly out of the dark mass of people. A water bottle burst on the windshield of their SUV, startling Elise who clung tightly to Axel's arm. The convoy pulled onto Delaware street and rapidly accelerated to escape the mob. They heard a large crash behind their vehicle, but all of the cars in the motorcade continued unabated toward the airport.

"I hope the attendees get out safely," Elise stated with concern.

Congressman Ambrosia turned to his head of security and requested an update. When he radioed to the security team at the Fieldhouse, they reported that the distraction of the motorcade enabled them to escort many people to their vehicles and others to their hotels. Some people chose to walk, and there were reports of clashes between the rioters and the attendees.

"Have your men do everything possible to protect our people," Congressman Ambrosia commanded. "And tell them to avoid, if possible, direct conflict with the rioters. The media will certainly blame our people in an attempt to further marginalize us."

"Yes sir," the head of security replied before conveying the instructions to his team.

They arrived at the airport and were driven expeditiously to a special security entrance. When Axel and Elise exited the SUV, it was apparent that the rear vehicle had been assaulted by more than a water bottle. The front passenger window was completely shattered. As they examined the damage and checked on the passengers, Axel turned to the congressman and said, "It seems like the war has begun."

"It has indeed," Congressman Ambrosia replied. "It's time to reclaim our country!"

19

HATE SPEECH

President Nagila Rao was incensed by the events in Indianapolis. Large scale riots erupting just months into her administration made her seem weak and out of control. Her team promptly scheduled a press conference so that she could speak directly to the American people. There was a considerable buzz as reporters assembled in the White House Press Briefing Room. She had generally delegated her relations with the media to the Press Secretary, so her decision to address reporters directly suggested she had something important to say.

The President entered a packed Press Briefing Room about fifteen minutes after the scheduled start time. She was flanked by her Press Secretary, the Attorney General, and the Director of the FBI. Given the team she had assembled, the reporters anticipated some significant legal announcements. President Rao stepped behind the podium and addressed the room.

"Good afternoon. My administration and sensible people across this country were deeply troubled by the events Saturday night in Indianapolis. A group of white nationalists, led by a racist congressman from Arizona, held a large rally that ultimately incited violence in the streets. Police shut down part of downtown Indianapolis to contain the violent mob, yet there were numerous injuries and significant property damage. I stand before you today to announce that we will not permit hate and intolerance to sweep across our country. We are a diverse nation that cherishes people of all cultures and backgrounds.

"I have instructed the Attorney General and the Director of the FBI to vigorously apply hate crime laws against anyone engaged in rhetoric that foments division or encourages violence. We will also be working with

Congress to strengthen our laws to enhance penalties for hate speech motivated by race, nationality, or immigration status. From this day forward, anyone who participates in a rally such as the one in Indianapolis will be prosecuted to the fullest extent of the law. Justice will be swift and severe. With that, I will take a couple of questions."

A reporter in the front row raised his hand and asked, "Madam President, are you suggesting that the participants of the rally instigated the violence?" He looked at his notes and continued, "Reports from Indianapolis suggest that a large group of masked protesters had gathered outside of the Fieldhouse during the rally and became violent as people left the venue."

"People were rightfully upset that the city permitted hate-filled people that are hostile to this nation to gather and openly promote their White supremacist ideology. Hate has no place in this country and is likely to elicit an emotional response."

"So are you condoning violence against the rally-goers?" he blurted out in response.

"Next question," the President replied.

"President Rao," a female reporter interjected, "what recourse do you have against Congressman Ambrosia, the organizer of the rally, given that he is an elected Representative?"

"Congressman Ambrosia is subject to the same laws and regulations as all Americans," President Rao replied. "Additionally, I have requested that the House of Representatives officially censure Congressman Ambrosia for his hateful rhetoric and behavior that is unbecoming of an elected official."

"Last question," the Press Secretary instructed the media from the corner of the room.

"Madam President," a Latino reporter in the middle of the room said loudly. "As an Indian American, how does it make you feel that so many people passionately believe that multiculturalism has degraded American society?"

"My parents immigrated to this country with nothing and watched their child ascend to the Presidency. America has always been a country of immigrants and a nation where anyone can achieve the American Dream. Immigrants enrich our culture and bring new vitality to the country. Diversity is our strength, and anyone who resists increased immigration is on the wrong side of history. Thank you all."

When President Rao concluded her remarks, she left the room followed by her entourage. Everyone in the room quickly scrambled to go live or to relay their notes to the newsroom. The President had vociferously condemned not just those that attended the rally but a sitting congressman. Congressman Ambrosia's response would inevitably be provocative.

The congressman was in his office when the press conference aired. He immediately asked his secretary to invite some reporters to his office so he could formally respond to the President's comments. Within a few minutes, more than a dozen reporters were gathered outside of the office to observe the congressman's response. His staff made room for all of them, and Congressman Ambrosia sat at his large stately desk as he made his remarks.

"Fellow Americans, today President Rao besmirched my reputation and slandered millions of patriotic Americans. Her loyalties unambiguously are not with the American people. She, therefore, is definitively unfit to be President of the United States. America is not an idea. It is not a melting pot where people of varied cultures and ethnicities come together and form one unified country based on principles of diversity and inclusion. America is a nation where people have toiled and sacrificed for generations to cobble together a home that is uniquely theirs. From the novel traditions to the quintessential experiences, there is an established American culture that is unlike any other. Americans' love for their country pulses through their veins and unites them in a common bond. The strength of this bond and the national pride it engenders is what makes America exceptional. Nevertheless, President Rao seeks to sever that bond and replace it with a concept completely foreign to America.

"President Rao and her globalist acolytes suggest that equality, opportunity, and diversity are the hallmarks of American society. In their minds, they owe no duty or obligation to serve and protect the American people. They believe we are all just self-interested actors competing for scarce resources in a global economy. In the minds of the corporate oligarchs, there is no America but just a free and open economy that can be exploited to maximize profits. They eagerly import cheap foreign workers to act as economic mercenaries whose sole mission is to displace American workers and destroy the American Dream. As for the globalists, they seek to undermine American hegemony by diluting the voice of historical Americans with millions of culturally and politically incompatible immigrants. With every passing day, the fabric of America slowly unravels until this nation is nothing more than a shadow of its former self.

"We patriotic Americans can no longer ignore the threat that these people pose. For decades they have promised reforms while accelerating the dilution of our people and the decay of our nation. We must act now to end this treachery before it is too late. Rest assured, in President Rao's America we must submit to the multicultural globalist agenda or be economically disenfranchised and socially ostracized by our peers. The time is upon us to stand up and declare, without hesitation, that America is a strong and proud nation that will not submissively acquiesce to cultural genocide and the repopulation of our nation. From this day forward, it will only be America First."

As Congressman Ambrosia finished, the room lit up with energy as everyone wanted more. A reporter blurted out, "Congressman, are you concerned that President Rao will weaponize the Justice Department against you or your supporters?"

"I am more concerned that she will facilitate the colonization of America by her native India," Congressman Ambrosia replied curtly.

"Congressman Ambrosia," another reporter inquired, "how do you respond to President Rao's assertions that your positions and supporters are racially motivated?"

"I don't," Congressman Ambrosia replied. "Her statements are inane and baseless. I am a United States Congressman who is loyal to no other nation. I represent the American people. Can the same be said about our President? I think not."

"Are you asserting that the President is not loyal to America?" the reporter asked seeking clarification.

"Does her rhetoric leave any doubts?" Congressman Ambrosia replied. "She is there to orchestrate the final stages of the fundamental transformation of America, not to represent the American people."

A reporter in the back of the room shouted, "Sir is it correct to assume that your call to action indicates that you believe the situation is dire?"

"The day when political solutions are no longer feasible is imminent," Congressman Ambrosia concurred. "The clout of the American people is diluted every day. Soon we will be a minority in our own country. We must fight to protect the Historic American Nation, or there will be nothing left to fight for. Thank you, everyone, and please keep America in your prayers."

20

I FOUGHT THE LAW

The war of words did not cease following the initial volleys between President Rao and Congressman Ambrosia. The President continued to threaten to use hate crime laws to prosecute Americans who supported curbs on immigration or openly challenged the value of ethnic and cultural diversity. In open defiance of her edicts, Congressman Ambrosia held three additional rallies across the Midwest and the Southeastern United States. Support of the America First Network continued to swell despite President Rao's intimidation and threats because the message of a resurgent American nation continued to resonate with many disenfranchised Americans. Years of economic decline had taken its toll, and these patriotic Americans knew that drastic change was their only path to salvation.

Axel returned to Los Angeles to spend some time with Elise. She was worried about the implications of the President's rhetoric and took her threats seriously. It was clear that President Rao was a devoted globalist who was intent on fundamentally and irreversibly transforming America. She did not share the cultural norms or traditions of Americans and had totalitarian impulses stemming from her familial heritage in India's Brahmin caste. Decades of rampant immigration have diluted the power and status of historical Americans to the point that an Americanized caste system had emerged. The corporate oligarchs and globalist elites now reigned supreme over the plebeian American working class. Elise was convinced that President Rao would not hesitate to mobilize the full force of the American investigative and legal system to crush her opponents and protect the power and status of the elite in the United States.

Elise had made her feelings clear and implored Axel to assume a less public role in the America First movement. The violent mobs in

Indianapolis had rattled her and weakened her resolve. She thought of Henry and the tragic events at the Harvest Festival, and she knew that they were up against a powerful, perhaps unstoppable, force. Elise had dreams of a family and a future together with Axel, so she could not stomach the thought of such a dire fate.

Her pleas had registered with Axel, but he also knew that the intention of the legal threats and the violent mobs was to intimidate and discourage opposition to the globalist agenda. President Rao and her administration sought to make it socially unacceptable to express dissenting views by threatening economic and social ostracism. They wanted to ostracize anyone who expressed nationalistic beliefs by making it impossible for them to exist in the modern digitally interconnected society. Axel knew all too well how the totalitarian impulses of the globalist elite could be actuated to deprive people of employment opportunities and social standing as retribution for challenging the existing orthodoxy. Surrendering to such forces would only legitimize the tactics and further embolden authoritarian actors to mandate conformity with the globalist agenda.

Elise's passionate arguments persuaded Axel to agree to a brief hiatus from public speeches and rallies. He would support Congressman Ambrosia's rallies from California and continue to enroll new volunteers in the America First Network. Axel was quite clear that he was not abandoning the cause, but merely pulling back until the rhetoric out of the White House became less threatening. The congressman had just wrapped up the final planned rally in Houston, which had been quite a success. With the momentum behind their movement growing, the team agreed to host one additional event in Jacksonville, Florida before returning to Washington. Axel immediately got busy generating interest in the event and trying to secure an appropriate venue.

Demand for the final rally was off the charts, so Axel booked the Jacksonville Arena and arranged for the team to stay at a hotel on the riverfront. All of the previous events had received significant media coverage, but no network would broadcast the rallies live. Axel had been negotiating with an upstart network from nearby Alabama to provide live nationwide coverage of the rally. They first covered the Birmingham event and seemed receptive to the idea, but they were intimidated by the President's recent saber-rattling. Ultimately they agreed to broadcast the rally in exchange for an exclusive interview with Congressman Ambrosia and Axel.

On the morning of the rally, the network set up its equipment for the live broadcast from Axel's living room in Los Angeles and Congressman Ambrosia's suite at the hotel. Chuck Woolford, the network's lead political anchor, would interview Congressman Ambrosia in person and Axel remotely. After a few hours of prep work, it was time for the interview to commence.

"Good morning from Jacksonville, Florida," Chuck said to the camera. "Today we will be speaking to firebrand Congressman Pete Ambrosia and his partner Axel Berg who single-handedly have rekindled nationalism in America. Gentlemen, welcome to the show."

"Thank you, Chuck," Congressman Ambrosia replied.

"Congressman, let me begin with you," Chuck said. "Your rallies have garnered impressive crowds but also have elicited an emotional response from your opponents. At your first rally, your motorcade was physically attacked by protesters. Does this opposition give you pause or make you question the righteousness of your message?"

"No, not at all," the congressman replied. "In fact, the magnitude of the response validates my message and strengthens my conviction. Our rallies have mobilized the forgotten men and women of America and directed their ire at the true cause of their disenfranchisement. The globalists and open borders activists have debased our country, degraded our culture, and displaced our people. No amount of opposition will silence me or our movement."

"Axel, you have withdrawn from recent events," Chuck continued. "Are you having second thoughts?"

"Not in the least," Axel replied emphatically. "I have been focusing on the America First Network and ensuring that the rallies are a success. After many months of traveling with the congressman, I needed some time with my family, so I have been working from my home in Los Angeles."

"The President has threatened to prosecute you for hate crimes Congressman Ambrosia," Chuck continued to probe. "Is she justified in suggesting that you are promoting hate? Are you indeed racially motivated?"

Congressman Ambrosia laughed. "Chuck, I expected more from your network. Since when does expressing loyalty and love for America constitute hate? Does standing up for my fellow Americans make me a racist? I will not apologize for putting America First, and neither should any patriotic American. When did Americans become second class citizens in their own country? We allowed weak leaders to open the doors to massive waves of immigrants which diluted and displaced our people. While I am in Congress, passive and feckless leaders will be held to account and will not be allowed to sell out the American people."

"Axel, what role does the America First Network have in the movement?" Chuck inquired as he pivoted to a new topic.

"We have built the America First Network into a powerful activist community with over one million members across the country. The inspiring message of Congressman Ambrosia and the desire to restore American Exceptionalism is an extremely effective recruiting tool. Our movement grows and becomes stronger with each successive rally, and we expect great success tonight in Jacksonville."

"How would you define success for tonight's rally, Congressman Ambrosia?" Chuck asked.

"The rally is already a success," the congressman replied confidently. "We have motivated thousands of patriotic Americans to come together in Jacksonville to take back their country. The public demonstration of their commitment to restoring the Historic American Nation informs our opposition that they have encountered an insurmountable force. Patriotic Americans are filled with a spirit and determination that ensures that we will not surrender without a fight."

"Thank you both for your time," Chuck replied. "As we conclude, I leave you with one last question. It appears that your nationalist movement is destined to collide with the globalist forces that control our government. Can the opposing ideologies be reconciled? Is there a resolution that doesn't involve direct conflict?"

"The American people have bled and sacrificed for the virtue of our great nation," Axel replied. "Our leaders have allowed immigrants that do not share our values, do not embrace our culture, and are disloyal to our nation to supersede the American people. America will never be colonized and we will never yield our legacy to foreign interlopers."

"We do not pursue a confrontation," Congressman Ambrosia added. "But America is our home, our community, and our nation. We will surrender it to no one. America First is our destiny!"

"Gentlemen, thank you very much. I am looking forward to what you have in store this evening." Chuck Woolford concluded politely.

After the interview, Axel connected with Congressman Ambrosia. "Dr. Pete, are you all set for this evening? We are expecting a massive crowd."

"Yes, I am looking forward to it," the congressman replied. "I will give you a call to debrief when I get back to the hotel. Axel, you did a great job securing live media coverage that will help to expand our reach. Now we just need to make this the most memorable rally yet."

***

Congressman Ambrosia delivered on what was his most inspirational and compelling rally yet. Axel had watched live on TV and monitored the number of people live streaming online. At their peak, they had more than one million people watching online and countless more on the TV broadcast. It indeed had been a great success to partner with the fledgling network and broadcast the rally nationwide. He was looking forward to his call with the team to share the news.

While Axel awaited Congressman Ambrosia's call, he continued to monitor the TV as they broadcast aerial shots of the massive crowds and conducted onsite interviews with some of the attendees who were leaving the arena. More than an hour had passed, and Axel was still waiting patiently for the congressman's call. He was scheduled to arrive at the hotel by now, but security might have delayed his departure to accommodate the crowds.

Moments later, the network broke away from their live broadcast at the arena for breaking news. Chuck Woolford appeared live from the studio to make the announcement. "While the exact details remain unclear, we know at this hour that a massive FBI task force interdicted Congressman Ambrosia as he arrived at his riverfront hotel following the rally. He was taken into custody by heavily armed agents along with a handful of his staff. More than forty agents were at the scene to take the congressman into custody and confiscate all laptops and documents that Congressman Ambrosia had in his possession. The charges are yet unclear, but this likely marks an escalation in the battle between President Rao and the outspoken congressman who has been agitating for change. Earlier today, I interviewed Congressman Ambrosia who made his disdain for the President clear and vowed to never surrender to those that he believes are corrupting and colonizing America. We will continue to monitor this situation closely and will keep you informed of any developments."

Axel was flabbergasted. President Rao, as the ultimate authority overseeing the FBI, had escalated the debate into a full-fledged conflict. He immediately called Congressman Ambrosia's legal counsel to inform them of the situation. Shortly after that call, he made some additional calls to the staff that remained on-site at the arena. It was time to activate the America First patriots.

He requested that staff members use the public address system at the arena to announce the developments to the people outside. They quickly broadcast the news of Congressman Ambrosia's arrest, and the animated crowd immediately morphed into a spontaneous protest. Thousands of people took over the streets surrounding the arena, where a large media presence remained after the rally. All of the national news networks went live with the coverage of the America First patriots flexing their muscle.

As news helicopters and police descended on the scene, the protest evolved into a march toward the riverfront hotel where the congressman had planned to stay. The rowdy procession was peppered with American flags and was identifiable by the vociferous chants of "America First." The silent majority would be silent no more. It had been clear to all intelligent observers that the war of words between Congressman Ambrosia and President Rao would escalate beyond a mere rhetorical clash, but his arrest definitively marked the first battle of an inevitably protracted conflict.

With the America First patriots activated in service to the cause, Axel returned his focus to liberating Congressman Ambrosia. After many calls, he determined that the congressman was being held in FBI custody at an undisclosed location but would later be transferred to Washington, D.C. for further interrogation. His staff had been questioned by the FBI but was scheduled to be released. They were ordered to return to Washington, D.C. and would be restricted from travel outside of the region. Despite dozens of inquiries, Axel was unable to obtain any additional information about Congressman Ambrosia, including the basis for his detention. Axel hoped that the congressman's attorneys had been able to reach him, but he concluded that he was helpless to further assist the investigation this evening.

The next morning, Axel woke to find Elise at the dining room table watching a recap of the evening's events. "See, Axel," she said anxiously. "I told you that the situation was getting too heated and the President would be forced to act. I am so glad I talked you out of attending this rally."

Axel agreed with his fiancée about his own legal jeopardy, but he vehemently disagreed with the premise of her statements. "If everyone backed down to people with power, we would be a nation of conformists and drones that live simply to serve their masters. President Rao and her globalist regime are authoritarians that seek to forcibly suppress dissent, silence the opposition, and intimidate American patriots. Withdrawing from the fight will only lead to the subjugation of our people and the end of the Historic American Nation."

Elise was not backing down. "The federal government is extremely powerful, Axel. They will steamroll you without blinking. What good would it do to fall as a martyr?"

"We must all hang together, or we shall surely hang separately," Axel replied. "Wiser words perhaps were never uttered. I have no intention of plunging emotionally and foolishly headfirst into the government sword, but if individually we are all afraid to act, then collectively we are doomed to fail. It takes brave leaders to organize a movement for change, and I cannot cower in fear when critical battles are upon us."

"So what do you propose doing, Axel? I hope you are measured and deliberate in your approach."

"I must stand with Congressman Ambrosia," Axel replied. "We must stand tall and demonstrate to all of the authoritarian globalists that we will not back down. We persuaded more than one million Americans to join the America First Network at great risk to their liberty and economic future. These people trusted us to lead, and we must deliver. We must continue to fight despite all the adversity we face from the wealthy and powerful interests that want us eradicated. "

Elise remained unconvinced and continued to argue her point. "Axel, the President has mobilized the Justice Department against a sitting congressman. Do you honestly think she will hesitate to crush you or anyone in the America First Network? Some opponents are just too powerful to overcome. President Rao has support throughout the corporate community and the bureaucratic administrative state. What levers of power do you possess? The odds are stacked against you."

Elise, like many Americans, had long ago surrendered hope and resigned herself to work within the system. She would rather play their game and try to carve out some adulterated version of the American Dream than pursue what she considered to be unrealistic ideals.

"What kind of nation, no what kind of existence, do we have if men of principle back down in the face of adversity? Should we kneel and surrender to globalists and corporate oligarchs? Our ancestors fought and died for liberty and freedom around the world, yet now you suggest we should withdraw from the fight. Should we surrender the Historic American Nation to immigrants who don't share our culture or values? I want to live in America, not India. I want to live in a country that cherishes individual liberties, not a country like China that arrests political opponents and imprisons them in forced labor camps. I will not stand idly by as the foundational principles of our nation are undermined and the American people are replaced. We must prevail."

21

JUSTICE

The next morning, the arrest of Congressman Ambrosia continued to dominate the news. The congressman was being detained in a secret location, and his legal team was being denied access to their client. Rumors and conspiracy theories were running rampant with some suggesting that he was being classified as an enemy combatant and being denied due process for fomenting an uprising against the current administration. Others suggested that an irate President Rao ordered the FBI to arrest Congressman Ambrosia due to his defiance of her edicts and the continuation of the rallies. The reports also suggest they were now struggling to establish a legal justification to detain the congressman and were working with the Department of Justice to develop a legal interpretation that would validate the arrest.

Axel and the congressman's team worked feverishly all day to locate Congressman Ambrosia. After being stonewalled by every reliable source, they held a conference call to discuss how they should proceed. It was decided that the legal team should bring the fight to the media and demand due process for their client. Either he should be charged with a crime or released from custody. The lawyers were preparing a statement for the next morning, and the congressman's staff would continue to try to locate him.

The staff worked diligently throughout the night and exhausted all leads. Just as despair began to take hold, the media announced a 10 A.M. press conference by the Department of Justice and the Attorney General. Axel and the team requested that Congressman Ambrosia's legal team respond publicly after the press conference. It was unprecedented to arrest a sitting congressman and deny him legal counsel. Even more, they suspected he was being detained at a black site outside of the purview of the judicial system.

The Attorney General appeared promptly to address the media. "Good morning. Two nights ago, the FBI carried out an operation to take Congressman Ambrosia into custody. The continuation of his rallies in direct defiance of President Rao's executive orders and his penchant for hateful and divisive speech could no longer be tolerated in a civil society. Freedom of speech is not absolute in the United States, and any speech that advocates for immediate or imminent lawlessness is not protected. We hold that Congressman Ambrosia violated hate speech laws, advocated for violence and discrimination against immigrants, and incited an uprising against the U.S. government. Such behavior will not be tolerated in President Rao's America. We have secured a grand jury indictment against the congressman for violating hate speech statutes. Additionally, Congressman Ambrosia's willful and repeated violations of the law, despite ample warnings, have led the judge to issue a gag order against the congressman barring him from discussing the case or making further incendiary comments. At our request, the judge agreed to remand the congressman into the custody of the Metropolitan Correctional Center in New York City pending trial. No bail was granted. We won't be taking any questions at this time, but we will provide additional details in the coming days. Thank you." With that, the Attorney General and his staff swiftly exited the room.

Axel was stunned. Congressman Ambrosia was deprived of adequate legal representation, denied bail, and imprisoned on a sham charge orchestrated by President Rao. At least the location of the congressman was finally made public, but it was unclear if he would be allowed visitors or if he could consult his legal counsel. It was of critical importance that the congressman's lawyers assumed control of the case and secured bail pending trial.

As agreed, Congressman Ambrosia's legal team addressed the media following the DOJ press conference. Stuart Schwartzman, senior legal counsel for the congressman, spoke for the team. "Thank you for gathering here today in light of the egregious injustice that our client, Congressman Ambrosia, has suffered at the hands of a vindictive and anti-American President. Our client has been denied due process and has been unjustly detained without access to legal counsel. The charges leveled against our client are specious and without merit. In the 1969 case of Brandenburg v. Ohio, the Supreme Court unanimously ruled that freedoms of speech and press prohibit the State from criminalizing the advocacy of force or lawlessness unless it imminently incites lawless behavior. Based on this decision, inflammatory speech and hateful rhetoric as defined by a legislative body is insufficient cause for arrest or prosecution. The Attorney General must surely be aware of this landmark case, which raises questions about his objectivity in leveling these charges. Clearly, the prosecution of Congressman Ambrosia is politically motivated and without a basis in law. The government is attempting to silence the congressman to facilitate his prosecution in the media rather than a court of law. We will not be silent, and we will not allow this egregious miscarriage of justice to endure. As Congressman Ambrosia's legal counsel, we demand to speak with him without further delay. These charges are unjust, without merit, and representative of the authoritarian impulses of President Rao's administration. They will not stand."

Axel felt reassured by the arguments presented by Mr. Schwartzman. It seemed unambiguous that Congressman Ambrosia was on a solid legal footing, but without access to his legal team, he would continue to be detained. The congressman's staff and legal team were actively reaching out to the Federal Bureau of Prisons to inquire about the status of Congressman Ambrosia and to determine the visitation schedule. They were informed that the Metropolitan Correctional Center was currently closed to visitors, but the congressman's legal team could visit their client tomorrow at 8 A.M. He was being held in the special housing unit where he would be heavily monitored and would have a cellmate as determined by the Bureau of Prisons.

Mr. Schwartzman and the team were waiting at the Metropolitan Correctional Center fifteen minutes before their scheduled visit. When they announced their presence and requested to see Congressman Ambrosia, the correctional officer instructed them to wait while they retrieved the prisoner. More than a half-hour passed as they waited to see their client, and Mr. Schwartzman was growing angry. He approached the correctional officer that he spoke to earlier and demanded an explanation.

"Our client has been denied legal counsel for almost three days," he said. "We demand to see him immediately."

The correctional officer picked up the phone to check on the status of the prisoner. "Uh-huh... ok... got it," the officer said to the person he called. When he hung up the phone, he turned to Mr. Schwartzman and said, "The prisoner is currently unavailable."

"What do you mean unavailable?" Stuart replied heatedly. "We scheduled an appointment and followed the Bureau of Prisons protocol, so we demand to see our client immediately. Is there some reason that you cannot produce our client?"

"Sir, I was told that the prisoner is currently unavailable. That is all the information that I have."

"I need to speak to a supervisory officer," Stuart replied. "We must be allowed to speak to our client."

"One moment please," the correctional officer said as he picked up the phone again. He stepped away from Mr. Schwartzman to prevent his conversation from being audible. After a few moments, he returned and said, "A supervisory officer will be here to speak with you momentarily."

"With my client, I hope," Mr. Schwartzman said emphatically. He stepped away to inform his team of the situation. It certainly seemed like the Bureau of Prisons was continuing the deception and obfuscation that had been the norm since the congressman was taken into federal custody.

A large overweight man with a look of authority came to address Mr. Schwartzman and the team. "Counselor, I understand you are here to see Congressman Ambrosia?" he asked even though he was fully aware of the answer.

"Yes, where is my client?" Stuart replied impatiently.

"I am sorry to inform you that the inmate cannot be produced at this time."

"Why the hell not?" Stuart replied furiously. "We had an appointment an hour ago and our client has been denied counsel since he was detained."

"The inmate is currently being transported to the New York City Hospital for emergency treatment. That is all I can say at this time."

The supervisory correctional officer was obviously withholding information, but Mr. Schwartzman was anxious to get to the hospital to assess the condition of the congressman. He asked a junior member of his legal team to stay at the correctional center to obtain more details about the circumstances of Congressman Ambrosia's health emergency and to ensure that all relevant evidence was preserved.

When Stuart Schwartzman and the team arrived at the hospital, the attending emergency room physician met them to address their concerns. "Mr. Schwartzman, your client is currently unconscious and suffering from significant internal bleeding and numerous bone fractures consistent with a violent assault or beating. We are doing everything possible to stabilize him, but he has swelling of the brain and elevated intracranial pressure. We need to drill into his skull to drain the fluid and relieve pressure resulting from the trauma."

Stuart was dejected and quite frustrated. "What is his prognosis?" he inquired.

"Not good," the emergency room physician replied. "The patient's age and the extent of the physical injuries suggest that it will be difficult to overcome the trauma. There is a high probability of permanently impaired motor functions and diminished cognition as a result of brain injuries. I must return to my patients, but I will keep you informed."

"Thank you, doctor," Stuart replied. "Please preserve all evidence and document any medical findings. We must determine how a sitting congressman can end up in such a predicament."

"Absolutely," the doctor said as he went to check on the congressman.

Stuart quickly called Congressman Ambrosia's staff to provide an update. They were devastated. Just a few days ago, they were celebrating their most successful rally yet. Out of nowhere, the congressman was abducted and imprisoned by the FBI, and now he is fighting for survival. This seemed all too convenient. Congressman Ambrosia had been a thorn in the side of President Rao and the transnational elite, as they sought to fundamentally transform America. Now he was out of the picture, perhaps permanently.

The congressman's staff asked Stuart Schwartzman and his team to continue to look into the circumstances surrounding the arrest, detention, and apparent assault of Congressman Ambrosia. Immediately after their call, Stuart got to work. He conscripted his entire team to pursue all angles and sources. Not only were there multiple avenues for lawsuits in this case, but there was possibly a coordinated attempt by the government to eliminate a political opponent and silence dissenting voices. The coincidences strained credulity. They needed to gather the evidence before it could be destroyed.

Schwartzman and Spears was the preeminent law firm in New York and Washington, D.C. They had over a hundred lawyers on staff who specialized in criminal, constitutional, and tort law. All available resources were assigned to investigate the events surrounding the detention and assault of Congressman Ambrosia. Mr. Schwartzman emphasized that the outspoken congressman was their primary concern and that all legal channels should be pursued. The team immediately started filing Freedom of Information Act requests, calling sources within the DOJ, and subpoenaing records germane to the criminal case. They were sure that a paper trail must exist linking the President directly to the arrest of the congressman, and the Bureau of Prisons must have video or records that shed light on the assault.

Aside from superficial reporting on the incident, the media remained relatively silent and uncurious about the events leading to the congressman's hospitalization. It seemed rather obvious that they were either secretly happy about the attack on Congressman Ambrosia, or they lacked the will and integrity to investigate further. While the media parroted the narrative from the government, Congressman Ambrosia was struggling to survive. His condition had deteriorated leading his physician to place him in a medically induced coma. The medical staff wasn't very optimistic about his prognosis, and his family and staff were told to prepare for the worst.

The official report was that the congressman had been assaulted by an illegal immigrant inmate that took offense to the congressman's rhetoric. According to the Bureau of Prisons, all of the cameras in the area had malfunctioned leaving only two correctional officers with direct knowledge of the assault. Both were veteran officers of the Metropolitan Correctional

Center and had been assigned to Congressman Ambrosia by the Warden of the prison. They had been suspended pending investigation of the incident, and the Bureau of Prisons would not provide any additional information until the investigation was complete.

The team at Schwartzman and Spears was unconvinced by this explanation. They were uncovering bits and pieces that were beginning to paint a more sinister portrait of events. Stuart consulted with his senior legal team and decided that they would gather enough information to compile a compelling case before holding a press conference announcing their findings and any legal actions on behalf of the congressman.

That evening, Stuart received a call from Congressman Ambrosia's chief of staff. Dr. Pete, beloved by millions, had succumbed to his injuries and passed away. The damage to his brain had been too significant and he was unable to recover. Stuart knew that it was essential that they get ahead of the news cycle before false media narratives became commonly accepted by the public as fact. He told the chief of staff that his team was close to uncovering the truth, and they would hold a press conference tomorrow morning to announce their findings.

The next morning, Stuart Schwartzman addressed the media outside of the Schwartzman and Spears offices in Manhattan. "Good morning. As many of you know, Congressman Ambrosia, a great American hero, passed away last night, surrounded by friends and family. Our firm has been vigorously pursuing the truth about the incidents leading up to his untimely death. Reality is not what the government wishes you to believe.

"Congressman Ambrosia was arrested in his Jacksonville hotel following his final rally by over forty heavily armed FBI agents in tactical gear. The congressman was quickly escorted to FBI headquarters where he was interrogated without legal representation for almost thirty-six hours. FBI supervisory agents instructed everyone involved that they were forbidden to disclose the congressman's location or any details about the investigation. This was by direct order of senior FBI leadership on the seventh floor. Despite our subpoenas and FOIA requests, no notes or details of the interrogation have been produced.

"After brutally interrogating a sitting United States Representative, the FBI filed charges against Congressman Ambrosia in federal court and transferred him to the Metropolitan Correctional Center in New York. Throughout this process, Congressman Ambrosia was denied legal representation in violation of his Sixth Amendment rights. Despite inquiries from my firm, the Department of Justice maintained a shroud of secrecy and would not confirm the status or location of our client. The government violated due process when they carried out a clandestine operation to detain an elected official, interrogate him at a secret location, and deny him legal representation.

"Once transferred to the MCC, Congressman Ambrosia was under the custody of a Warden who is a close friend of the Attorney General and a major campaign donor of President Rao. The Warden maintained the secrecy of the government operation against Congressman Ambrosia with our team learning about the arrest and detention of our client via a press conference by the Attorney General. It is our assertion, based on evidence gathered, that the delay was necessary to afford the Warden time to coordinate the assault on Congressman Ambrosia. The Warden assigned two officers to monitor the congressman at all times and ostensibly ensure his safety. Both officers, however, have previously been reprimanded for failing to maintain control of inmates, falling asleep while on duty, and allowing a riot to break on their watch. It is quite curious that the Warden would select these two officers unless you consider their true motives.

"We have uncovered evidence that suggests that the Warden, at the direction of his associates at the Department of Justice, orchestrated the attack on Congressman Ambrosia. Bank records will show that the two suspended officers were paid for their involvement through shell companies located in the Cayman Islands. Additionally, audiotapes will prove that the officers were promised early retirement by the Warden following a sham investigation into their actions. While we currently have no direct evidence linking President Rao to Congressman Ambrosia's assassination, you can be assured that it was the outcome that her administration desired.

"We cannot let the assassination of a respected United States Congressman go unpunished. Our legal team will be pursuing civil action against the parties involved where appropriate, but there must be accountability for those participating in the government plot against Congressman Ambrosia. We are not some third world dictatorship where the power of government is used to intimidate or imprison our political opponents. In America, we do not assassinate elected officials for opposing the prevailing political dogma. Justice must be served."

22

UPRISING

Axel was stunned and devastated when he heard the news. Dr. Pete had generously taken Axel under his wing after Henry's murder and had helped Axel find purpose and direction. His assassination was a true come-to-Jesus moment. Axel was now confronted with the choice between continuing to fight for the Historic American Nation and acquiescing to the fundamental transformation of America. He could submissively conform to the new globalist doctrines and be subservient to the transnational elite, or he could fight for the American Dream and preserve the legacy of his ancestors. Generations of Americans built this nation and fought for its principles, yet now their ancestors would be cast aside and left to squabble over the scraps of the transnational elite. Axel could not bear the thought.

America was rapidly changing. President Rao had consolidated power and embarked on a crusade to marginalize all remaining patriotic Americans. Her willingness to unabashedly wield power to suppress dissent was consistent with her elitist and authoritarian impulses. America was her country now, and any resistance to her transformational agenda would be met with decisive opposition. President Rao and the transnational elite would reinvent the nation in their image, with immigrants and quislings in positions of privilege and power. The Historic American Nation, undermined by decades of globalism and unfettered immigration, was teetering on the brink of extinction.

The weight of this realization was monumental for Axel. For decades, many Americans were so naïve and complacent that they willfully embraced a globalist agenda that allowed soulless multinational corporations to amass overwhelming power while anti-American immigrants repopulated the country. As foreign-born residents began to dominate the population, discrimination against patriotic Americans became normalized. Anyone who expressed nationalistic impulses was ostracized and denigrated. White Americans were accused of white privilege and forced to publicly denounce their race and identity. The traditional American people were psychologically neutered until they were completely reprogramed and would blindly submit to the new multicultural globalist regime. They were destined to become a permanent servant class for the transnational elite.

With the gravity of Congressman Ambrosia's assassination weighing heavily on his mind, Axel wondered if there was still hope for the Historic American Nation. There was no prestige in martyrdom. The murder of his father would be an insignificant blip in the history of Crystal Springs, one that would perhaps be forgotten altogether when the founding families were all finally replaced by immigrants. Surrender, however, assured an equally dire fate. All that he held dear – his identity, his values, and his family – would be targeted for elimination because they were fundamentally at odds with the new America. In such a world, he could not live.

With Congressman Ambrosia gone, it was incumbent upon Axel to direct and inspire the America First patriots to resist the fundamental transformation of America. All of the hard work during months on the campaign trail would now pay dividends. The America First Network had exploded in popularity with each successive rally. This was the legacy that Congressman Ambrosia left behind, and it would be instrumental in mobilizing patriots across the nation. For months they had encouraged people to maintain their anonymity and only engage in discrete acts of subversion, but the time for visible mass action had arrived. The assassination of their spiritual and inspirational leader must now awaken the silent majority.

Axel recorded a video message to all America First patriots. "Good evening fellow patriots. For years, we have watched idly as leaders who feign loyalty to the United States put their interests, as well as those of foreign lands and multinational corporations, ahead of Americans. We sat silently as they deprived us of employment opportunities and opened the doors to immigrant workers. We stood helplessly as our children were told to feel guilty about the color of their skin or the deeds of their ancestors. We waited patiently for a leader who would make us proud to be Americans once again. We longed for a leader who would give us hope after years of despair. We dreamt of a leader who would fight for us, not for the transnational elite and corporations. We found that leader in Congressman Pete Ambrosia. Now, thanks to the vile anti-American animus of President Rao, our inspirational leader is dead.

"America is at a crossroads. Either we fight for the Historic American Nation, or we surrender to the transnational globalist elite who wish us dead. Emboldened by their brazen assassination of a sitting congressman,

President Rao and her brethren will not hesitate to use the full power of the government against us. The odds against our success are daunting, but submission would ensure that our people and our nation will not survive. I ask you today to stand with me and make your voices heard around this great nation. We are the silent majority, and we will be silenced no more.

"Together, we will fight for our families. We will fight for our people. We will fight for our nation. My brothers and sisters, we will fight for our survival. We shall prevail because America First is our destiny."

Within twenty-four hours, the video had been disseminated around the country and had over one million views. Axel was now the public face of the movement, and he was sure that he had just become a target. Paranoia began consuming him as he considered that President Rao's secret police and the FBI had almost certainly infiltrated the America First Network. He had to be extra careful about who he allowed into his inner circle. Axel advocated for a decentralized network of local America First groups that would organize their own actions and maintain independence from each other to protect the network as a whole.

Almost immediately after the video broadcast, local protests began to erupt. Police were dispersed to quash the protests, but the patriots had well-planned escape routes and would regroup in other areas of the city. This game of whack-a-mole continued for days and received national media attention. President Rao was frustrated by the growing discontent, so she established curfews in an attempt to silence the increasingly popular protests. While her directives gave the police more power to arrest protesters, it only emboldened the malcontents who advocated for the revitalization of the American Dream and an end to her globalist policies.

President Rao and the transnational elite were not about to relinquish power. In an escalation of her response to the protests, she invoked the Insurrection Act and activated the National Guard. Her directives were to suppress civil disorder and enforce compliance with her edicts. President Rao intended to break the will of the protesters to ensure that no one else dared to challenge her authority. If the death of Congressman Ambrosia wasn't enough to intimidate the protesters, then new examples must be made.

The National Guard was deployed to all major cities. They succeeded in intimidating the people and thereby restored order in the cities, but protests began to pop up in smaller towns across the country. When police or authorities swarmed a location, the protesters would disperse and reorganize in the next town. People grew emboldened by the successful implementation of these tactics, and the number of cells of protesters continued to grow. Lookouts would signal to block captains when the authorities were approaching so that the protesters could scatter before the authorities arrived. Protesters would then regroup in other preplanned locations, based on color-coded signals from the block captains. The sophistication and organization of the America First activists grew with experience, enabling them to stay one step ahead of the authorities.

After more than thirty days, the constant state of civil unrest was becoming a major embarrassment to President Rao. Her invocation of the Insurrection Act and deployment of the National Guard failed to quell the uprising, which made her look weak and inept. It was time, she decided, to ratchet up her response. The protests continued to gain momentum, and it would now take a massive show of force to suppress them. President Rao called for a meeting of her cabinet to discuss strategic options. If they didn't act now, they risked losing control of the situation.

That evening, the cabinet convened at the White House. President Rao was fiery as she opened the discussions. "This country is under siege. Everything we hope to accomplish is threatened by these racist radicals that seem entirely too adept at evading the police and the National Guard. When we invoked the Insurrection Act, you told me that you would dispense with these protesters forthwith and with maximum prejudice. We are over thirty days into this uprising, and they are making a mockery of us all. What are you going to do about it?"

"Madam President," the Secretary of Defense chimed in. "The military is ready to deploy at your command. We need to overwhelm the protesters with an insurmountable show of force."

"I am not sure if we are ready for tanks in the street," the President replied. "Not yet at least."

"Madam President," the Attorney General interjected, "the FBI has infiltrated the America First Network and has some informants in place–"

"That is too slow and too targeted," the President interrupted. "There are hundreds of cells around the country. Taking down one or two will have minimal impact and might only inspire more discontent."

"I agree," the Attorney General replied. "The only way to end the protests is to take out the entire organization in one fell swoop. We cannot do this without a significant coordinated action that will only be possible with actionable intelligence."

The President turned to the National Security Advisor. "Have you made any progress infiltrating the database of the America First Network? We need to know who is involved."

"Not yet ma'am," said the National Security Advisor. "We have our best team on the case, but they have done a good job encrypting their database and ensuring that each member has a unique identifier that helps maintain anonymity."

"We need answers, and we need them now," the President said angrily. "So far, all I have heard are half-baked ideas and excuses. What can we do NOW to curtail the protests?"

The Secretary of Defense was eager to get in the fight. "Madam President, may I suggest a three-pronged approach. First, we mobilize the military to further discourage protests and to desensitize the public to a military presence for the day when overwhelming force is activated. For now, the military will simply be a visible presence to mollify the public and intimidate protesters. Second, we expedite the acquisition of intelligence to prepare us for a decisive sweep. The NSA and FBI need to identify all members of the America First Network including known associates and collaborators. Finally, you should invoke the Defense Production Act to conscript the railroad operators and bus companies into the service of the Defense Department for the transportation of prisoners. We must be prepared to transport hundreds of thousands of insurgents to federal facilities for detention."

President Rao's eyes lit up with enthusiasm. "That's good, General. Now let's make it happen. The future of America is at stake."

23

THE INSURRECTION ACT

Saul Goldstein was a giant in the investment industry. The son of holocaust survivors, his family had immigrated to the United States following the war and quickly found success. His father amassed a small fortune through an art and jewelry business, which financed Saul's Ivy League education. He had led a privileged life and had been exposed to the New York elite from a very young age. Saul had become a leader in the corporate business community and was well known in political circles in Washington, D.C. He was never afraid to use his clout to advance his business or enhance his competitive advantage, but he knew how to grease the wheels in the political community as well.

Saul's knack for finance and extensive connections enabled him to transform a small insurance company into a multinational conglomerate of manufacturing, banking, insurance, and transportation businesses. One of his most visible divisions was the freight transportation business. It owned sixty percent of the country's freight rail lines, thousands of tractor-trailers, and hundreds of distribution centers nationwide. They were able to move freight with greater speed and efficiency than any other company in the world.

Following the cabinet meeting, President Rao gave Saul a call. He had donated generously to her campaign and was an ardent supporter. As one of the largest employers of immigrant workers, Saul shared her vision for the future of America.

"Saul, this is President Rao," she said when he answered.

"What a pleasant surprise," Saul replied. "To what do I owe this honor?"

"Saul, America needs you," she said. "My advisors have developed a plan to address the widespread protests and riots, but we will ultimately need access to your railroad. Can we count on your support?"

"Madam President, I am always here for our nation," Saul replied. "However, I am concerned about the public relations impact of my company's involvement. What assurances can you provide?"

"My advisors encouraged me to invoke the Defense Production Act to compel your participation," she said in a mildly threatening tone, "but I only want to do that as a last resort."

"I see," Saul replied. He was a bit offended by her aggressive posture. So far, he had been cooperative.

"While that may provide you cover from any blowback, I would prefer that we didn't have to pursue such a heavy-handed approach," the President replied. "I have to manage the perception of the people as well, and it would be beneficial if they observed a unified approach on behalf of government and industry."

"I very much agree, Madam President," Saul said. "You can count on our support."

"Thank you," President Rao said appreciatively. "I have always valued your support and counsel, Saul. The Secretary of Defense will coordinate details as they become available. Good night Saul."

President Rao called her chief of staff. "Tell the General that Saul Goldstein is on board. His railroads and trucking companies will facilitate transportation. They can coordinate needs directly."

The President wanted to maintain some distance from this plan. While she had ultimately approved the General's proposal, any missteps could severely impact her public approval ratings, and she wanted a fall guy to assume responsibility if things went awry. The General and the Defense Department had already begun to mobilize the troops and position them across the country. Soon she would be able to gauge public reaction to the military being deployed on American soil.

With the deployment of the military came nationwide curfews. No one was allowed on the streets after 9 P.M. or they would be subject to immediate arrest. The vast display of force had to be backed up by an enforcement mechanism, and curfews provided an ample excuse to detain anyone on the streets at night. While initial reports suggested that the military presence and curfews were reducing the incidence of protests, there was growing discontent among the general public. Many resented the show of force by President Rao, but almost all were too afraid to openly object. They silently stewed and went about their daily lives compliantly.

A week after the military was deployed, protests had been virtually eliminated. The America First patriots had been trained well and realized that martyrdom would do little to help their cause. Getting arrested would only end their ability to resist. To succeed, they needed to observe and adapt. Strategies and targets must be modified to account for the strengths and weaknesses of the enemy. The government had more people and military might, but the America First patriots were inspired by self-preservation and resolute purpose. Failure was not an option.

Now that open protests were no longer feasible, it was time to utilize guerrilla tactics to undermine the enemy. Instead of protesting, cells would form flash mobs that would strike institutions, companies, and government agencies that supported the replacement of Americans. The goal was to frustrate the opposition and disrupt their lives such that they became disenfranchised with the status quo. By targeting companies and organizations that were complicit in the displacement of American workers, the America First Network sought to inflict economic pain on the transnational elite and cause the public to question the efficacy of a globalist system.

For those that wanted a more subtle approach, large scale sickouts and work slowdowns were employed to economically disrupt multinational corporations. While they had succeeded in replacing many Americans and marginalizing others, they were still dependent on American workers to keep the businesses running. Those with greater access would engage in industrial espionage or sabotage. Leaks of embarrassing materials, confidential economic information, or personal contact information of corrupt corporate oligarchs became common. Hackers began to breach corporate networks to disclose source code, disable access, and disrupt economic activity.

Month after month, the America First Network wreaked havoc on the globalist economic system in the United States. The FBI was able to disrupt some cells, but the vast majority operated in the shadows with impunity. They were winning, and President Rao knew it. The stock market had declined over thirty percent, and corporate bankruptcies were rising. Some America First patriots were suffering personal financial losses, but they knew that complicity with the globalist system and the transnational elite was akin to making a deal with the devil. Just as America's founding fathers risked personal fortunes and business ties with Britain, the modern-day patriots knew that sacrifices must be made to restore the Historic American Nation and the promise of a brighter future. The alternative was subservience to the transnational elite or, even more likely, ethnic and cultural genocide.

President Rao had grown so furious with the impotent attempts to squash the uprising that mass genocide was not far from her mind. The FBI and NSA failed to obtain any meaningful intelligence on the America First Network. As far as they knew, Axel Berg had distanced himself from the movement after Congressman Ambrosia's death, leaving no known leader orchestrating the insurrection. It was almost as if the America First

Network had splintered into thousands of local groups that acted independently and unpredictably. The FBI and Department of Justice advised the President that they could not justify any meaningful charges against Axel. Arresting him, they suggested, would risk fomenting additional discontent.

The President knew that she was losing her grip on the situation. She had already invoked the Insurrection Act, activated the National Guard, and deployed the military. For each of those actions, the America First Network had outflanked her and modified their tactics to exploit her weaknesses. History had proven that guerrilla warfare could be highly effective at disrupting a regime but seldom powerful enough to overthrow it. Her administration, however, could never withstand a protracted fight with a determined guerilla force. They would suffer a death by a thousand cuts. She must act decisively to eradicate the scourge that was plaguing the nation.

The next morning, she called a meeting of her cabinet. It was time to take drastic measures. Once they arrived, she laid out her plan for the group. "We have endured this uprising long enough. I can no longer worry about optics. We must act with overwhelming and vengeful force to eradicate these insurgents and thoroughly deter any residual inclinations toward dissent."

"General, this is a revolution," she said as she turned to the Secretary of Defense. "Under the Insurrection Act, the President has the authority to suppress a rebellion through extraordinary means if necessary. I am instructing you to plan a black operation to detain Axel Berg, the founder of the America First Network. He should be captured alive and transported to the Yucca Mountain Facility in Nevada for permanent detention. Have a team scour his residence for actionable intelligence and anything that would expose the members of the America First Network. We are going to cut off the head of the snake, gentlemen."

"We will be operationally ready within twenty-four hours Madam President," the General replied.

"Excellent," President Rao said. "Get it on my desk in the morning and prepare your men for deployment tomorrow evening. It is time to end this charade."

The next day, President Rao was briefed on the Secretary of Defense's operation plan for the arrest of Axel Berg. Former special operators who now were contractors for the Department of Defense would carry out the mission. They would storm Axel's house at four in the morning, detain him, and transport him via van to Yucca Mountain. The entire operation should take less than ten minutes after which a second team would search for intelligence. Upon reading the operation plan, President Rao signed off and said that she would be in the situation room to observe the proceedings.

President Rao entered the situation room thirty minutes before the operation commenced. The contractors were huddled in the back of a van and were clad in black clothes with matching ski masks. The driver was proceeding on route to Axel Berg's home in Los Angeles while the team checked their weapons and prepared for the assault. As they neared the residence, the team leader checked in with operation control. "Control, this is team leader confirming that we are a go for extraction?"

The General looked to President Rao who nodded with approval. Once the signal was given, the radio operator relayed the message. "Team leader, extraction is confirmed. Execute at your ready."

Immediately after, the back door of the van swung open. Eight men streamed out and organized into a tactical position with great precision. Once the team was in place, a battering ram was slammed into the front door which splintered off its frame. Six of the contractors streamed into Axel's house one at a time while the other two covered the rear exits. As quickly as it began, a stunned Axel Berg was detained while his hysterical fiancée wept in fear. The contractors had Axel kneel on the bedroom floor while they zip-tied his hands behind his back and put a black hood over his head.

Elise was screaming for Axel as he was dragged from the room. These men didn't look like police, and she was afraid they were there to kill Axel. As she watched helplessly, the men threw Axel in the back of the van and sped off. They were gone as quickly as they had arrived, with the entire operation lasting less than two minutes. Elise sat alone on the floor crying uncontrollably. Her worst fears had just been realized. Axel was gone.

The two contractors who had covered the rear exits guarded Elise as the intelligence unit descended on the house. They went through everything in the house, boxing up papers, computers, phones, and other potential sources of intelligence. For hours, they searched every nook and cranny for anything that might expose the members of the America First Network. The contractors questioned Elise about her involvement in the rebellion, her knowledge of Axel's activities, and the location of the membership roster. To their dismay, she obfuscated and misdirected them as Axel had trained her. They quickly grew frustrated and ultimately concluded that she had no useful intelligence. After eight hours of intense interrogation and exhaustive searches, they left her alone on the sofa, trembling in fear and wondering what would come next.

President Rao was pleased with the efficiency and precision of the operation, but she knew that it was all for naught if no actionable intelligence was secured. While Axel was a leader and the figurehead of the movement, simply arresting him would do little to derail the momentum of the insurgency. She needed a list of all the members so she could dismantle the America First Network once and for all, thereby securing complete control of the nation. Her globalist policies would then be transcendent and her coalition with the transnational elite would be in control of the most powerful and prosperous nation in the world. America First must be eradicated with maximum prejudice.

24

MOBILIZATION

It took the FBI over two weeks to sort through all of the materials and devices that were confiscated from Axel Berg's residence. In all of that time, they had been unable to uncover information that exposed any member of the America First Network. The hard drives were heavily encrypted, and it would be nearly impossible to crack them. Even if they could obtain the data, there was no guarantee that any actionable intelligence would be uncovered. It seemed that the covert operation against Axel Berg was leading to a dead-end, and it very likely would reignite the insurgency if the America First patriots sought vengeance for Axel's arrest.

President Rao did not receive this news well. She was convinced that Axel was the key to toppling the America First movement and crushing all opposition to her globalist ambitions. Immediately upon receiving the preliminary report on the FBI's findings, she demanded a meeting with the Attorney General to discuss how they would proceed.

"The FBI has had over two weeks and has delivered nothing," she said. "What do you propose we do now? We need to expose those involved so we can crush the insurrection once and for all."

"Madam President, we have a few avenues to garner more intelligence," the Attorney General replied. "The slowest would be to continue to infiltrate the America First Network with undercover agents to garner first-person knowledge of the leadership structure and members. We have taken down a few cells this way, but it has never led to broader arrests. Another strategy would be to embark on a propaganda campaign that paints the activists as white supremacists and anarchists. This campaign would be designed to discredit the America First Network and paint them as enemies of the people. Then we can foment a vast network of citizen informants who will willingly help us eradicate these destructive elements from society. I would anticipate that this could build nationwide momentum faster than using undercover agents, but it may lead to a witch hunt mentality that falsely accuses many innocent people.

"Finally, and perhaps most dramatically, you leverage your powers under the Insurrection Act to strike fear into the hearts of the people. As we arrest activists, especially the ringleaders, we could publically prosecute them for treason and televise their execution. This may be a heavy-handed approach, but it sends the message that there will be no revolution and the only destiny of people associated with the America First Network is a brutal and untimely death. That should disabuse activists of the fantasy that they will be able to resurrect what they call the Historic American Nation."

"Thank you," the President replied, "that is a lot to think about." As President Rao contemplated the advice of the Attorney General, she quickly dismissed the first option because it seemed inadequate given the magnitude of the uprising.

"Of course, President Rao," the Attorney General said in agreement. "It is a tough decision and one that will have lasting implications for the future of America."

Given the options before her, President Rao believed that the choice was clear. "I am not yet prepared for the third option, but we need drastic measures. Let's implement the propaganda campaign and start recruiting a network of informants. We need to act fast because every day that passes will strengthen the nationalists' resolve."

"I will get started right away," the Attorney General replied. "I think this is the best choice, but I will also have my staff prepare for possible escalation if you deem it necessary."

President Rao thanked the Attorney General. As he was leaving, a breaking news report appeared on the television. The nationalists had disrupted the electronic payment system, causing the entire network to shut down. No one could use credit or debit cards, and electronic transfers were suspended. In response to the news, the stock market was down ten percent, and people were panicking across the country. She sighed and realized that time was of the essence. They were losing the battle.

The Attorney General coordinated with the White House communications department to craft suitable messages to influence public opinion. They enlisted a team of public relations specialists and leading psychologists to craft manipulative slogans that cast the America First Network as a rabidly racist mob that hates immigrants and people of color. Other slogans portrayed the insurgents as unhinged right-wing anarchists that want to destroy America and the American way of life. Finally, campaigns were developed to suggest that citizen informants were patriots that protected their country and preserved the American Dream. The citizen informants were depicted as the front-line defenders of security and prosperity in America. After a week, the campaign was ready to be deployed.

The national television networks and government-sponsored broadcasters were forced to air the commercials and disseminate the propaganda throughout the country. Millions of posters and billboards went up in cities far and wide, encouraging people to become citizen informants for the Civil Information Division. This would be a new division of the FBI that would analyze reports from citizen informants and offer rewards to those that provided actionable information regarding the America First Network. Over a thousand FBI agents had been assigned to collect and review tips from these informants and identify those that are most credible. Almost immediately, countless reports from informants began streaming into the Civil Information Division, quickly overwhelming the newly assigned agents.

The FBI began rounding up suspected nationalists that were allegedly part of the America First Network. Each was interrogated vigorously, often using enhanced techniques that had been deemed torture by former presidents. Despite this, the FBI found that many of the tips received from informants were questionable at best. The America First patriots were well versed in the use of technology, and they immediately began trolling the Civil Information Division with false information. Among those implicated were many of the transnational elite that had been complicit in the destruction of the country. While most of these reports were flagged as not credible, some were acted upon, and the President started receiving angry calls bemoaning the unjust treatment and authoritarian tactics used against supporters of her administration.

President Rao demanded an explanation from the Attorney General and wanted recommendations for improving the recruitment and vetting of informants. He suggested that they develop a social credit score where the civilian informants would receive positive credit for accurate information and demerits for false or inaccurate leads. They could even use the demerits as an indication of subversion and investigate those people further. President Rao liked the idea and ordered the Attorney General to implement it immediately. The current system wasn't getting them much closer to exposing the America First Network even though billions of dollars were spent disseminating the propaganda.

Once implemented, the social credit score immediately began paying dividends. The FBI was able to identify the most effective informants and prioritize their leads. Within weeks, the FBI was rounding up hundreds of potential America First activists and interrogating them with the hope of exposing the network. These American citizens were treated like animals and were tortured until they could take no more. After interrogation, they were locked in large holding pens exposed to the elements, with only bread and water to eat.

There was clear momentum behind the citizen informant program despite the questionable accuracy of the information. The growing number of captured activists, however, was making the ongoing incarceration of the alleged insurgents more complicated. The holding pens had been conceived as temporary solutions, and the FBI needed a more permanent option suitable for mass detention. The Attorney General described this problem in detail to the President and eagerly proposed a solution.

"Mr. Attorney General," the President said upon answering his call. "We have made great progress with the Civil Information Division."

"Thank you, Madam President," the Attorney General replied. "I was calling because we have a new problem. Our holding pens were designed for temporary intake and are overflowing with insurgents."

"A good problem to have," the President replied.

"Indeed, but it is untenable at this point. Given that this is an operation governed by the Insurrection Act, I suggest we begin transporting the detainees to the Yucca Mountain Facility and to military bases where they can be properly supervised."

"That seems like a good idea," the President replied, "and I know just the man to make it happen."

"Excellent," the Attorney General said proudly. "Before I go, I would also suggest that the cost that these people have imposed on our nation must be repaid. I suggest we create work camps where the detainees will be forced to engage in hard labor to productively support the society they sought to destroy. Not only is it a fitting punishment, but it would send the message that we are one united country that works toward singular goals."

"I like it," President Rao replied. "Draft a proposal for me to review, and I will take it under advisement. That could be the catalyst to rebuild America and put this chapter of ethnonationalism behind us."

"Absolutely, Madam President," the Attorney General replied.

Immediately after she spoke with the Attorney General, the President asked her assistant to organize a call with the Secretary of Defense and Saul Goldstein. Within an hour, she had them both on the line.

"Thanks for connecting so quickly. We have some important things to discuss."

"Absolutely, Madam President," the General replied.

"Saul, we had previously discussed access to your railroads and transportation networks, and now it's time to put that plan in motion. The success of the Civil Information Division is overwhelming the capacity of the FBI to house detainees. We need your trains to transport these terrorists to military bases around the country that will serve as detention facilities. Through vigorous interrogation, we have certified that the detainees are enemies of the state and must be eliminated. These people are filled with hate and xenophobia. They are not suitable for the new multicultural America. Quite simply, they are subhuman. We must make a clean sweep and remove them from society."

"My companies are at your disposal, Madam President," Saul replied.

"Thank you, Saul," the President replied. "The General will reach out to you to start scheduling transportation to begin relocating these racist nationalists to their permanent home. We will exterminate this scourge once and for all."

"I am looking forward to working with the General," Saul confirmed. "It has been great talking to you, Madam President. Congratulations on your success. Good night."

After Saul hung up, the President spoke directly to the Secretary of Defense. "General, after reviewing proposals from the Justice Department, I have decided that all of the detainees will be sentenced to forced labor while incarcerated. Please have your military police work with the Attorney General's team and the Commerce Secretary to identify suitable work assignments and plans for implementation. The base commanders will have wide latitude in assigning work and enforcing work schedules. These people will be forced to atone for their insurrection and recant their support of America First ethnonationalism."

"Understood, Madam President. We will begin transporting detainees immediately and will develop work programs in coordination with Justice and Commerce. How long should we anticipate housing these detainees?"

"Permanently," the President replied definitively. "These work camps will be their new existence. Their dream of the Historic American Nation will be lost forever. Instead, their new reality will be a life of hard labor in support of a multicultural globalist society that welcomes all."

"We will prepare accordingly," the General acknowledged. "I will keep you informed of our progress. Good night."

Within days the Secretary of Defense and Saul Goldstein had orchestrated the mass transportation of America First detainees via bus and rail. From four regional FBI detention centers, the detainees would be transported by bus to the freight rail yard. They would be processed in Saul's warehouse facilities, implanted with a tracking chip, and loaded into boxcars for transportation to either the Yucca Mountain Facility or one of the regional military bases that were designated as an internment center. The Department of Defense and the Commerce Secretary were working rapidly to prepare for an influx of detainees that would need to be permanently housed and assigned to hard labor. Each internment center would have specific industrial purposes based on location and resources.

The first trains of detainees left for the camps only three days after the plans had been confirmed by the President. In less than two weeks, more than a quarter-million were consigned to the internment centers. They were housed in cramped makeshift facilities that had little protection from the elements and were extremely overcrowded. Anyone who complained learned a brutal lesson that they were there to atone for their sins. Those who didn't learn the lesson were not seen again.

All America First patriots that had evaded capture knew that they were now surrounded by people who would be eager to report them to the Civil Information Division. The entire movement was forced to go underground. Fear became widespread. Any White American, regardless of beliefs, was immediately a suspect and a target for investigation. If a White American was reported to the Civil Information Division, they were assumed to be an America First collaborator unless they had proof to the contrary. The great replacement had accelerated. Soon, historical Americans would be eradicated once and for all.

President Rao had succeeded. She suppressed the uprising and systematically neutered the insurgents. Anyone who might oppose globalism or the transnational elite was being sent to internment centers without trial or proof of guilt. While some of the early detainees certainly were part of the America First Network, the witch hunt engendered by the propaganda campaign engulfed many innocent people. The President had struggled for so long to quash the uprising that she didn't care if innocents were caught up in the operation. In her mind, White Americans had the most to lose from the fundamental transformation of America and expansion of globalism, so an assumption of guilt was justified. They were the greatest threat to her agenda and must be neutralized.

Soon the internment centers amassed one million detainees. Fear and paranoia were rapidly overwhelming the public psyche. Informants began accusing others simply to portray themselves as loyal and compliant subjects. The Civil Information Division was receiving so many tips that they started labeling them as probable or doubtful without a rigorous investigation. The number of detainees grew exponentially, and Saul Goldstein's trains were running multiple trips daily to the internment centers.

Since many companies began to lose some of their most valuable and experienced employees, President Rao signed an executive order instructing the Department of Labor, the State Department, and the Department of Homeland Security to process as many immigrant work visas as companies demanded. There would no longer be restrictions requiring that competent American applicants are considered for an opening, and country caps would be removed so that companies could access the virtually unlimited pool of Indian and Chinese applicants. The entire southern border would be opened to an unlimited and unchecked flow of migrant workers who could come and go as they pleased.

The corporate oligarchs and transnational elite were ecstatic. They had aspired to these ends for decades, but now they could use the world's masses to suppress wages and permanently displace American workers. Profits would soar, and their grip on power would be insurmountable. This is why they had backed President Rao. She delivered what no one else could. The Great Transformation had begun, and the economic and cultural landscape of America would never be the same.

25

THE GREAT
TRANSFORMATION

In just a matter of months, America resembled nothing of its former self. The multinational corporations acted quickly to transfer foreign workers from their offshore facilities to domestic locations. Many engaged staffing companies specializing in Indian and Chinese immigrant workers to further bolster their rosters. States like California and New York were now virtually devoid of White Americans, and schools began teaching classes in Mandarin and Hindi. Entire neighborhoods were repopulated by the new arrivals who found plenty of available housing that had been left vacant when Americans were sent to internment camps. Furniture, heirlooms, and even photos were left behind due to the rapid depopulation conducted by the Civil Information Division.

It didn't take long to erase all memories of former neighbors. Those lucky enough to remain were always mindful of the proverb "There but for the grace of God go I." After the Great Transformation, the remaining Americans knew to keep their heads down and their mouths shut, or they might be next. People focused on keeping their employer happy and their family safe without giving neighbors reason to report them to the Civil Information Division. Never before had the American people been so compliant and servile, bringing great satisfaction to the multinational corporations and transnational elite.

Most White Americans that evaded the culling had quickly fled the cities. Those who remained were primarily corporate oligarchs and the political elite who were exempt from the inquisition. The White Americans fortunate enough to avoid internment were cognizant of the President's motives and the sinister objectives of the Civil Information Division. Elise had been one of the few that escaped the wrath of the eradication squads. She fled Los Angeles shortly after Axel's arrest to hunker down in Henry's house in Crystal Springs. It was very fortunate that Axel's busy schedule with Dr. Pete and the American First Network distracted Axel from the sale of his father's home because it now served as a sanctuary from the citizen informant mobs.

Elise was afraid. She was alone in a relatively unfamiliar town with limited resources. Those flagged by the Civil Information Division for internment had all of their assets frozen and confiscated by the State. Since Elise remained a free woman, her assets were unencumbered, but she was quickly burning through her cash. Fearful that the use of debit or credit cards would expose her location, Elise had subsisted on canned food and nonperishables that she had found in Henry's cellar. A life-long inhabitant of Los Angeles, Elise had no experience in a farming community and not the slightest clue about self-sufficiency. Living a self-sustainable lifestyle was as foreign to her as the immigrants flooding America. She was lost, but at least she was free.

After a few weeks holed up in Henry's house, Elise was beginning to run out of food. Desperation forced her to leave the security of the house and pursue a more reliable means of survival. She ventured into town and found that the Crystal Springs Diner was still open. When she entered, an older woman was wiping down the counters with a sullen look on her face. Since every bar stool was unoccupied, Elise selected the one nearest to the woman and sat down.

The old woman perked up slightly and asked, "What can I get ya?"

"How about a burger and a job?" Elise asked with a hint of desperation.

"Honey, look around," the waitress replied as she gestured to the empty restaurant. "We ain't exactly busy around here."

"I will do anything," Elise answered. "I can bus tables or clean dishes or mop floors. I just need a little money for food."

The waitress sighed and looked Elise up and down. It was obvious that Elise wasn't from Crystal Springs, and she looked desperate. "I'll tell you what. I will give you a chance for a few hours a day, but we can't pay much. How does twenty dollars a day and a free lunch sound?"

Elise didn't hesitate before reaching out her hand and proclaiming, "Deal!"

The waitress shook her head in acknowledgment of the despair afflicting many Americans. "Grab an apron, honey," she said without emotion. "I will get you a burger."

Elise quickly grabbed an apron from behind the counter and reported for duty. Her first day at the diner involved mostly bussing tables and cleaning, but she was grateful for the opportunity. While she mostly kept her head down and focused on the task at hand, she found that working at the diner offered a unique window into the community. Almost all of the customers that day were Hispanic farmworkers, with a few older White farmers disrupting the ethnic monotony.

As she wrapped up for the day, the waitress turned to her and said, "You did alright, so come back tomorrow at noon."

"I can't wait," Elise said with a smile. "I am Elise by the way."

"Betty," the waitress replied curtly.

Over the coming days, Elise slowly chipped away at Betty's gruff exterior. Betty proved to be a fountain of knowledge, which she slowly shared with Elise as time went by. Ever since Henry's death, Crystal Springs had taken a turn for the worst. Henry had been the last leader in Crystal Springs that was capable of captivating the people and attracting a broad coalition of voters. When he was elected, there had been great hope and optimism about the future of the town and a potential resurgence in jobs and economic growth. That all ended when the previously deported illegal alien murdered him.

"The death of Henry led to the death of Crystal Springs," Betty told Elise during a lull in customers. "The coalition of voters that he built and the hope he instilled in a demoralized population could never be replicated. After his death, Pedro Guerrero took over as mayor, and all hope and optimism faded. Pedro was responsive to the large corporate farms and the immigrant community. The trend toward the disenfranchisement of Americans accelerated. Those that didn't leave were often too old to make a fresh start and were left behind to die in a town where they no longer belonged."

"Well you are still here," Elise said to Betty. "Why is that?"

"All of our savings was in this diner. We have nowhere to go, especially now that our revenues are half what they used to be. All of our regular customers are dead or long gone. Now my husband and I join the dying breed of Americans who have no place in the country of our birth. We will live out our remaining days here in Crystal Springs, cherishing the memories of our youth and mourning the end of the American Dream."

Elise could feel Betty's pain but remained guarded. It was obvious that Betty was suspicious of a strange White female who showed up in a dying town. She could not let Betty know her relationship with the Bergs for risk of being arrested by the Civil Information Division.

"I am just trying to put my life back together before I figure out my next move," Elise said in an attempt to quell her curiosity.

"Honey, that's just about everyone nowadays," Betty replied casually. "Unless you are among the wealthy elite, you are just searching for your next meal. I am glad you came along, and you stay as long as you like."

Elise was happy to have a friend, and being in Crystal Springs made her feel connected to Axel. She missed him dearly and was constantly searching for any information about what happened to him. Rumors were spreading about the harsh treatment of the detainees at the internment centers. Meanwhile, the President was boasting about the industrial might of her new labor camps, which were inundated with requests from multinational corporations seeking to exploit this new source of free labor. Elise wondered if Axel was currently subjected to hard labor in support of the enemy. If so, at least he was still alive.

After President Rao partnered with the corporate oligarchs, Americans confined at the internment centers began to manufacture virtually all American steel, mine the majority of American coal and iron ore, sort and manage the trash, and mill most of the lumber and pulp originating from the United States. Basic industries were now entirely staffed by conscripted laborers housed at internment centers. American industry was operating at an unprecedented level of productivity, lavishing the transnational elite and corporate oligarchs with unfathomable wealth. They had repopulated America with armies of compliant and subservient workers who would do as they were told or risk being sent back to whatever third world hellhole that they came from.

Despite the ruthless oppression of the Naglia Rao regime, pockets of America First patriots remained in the shadows. Like pesky mosquitos, they located easy targets and struck out opportunistically just to let President Rao know that she had yet to exterminate them all. Elise often dreamed that somehow Axel was still involved, leading his patriotic followers in a virtuous fight against the fundamental transformation of America. She knew, however, that this was likely far from the truth.

The next day at the diner, Betty had a long look on her face. That wasn't unusual, but today something seemed to be deeply troubling her. While Elise was putting on her apron and preparing for her shift, Betty approached as if she wanted to share a secret.

"Elise, three White farmers who had lived in Crystal Springs for over seventy years were taken away last night by the Civil Information Division."

"Betty, no!" Elise said surprised. "What had they done?"

"Nothing of course," Betty answered. "Rumor has it that George McLennan of the Crystal Springs Farm Bureau coveted their land and filed false information with the Civil Information Division. George's report was deemed credible because he is a wealthy corporate farmer. He has an impeccable social credit score and is held in high regard by the corporate oligarchy, so the government did his bidding despite the lack of corroborating evidence. The accused are small family farmers, like the ones that once thrived in Crystal Springs and were the backbone of a vibrant community. They were powerless when confronted by the overwhelming might of the government."

"How scary," Elise replied. Memories of the raid that resulted in Axel's abduction began to resurface in her consciousness.

"Be careful Elise, you don't know when someone will turn on you. We are all targets, and they won't stop until they have eradicated us all. Those of us that remain are just a reminder of the past and a threat to their future."

"Thanks for the warning," Elise responded with concern. "I will keep my head down and stay off their radar."

"We must look out for each other," Betty said genuinely. "There ain't many of us left."

After the arrest of the farmers, there was a lot of tension around Crystal Springs, but especially in the White community. Everyone was suspicious about what happened and fearful that they might be next. People noticed that Elise was living in Henry Berg's old house, and she began to fear that her presence in the town would invite false reports by desperate citizen informants. Unfortunately, she didn't have much choice. She could not return to Los Angeles, and there was nowhere else to go.

Elise kept a low profile for weeks, desperate not to draw unnecessary attention, but it was becoming more difficult. That Friday, Betty came up to her at work and said, "Honey, is there something you want to tell me?"

Shocked by the forthrightness of the inquiry, Elise was evasive. "What possibly could you mean?"

"You can't hide it from me," Betty replied. She then leaned over toward Elise and whispered, "You are pregnant!"

"How could you tell?" Elise replied in a hushed tone. She had purposely been wearing baggy clothes and disguising her condition with great success for months. It appeared that it was no longer working.

"Honey, I have six kids and twenty-two grandkids. I have seen it all before."

Elise looked concerned that her secret was exposed. She was all alone and vulnerable in the current environment. She looked at the floor nervously.

Sensing the concern, Betty sought to alleviate her anxiety. "Don't you worry, honey. I have delivered many babies in my day, and we will take good care of you. Children are the future after all."

Still concerned, Elise looked at Betty and uttered a simple phrase. "Thank you."

"My pleasure," Betty replied. "Your secret is safe with me."

For the next four months, Elise was either at the house or the diner. She was too afraid to venture anywhere else. Her secret was now obvious to the world, and she wanted to avoid interaction with any unnecessary people who might not share Betty's goodwill.

After hiding out for months, the time had come. Her baby would arrive any day. Betty made preparations and began spending evenings with Elise at Henry's house. After two weeks together anxiously awaiting the baby's arrival, Elise gave birth to a healthy baby boy.

Betty was beaming with pride when she asked, "What will you name him?"

"I will name him Caleb," Elise replied smiling. "Like his namesake, he must be fearless when confronting the seemingly insurmountable odds against him."

"A fitting name indeed," Betty replied. "May God give him strength and courage to overcome the obstacles ahead!"

"Amen," Elise agreed.

26

INDUSTRIAL SUPREMECY

Saul Goldstein, through his railroads and freight transportation system, had played a pivotal role in suppressing dissent and crushing the momentum of the America First Network. His trains had expedited the transfer of detainees to work camps, enabling what was the greatest mobilization of people since the Second World War. At least thirty million Americans were relocated to the internment centers since the first wave of arrests. While he had profited handsomely from his contract with the government, Saul felt that his pivotal role in the Great Transformation should earn him additional privileges.

Saul's cooperation with President Rao was instrumental to the implementation of her plan and made critical transportation assets available for the relocation of America First activists. Many corporate oligarchs, while sympathetic to President Rao's agenda to fundamentally transform America, would have balked at jeopardizing their corporate image in such a public and risky endeavor. Saul never hesitated and radically reorganized his rail business to accommodate the government's significant demands. Now it was time to call in his chits.

At his request, Saul's executive assistant reached out to the White House to schedule a meeting. The White House conveyed that President Rao was very busy, but she could always find time for her friend Saul Goldstein. They agreed to schedule a call that afternoon.

Saul was sitting comfortably at his massive antique desk reviewing real-time revenue and sales volume data for his various businesses when his phone rang. He answered, leaned back in his chair, and turned to look out the windows of his office high above Central Park.

"Please hold for the President," the voice on the other end of the line said.

A few seconds later, President Rao greeted her old friend. "Saul, it is so great to hear from you."

"Madam President, I appreciate you taking this call on such short notice," Saul replied politely. "Congratulations on your great success in suppressing the America First uprising and accelerating the Great Transformation."

"I couldn't have done it without your help," she replied.

"I am glad that my railroad company could be of service," Saul said in preparation for laying out his demands. "Now that the transportation needs of the operation are waning, I wanted to discuss how my companies could play a greater role in the ongoing execution of the work camps. My waste management and trucking companies could be much more efficient if we were able to build facilities close to the internment centers and utilize the work crews to sort trash, recover valuable materials, and load trucks for distribution. We could even build highly efficient waste-to-energy facilities to incinerate the garbage and generate electricity to power the internment centers. All of this could be billed as a major green energy initiative that seeks to maximize the recovery of valuable materials and efficiently dispose of waste, all far removed from civilized society."

"I like the idea," President Rao responded. "I will have the Commerce Secretary reach out to coordinate details. Your commitment to the endeavor will not go unrewarded."

"Thank you Madam President," Saul replied. "Your visionary strategy to suppress dissent and reinvent America will usher in a new era of American economic supremacy. The sky is the limit, and my companies are committed to standing by your side to build a brighter future."

As Saul concluded the call, he triumphantly looked out his office windows at the impressive skyline of the city. Generations of immigrants had built this city into a global financial and economic hub. Now, their ancestors would be working in labor camps across the country to build a new America as the nation welcomed a fresh wave of immigrants. These immigrants, however, weren't here to become Americans but to replace them. There would be no assimilation, just eradication. Saul couldn't help but notice the irony.

Multiculturalism was always a myth that was used to lull people into complacency. Enticed by a new ethnic restaurant or cultural novelty, the American people embraced diversity and watched silently as their culture was diluted and the nation devolved into an unrecognizable transnational amalgamation. Diversity was never a source of strength but was, instead, divisive and polarizing. Now, this destructive force was devouring the Historic American Nation.

Saul Goldstein was acutely aware of how propaganda and stereotypes could be used to marginalize a group of people in a divided country. In a society that lacked cultural cohesion, fissures would develop enabling the shrewd manipulator to marginalize threats, eliminate resistance, and concentrate power. In America, globalists portrayed anyone who questioned the value of diversity or resisted multiculturalism as a racist, a bigot, or a xenophobe. The transnational elite made it socially unacceptable to be a proud American that wanted to preserve the Historic American Nation, and now President Rao has completed a silent coup and eliminated all political opposition to a multicultural America.

Saul recognized this development early on. His ancestors had been nomadic and were forced to survive under various regimes often hostile to their beliefs. Even in his youth, he had developed a shrewd instinct for identifying trends and aligning himself with the prevailing tides. Saul built a corporate empire by being opportunistic and capitalizing on the misfortune of others. For Saul, the Great Transformation was the biggest economic realignment of his lifetime, and he was determined to come out on top.

The Commerce Secretary called Saul later that week to discuss his proposal. "Saul, I have discussed your plan with the President, and we are eager to see if we can get it off the ground quickly. What do you need to get started?"

"Mr. Secretary, we could get up and running immediately with a manual processing facility, but we would want to ramp up to a full-scale operation quickly. For that, we would need some land to construct industrial sorting facilities, environmental permits for waste handling, and authorization to build waste-to-energy facilities or chemical plants. If we can agree to a long-term capacity reservation contract for the transportation of detainees, then my company would be willing to cover all costs of the new infrastructure required. We would just want to secure a guaranteed minimum payment for the transportation of detainees, regardless of actual utilization."

"That can be arranged," the Secretary replied confidently. "I think we have a good plan here, and I want to get started right away. We need to make sure there are no idle hands and that all detainees are set to a purpose."

"We will get started immediately," Saul agreed. "Trucks will begin making deliveries on Monday."

"Excellent," the Commerce Secretary said enthusiastically. "I will let the General know to expect them and to prepare the detainees."

Saul had big plans. His most labor-intensive subsidiaries could greatly benefit from a subservient workforce that had no rights and worked for free. If he could get the waste management plans off the ground, then he could expand into recycling facilities, waste-to-energy plants, and perhaps raw materials production. This could be a multibillion-dollar expansion of his existing business and would provide a steady flow of cargo for his established rail and trucking companies. It would solidify his societal standing among the corporate elite and render him immune from oppressive regulations and executive orders.

Early in Saul's career, he learned that size meant power, and with power came clout. Rather than be wedded to principles or values, Saul learned to be adaptive and to play the hand that he was dealt. He had no sympathy for the Americans caught up in President Rao's cultural cleansing. Quite the contrary, he despised them. They allowed their values and beliefs to guide them on a hopeless crusade that ultimately led to an untenable predicament. Their idealism and longing to maintain their place in the world ultimately led to a foolish quest to preserve a legacy that was already lost. In Saul's opinion, surviving and adapting in pursuit of personal enrichment was the name of the game.

Saul's parents had been survivors. They did what was necessary during their time at Auschwitz to make it out alive. Out of that experience, they always carried with them the lesson that life is always an existential crisis. Even when you feel comfortable and complacent with your life, forces are conspiring against you to displace you from your perch and take all that you cherish. His parents would constantly tell Saul to never be complacent and to always adapt to the situation at hand. Sometimes it is necessary to partner with people that hate you or wish you dead in order to persevere and perhaps even prosper. The man that can survive and thrive under any regime, they would say, is the man that will endure the test of time.

Long before President Rao took power, Saul could sense that globalism was ascendant and the transnational elite were gaining control of America. As a successful businessman with subsidiaries in a variety of industries, he knew better than most that the American worker was being left behind in this new regime. Rather than help his fellow Americans, he focused on boosting profitability by hiring immigrant workers and outsourcing technology jobs. He accelerated his acquisitions of distressed companies, capitalized on their assets, and burdened them with additional debt. As his business grew, so did his power and influence.

It took Saul Goldstein just six months to get fully operational at the internment centers. Large industrial trash sorting facilities that could handle dozens of truckloads per hour were immediately profitable upon construction. The detainees manually sorted through the smelly soiled trash to divert recyclable materials from landfills. Trains that previously transported millions of Americans to the work camps were now also conveying hoppers full of garbage to the sorting facilities and delivering recyclable materials to end markets. For Saul, this was just the beginning.

He began working feverishly to fabricate industrial-scale waste-to-energy plants at every location. Given his cozy relationship with the administration, environmental permits were fast-tracked and regulations were suspended to facilitate construction. Saul was able to ship construction materials to the internment camps via his railroads, enabling him to quickly build six massive electrical generation facilities that are fueled by incinerating trash. These facilities went into full production immediately, operating around the clock with a consistent feedstock of garbage that was sorted at the camps.

Trains were now unloading tons of trash at the facilities with multiple deliveries each day. Almost overnight, Saul had captured more than half of the waste management business across the United States and had increased recovery rates for recyclable materials to over ninety percent. With the incinerators operating at full capacity, they were able to provide abundant cheap power for the internment centers and the surrounding areas, so Saul began planning the next phase of his new enterprise.

The President and the Commerce Secretary were extremely happy with the success of Saul's businesses at the internment centers. He was generating an abundance of productive work for the detainees while addressing societal needs. When Saul approached them with a proposal for the next phase of his industrial plan, they quickly authorized it without scrutiny. Now that he had abundant cheap power and a steady feedstock of raw materials, Saul planned to vertically integrate and begin processing recyclables into raw materials. He would build a plastics facility and a metals plant at each of the internment centers. Soon he would be getting paid to process trash that would be used to generate electricity and to power his recycling facilities. These recycling plants would create valuable raw materials for his manufacturing businesses upstream. His railroad and trucking businesses would provide transportation throughout this value chain, ensuring that he retained all the profits.

In just thirty-six months, Saul had built an extremely profitable industrial empire that exploited the forced laborers at the work camps. His industrial conglomerate now operated throughout the product life cycle from processing waste through finished goods. The raw plastics created from recyclable materials were used at Saul's carpet mills, while the aluminum and steel were crafted into appliances at his factories. By leveraging a servile workforce at the internment centers, he had developed a pipeline of virtually free raw materials and doubled his company's profitability. In Saul's mind, that achievement alone justified all of his prior actions. He had been prescient enough to align himself with the globalist movement and now was reaping the rewards.

Saul looked to the heavens and thought of his parents. They instilled in him values of adaptability and opportunism, and he carried these lessons with him throughout his life. His parents had survived Auschwitz, immigrated to the United States, and established the foundations of Saul's industrial empire. Saul had followed their lead and aligned himself with anyone that would help him build his empire. When he reflected on all that he had accomplished, he felt validated. If they were still here today, Saul knew that they would be overwhelmed with pride.

27

THE STRUGGLE CONTINUES

With the Great Transformation nearing its final stage, President Rao solidified her grip on power. With more than thirty million Americans detained at work camps, she won re-election in the largest landslide in United States history. It was surprising to many that she even faced an opposition candidate because most Americans lived in fear of the Civil Information Division. No one dared to question the internment of American citizens publicly because they feared that they would be whisked away in the dead of night and thrown in a boxcar destined for the nearest work camp.

President Rao had nearly eradicated the America First movement by ruthlessly leveraging the overwhelming power of the government. The United States was now comprised of the transnational elite, American quislings, and a subservient and compliant immigrant working class. All that remained of the America First Network were small splinter cells, hiding in the shadowy underground to evade detection. Riotous and disruptive activity had been almost eliminated following the introduction of the Civil Information Division and the creation of work camps. Peace and prosperity had been restored for the transnational elite.

For American citizens, life had become a constant struggle. White Americans who evaded life in a labor camp were virtually excluded from society, with most struggling to find work. Only White Americans who accrued sufficient social credit scores and fully embraced the Great Transformation were immune from oppression. All other White Americans were viewed as racist oppressors who didn't deserve a place in the new multicultural America. They were the Dalits in the new American caste system.

Non-White Americans found themselves competing with an unlimited supply of cheap immigrant labor. Wages plummeted, especially for manual labor, due to the abundance of servile laborers at the work camps. Those who were able to secure work were viewed with suspicion and faced discrimination, especially if they only spoke English. They were forced to accept the most undesirable positions at already suppressed wages, and if they complained, they would be fired and replaced with an immigrant who knew not to speak up or risk deportation. Labor had become a commodity that was exchanged in a global marketplace where billions of people would accept almost any terms to work in America. The transnational elite were now firmly in control, and the fundamental transformation of America was nearly complete.

Life was extremely difficult for most Americans after the Great Transformation. Everyone outside of the transnational elite and the corporate oligarchs had to make do with less. Gone were the days where hard work and personal responsibility would enable you to climb the ladder of economic prosperity. America was no longer a nation with a prosperous middle class emboldened by the American Dream. Now, Americans worked to survive.

After the systematic culling of the America First patriots, the American people were adrift without direction or leadership. It had been months since President Rao was re-elected, and there were no further dissident acts of resistance. It was smooth sailing under the new hierarchical system, which was good for business. Comfortable atop their societal perch, the transnational elite enjoyed wealth and luxuries that were unfathomable to average Americans. The abundance of cheap labor ensured that they all could maintain a large domestic staff to take care of their expansive estates and household needs. They lived a life of decadence and privilege while the rest of America suffered in despair.

That was the new status quo until the fifth anniversary of Congressman Ambrosia's death. It was then that all hell broke loose and the first major blows against President Rao's globalist regime landed with devastating effect. The last remaining cells of the America First Network coordinated an attack on major multinational corporations that collaborated with the government to send Americans to internment centers. In the dark of night, a half dozen trucks loaded with ammonium nitrate and nitromethane drove to the headquarters of the Chinese tech company that developed and maintained the social credit score, the Civil Information Division, and other international companies involved in the exploitation of detainee labor. All were detonated with devastating effect.

The explosions occurred virtually simultaneously even though they targeted facilities in different locations across the country. Within minutes, it was all over, but the aftermath was enduring. The Chinese technology company completely imploded, destroying their primary servers and knocking the social credit system offline for two days. A pivotal transportation hub in Saul Goldstein's rail network was obliterated, leaving a thirty-foot deep crater covering the area of a football field. Traffic to and from half of the internment centers would be curtailed for months until the tracks and infrastructure could be rebuilt. The Port of Los Angeles in San Pedro, California suffered extensive damage disrupting shipping activity from the Asia Pacific region. On the other side of the country, a blast took out critical power infrastructure owned by a French conglomerate, causing a power outage in the Washington, D.C. metro area for two weeks. The devastation was widespread, but it was trivial compared to the damage that President Rao had inflicted upon the country.

The President was briefed about the blasts in the early morning hours. She was furious and immediately demanded retribution. The Civil Information Division building had been badly damaged, but the informant data and target profiles were electronically stored offsite, so the investigators suffered little impairment to their operational capabilities. President Rao ordered an immediate escalation of investigations and arrests. She believed that a show of force was necessary to deter additional attacks and to reinforce her zero-tolerance policy toward dissent. The only deterrent that had been effective so far was the ruthless eradication of dissidents and the swift internment of suspected America First sympathizers.

Later that morning, news broadcasts led with coverage of the blasts. After describing the devastation that had occurred, the news anchors on every network announced that they had breaking news on the attacks. They had all received a manifesto declaring that the America First Network was responsible for the bombings and that additional attacks would be forthcoming unless Axel Berg and all illegally detained Americans were immediately released. As a caveat, the news anchors announced that they were unable to verify the provenance or authenticity of the manifesto but believed it to be legitimate. This strike was a bold move that reinvigorated the battle for the soul of America.

For the next two weeks, the Civil Information Division went on an all-out offensive to round up suspected insurgents and relocate them to internment centers. Snatch and grabs became commonplace. Government vans would roll up on unsuspecting targets who were quickly apprehended and transported directly to a processing facility. Vigorous investigations became a relic of the past after President Rao authorized the internment of suspected dissidents based on plausible suspicion of anti-government behavior. Additionally, Civil Information Division officers were authorized to arrest White Americans if they reasonably resembled a potential suspect. People were paralyzed with fear and afraid to leave their homes lest they be swept up in a raid. The country, once proud of its individual liberties, had become a militarized police state.

A month after the explosions, President Rao had yet to release any detainees and instead had transported over two million more Americans to internment centers. She was proud of her response and felt confident that the maximum pressure campaign had been effective in disrupting the America First Network and deterring additional attacks. The country was beginning to return to normal. Electrical power in the nation's capital was restored and repairs were completed at the heavily damaged rail hub, which enabled train traffic to the eastern work camps to resume. Cargo from China and other Asian hubs had been redirected to Long Beach, Oakland, and Seattle for processing while repairs in San Pedro were underway. President Rao had once again demonstrated her ability to suppress opposition and restore the social order through force.

As people returned to work, a sense of normalcy began to return amidst the chaos that characterized the new American nation. The paralyzing fear that gripped the non-immigrant community diminished as the Civil Information Division raids subsided. It was just two months since the attacks, but people began to believe that the coordinated explosions were only an isolated moment of rage by a disenfranchised segment of the population. And then, there was Henry Hub.

Exactly two months after the first round of attacks, a massive explosion occurred at the Henry Hub natural gas distribution and processing facility in Louisiana. That facility acts as a major pricing center for natural gas futures in the United States, due to the volume of gas that flows through the hub to major interstate pipelines that serve the entire Eastern United States. The explosion was so large that it sent shockwaves through towns that were two hundred miles away and sent fireballs soaring into the air. It took firefighters three days to put out the blaze, which disrupted power supplies throughout the East Coast. This one strike did more damage to the economy of the United States than the previous six combined. More than a quarter of Americans were without power, industrial production ground to a halt, and riots were erupting in the streets. This time, it wasn't fear that overwhelmed the people but desperation.

President Rao again had to pivot into crisis mode. Her usual heavy-handed approach seemed ineffective in this circumstance. The people needed food. They needed power. They lacked basic necessities, and they were expecting their leaders to come to their aid. President Rao called on the Federal Emergency Management Agency to coordinate disaster support to the stricken areas. The Federal government, however, was already stretched thin, given the need to provide subsistence to over thirty million detainees. A significant portion of the American population had been impacted by the recent attack, and there were inadequate supplies of basic necessities to care for everyone.

The Department of Agriculture advised that food supplies could support demand for about thirty to forty days before existing stockpiles were exhausted. Winter was fast approaching. Without power or natural gas, people would be left without heat and in some cases potable water. Since the pipelines were down, FEMA would have to transport liquefied natural gas and propane by train to the affected areas. This would be a massive undertaking that would strain the government to its limits. Drastic action must be taken to prioritize resources and protect the American people.

President Rao once again convened her cabinet to discuss the available options. Quickly a multifaceted consensus developed. First, any recent immigrants in the affected areas that were nonessential employees would be immediately deported to their native country. There was significant guilt among the cabinet that they couldn't uphold their multicultural ideals, but this was a disaster that required extraordinary measures. Second, aid would be granted according to a priority system in which people with the highest social credit scores and most distinguished social status would receive priority for aid while those lowest in the social hierarchy would be granted only the bare necessities. Finally, block grants of food and supplies would be made to the work camps to be rationed and distributed as the Secretary of Defense saw fit. He was granted exclusive domain and authority over the internment centers with instructions to prioritize efficiency over equity.

There would be difficult months ahead. While it was critical to provide necessities to the people, there must be a reckoning for the act of terror perpetrated against America. President Rao was determined to eradicate every remaining vestige of the America First Network and extinguish any hope for the resurrection of the Historic American Nation. She had orchestrated the Great Transformation of America, yet everything she had accomplished would be under constant threat unless she eliminated the opposition. Escalation was inevitable.

28

EXTERMINATION

Life was difficult across America following the attack on the Henry Hub gas distribution facilities. People were without electricity across much of the country, transportation networks ground to a halt, and millions of people were out of work. Nowhere was the impact more acutely felt than at the work camps. The American detainees at the camps worked more than twelve hours a day, lived in deplorable conditions, and now received only minimal food. It had always been a struggle to survive in the camps, but now people were dying every day.

At first, it was just the elderly. Soon, however, malnourished people of all ages were collapsing from exhaustion. These Americans toiled in grueling labor for the majority of their waking hours to maintain the lifestyle of the corporate oligarchs and globalist elite. Those that were no longer productive became merely a nuisance that could no longer be indulged. President Rao and the transnational elite were ready to move forward and put the country's struggle with the America First Network behind them. They were eager to permanently displace Whites, once and for all, as the predominant ethnic force in America.

Previously, the guards at the work camps would tend to the sick and the injured. Basic field medicine was commonly administered, and it was usually sufficient to triage the afflicted. Following the Henry Hub attack, the dire conditions outside of the camps changed everything. Medicine and supplies were to be conserved for the benefit of citizens with higher social status so the guards began to leave the sick and the injured to fend for themselves. Other detainees tried to help, but the guards would quickly force them to return to work. Productivity was now paramount. Anyone who couldn't contribute was expendable.

It didn't take long for the barracks to become overwhelmed with weak and sick detainees who were unable to work. Initially, the guards ignored those who couldn't work and forced the able-bodied to work harder in order to compensate for the lost productivity. Ultimately, it became apparent that the invalids were a distraction and were consuming resources that the work camps could not spare. To protect the able-bodied, the Secretary of Defense decreed that all sick or injured detainees would be transferred to the infirmary. As the weeks passed, few returned to the barracks.

Meanwhile, President Rao ordered the camps to operate the waste-to-energy facilities at full capacity to supply much-needed electricity to the grid. While Saul Goldstein's railroads were still able to keep a steady stream of trash flowing to the internment centers, his supplies were inadequate to meet the elevated demand for combustible materials. In response, the camps began incinerating anything available to keep the waste-to-energy plants working at full steam. Much of the generation capacity of the Eastern United States was offline, so full utilization of every operable power plant was essential to prevent a complete collapse of the economy.

While the pool of labor was depleted by the demise of infirm detainees, the internment camps were regularly repopulated with a fresh crop of able-bodied laborers courtesy of the Civil Information Division. Since the Henry Hub attack, the flow of Americans to the internment centers accelerated once again. President Rao ordered anyone plausibly involved in subversive behavior to be detained and transported to the camps. This usually meant that any White American would immediately be a suspect and the slightest hint of culpability was enough to seal their fate. The Great Transformation was embarking on its final phase, and it seemed no force was sufficient to stop it.

Axel had now been confined to his subterranean tomb for years. Deep inside the Yucca Mountain Facility was the highest security detention center in the country. Only those with top-secret security clearance even knew of this black site's existence because its primary purpose was to house enemy combatants and people being held without trial. Yucca Mountain was now filled with the most passionate activists of the America First Network. It was nearing capacity after years of systematic incarceration of suspected subversives. Outside the high-security facility was the largest internment center in the country. Almost ten million people from all across the Western United States were held at this camp, and the Secretary of Defense received orders to reduce the population to conserve resources.

When the Secretary arrived at the Yucca Mountain Internment Camp, it became apparent why he had received the orders. Barracks were overflowing with people, and there was complete disorder among the detainees. A hierarchy had been allowed to develop where the strong preyed on the weak, and people were forced to fight for food or shelter. Sick and injured people were left outside in the mud to die alone. It was immediately apparent that the facility was overpopulated, and a solution was necessary.

Drastic times require drastic measures, and the Secretary of Defense knew what must be done. He ordered the military police to round up all sick and injured detainees and take them to the infirmary. Those that were incurable would be given a quick death and incinerated in the waste-to-energy plant at the internment center. For everyone else at the camp, new productivity rules would be put in place. The detainees that were most productive would be allowed to eat first and would receive larger portions. This was meant to incentivize hard work and to cull the least productive from the population.

The new policies were extremely effective. Productivity rose even as the population of detainees began to decline. President Rao called the Secretary to congratulate him on his success. "Mr. Secretary, I appreciate your ability to quickly solve problems with acute decisiveness."

"Thank you, Madam President," he replied. "We have just begun, but we are showing great progress."

The President agreed and asked the Secretary to address another issue. "It is time to end the scourge of America First once and for all. Axel Berg is housed at Yucca Mountain, is he not?"

"Yes, Madam President. Axel is housed in the high-security facility."

"Excellent," she replied. "I think we need to exert some pressure on the leadership of the America First Network to publicly denounce the movement and their beliefs. This would go a long way toward discouraging additional attacks and would demoralize the few remaining Americans predisposed to taking up the cause. We must decisively convey that this has always been a fool's errand doomed to failure."

"What would you like me to do, Madam President?"

"You always have creative solutions," she said. "I will leave it in your hands."

"Understood," the Secretary acknowledged. "We will deliver."

Immediately after their call, the Secretary of Defense called the Yucca Mountain Facility and asked that Axel Berg be brought to the observation suite. Far above the depths where Axel had been imprisoned was a large control center carved into the mountain where you could observe the entire internment camp as well as the thousands of cameras that monitored the high-security cells. A team of operators and security personnel monitored everything that was occurring at the facility and could immediately deploy military police to address any disturbances.

As requested, an operator in the suite sent an elevator to retrieve Axel from his cell. Once it arrived, he barked orders to Axel over the intercom.

"Inmate 03041949, you are ordered to depart your cell and enter the elevator."

Axel looked around his cell perplexed. He had not left his cell or spoken to anyone in years.

"Inmate 03041949, immediately proceed to the elevator," the operator repeated demonstrably.

Axel stared blankly, like a deer in headlights, as the open doors of the elevator awaited his action. Unaware of anything that occurred in the outside world since his incarceration, Axel wondered if he perhaps would be set free. He had been detained for so long without a trial that it seemed likely he was boarding an elevator that would bring him to freedom or possibly his death. Axel hesitantly entered the elevator and watched as the doors closed behind him. It whisked him away as suddenly as it had arrived, traveling with such speed that it was impossible to gauge how far he had traveled. When the doors opened, he was greeted by four armed guards who motioned for him to exit the elevator. They walked silently down a hallway toward two locked steel doors. As they approached the doors, Axel saw a man in a highly decorated military uniform waiting for his arrival.

When they reached the end of the hallway, the man greeted them with an authoritative tone. "Axel, I am the Secretary of Defense of the United States. You have been detained by the order of President Rao for subversion and inciting a rebellion against the government. It is time for you to atone for your crimes and recognize the legitimacy of the new American nation. Please follow me."

The Secretary swiped his identification badge and opened the steel doors. As he led Axel and the armed guards into the observation suite, Axel could see masses of people spread as far as the eye could see. They were contained behind miles of barbed wire fencing and illuminated by countless floodlights, such that every action in the camp could be easily observed. Axel was speechless as he soaked in the magnitude of what was before him.

"Axel, this is the America First Network," the Secretary said as he gestured with his hand toward the countless detainees. "President Rao has systematically dismantled the resistance movement and now they labor in service of the new American nation. There will be no resurrection of the Historic American Nation. Your dream is dead. It is time that you finally acknowledge the new reality and embrace the virtues of diversity, inclusion, and globalism. Multiculturalism is the future."

Axel stood silently in disbelief of what was before him. Millions of his people – patriotic Americans – were milling around like cattle in a giant pen. It was as if he had awakened from a lengthy slumber just to find the world completely upside down. This was a nightmare that he had never imagined.

"If it were up to me, I would have left you locked away in your cell forever," the Defense Secretary continued. "But President Rao has other plans for you. While you were locked away, the America First Network has committed countless terrorist attacks against the United States. This cannot be allowed to continue. The most recent attack wiped out power for the entire East Coast and has severely threatened our food supply. President Rao is determined that loyal Americans do not suffer as a result of this terrorist act, so the brunt of the pain must be borne by the America First insurgents. Tonight will be the first step toward correcting the injustice."

As the Secretary of Defense was speaking, a large group of frail-looking detainees was ushered single file into the courtyard closest to the observation suite. Their faces were sullen, and they looked defeated as they stood limply along an exterior wall of a cinder block building. There must have been five hundred people lined up with bright floodlights illuminating their battered bodies.

"Axel, the President has made you an offer," the Secretary continued. "You can't save yourself, but you can save your people. All you need to do is agree to announce publicly on live television that you, the leader of the America First Network, renounce all violence against the United States and pledge your support to the new American nation. You must state that the Historic American Nation is a fantasy, and the true American nation is an idea founded on open borders, multiculturalism, and immigration. After all, it was immigrants that built America, and it will be the next generation of immigrants that lead us forward.

"In exchange for your cooperation, your people will be spared, and over time many will be released. You, however, must pay for your crimes of fomenting a revolution and inciting acts of terror, but we can certainly make your accommodations more comfortable. This is a very generous offer from President Rao, and we need an immediate answer. Resources are in short supply following the most recent attack, so drastic action must be taken."

Axel stared blankly ahead at the people standing before them. He knew the Secretary had something abhorrent planned, but there was no possible way that he could accept their offer. Axel watched them murder his father, assassinate Congressman Ambrosia, and detain his people in deplorable conditions. He would never bend a knee.

"I will not bend a knee," Axel replied defiantly. "America First is our destiny."

"I thought you might say that," the Secretary replied. He turned to one of the operators in the observation suite and nodded.

"Authorization has been granted," the operator announced to the guards at the internment camp.

Axel watched as two armored Humvees with fifty caliber rifles mounted on top drove into the courtyard. Four soldiers exited the vehicles armed with automatic rifles and two other soldiers manned the fifty caliber rifles up top. They lined up to face the detainees directly and opened fire. Hundreds of rounds of ammunition were unloaded on the frail detainees until there was nothing left but lifeless bodies and a blood-stained wall.

The soldiers got back in their Humvees and exited the courtyard. As they left, a large transport vehicle entered the courtyard and a half dozen soldiers began to load the bodies into the back. One by one they tossed the lifeless bodies into the truck until it could hold no more.

As the truck drove out of the courtyard, the Defense Secretary turned to Axel and pointed to four large smokestacks billowing clouds of gray smoke into the sky. "See that?" he said callously. "These dead traitors will power the growth of the real American nation. This is the actual destiny of the America First patriots unless you agree to President Rao's terms. Your people will be incinerated with the other trash unless you acknowledge the superiority of multiculturalism and the ascendance of the new American nation. Give it some thought, Axel. We will speak again soon."

As if on cue, the four guards escorted Axel back to the elevator where he was returned to his cell. Axel always knew that the open borders acolytes and the multicultural mob wanted patriotic Americans dead, but it took on a new significance to see it with his own two eyes. As he sat alone in his cell, he tried to forget the violent execution of all those people. The transnational elite were determined to repopulate America one way or another, and there may be nothing anyone could do to stop it.

Axel reflected upon the President's offer. He had always known that the America First Network was a dissident movement that faced long odds, but people had apathetically accepted the steady leftward drift in both cultural and economic policy for far too long. If they acquiesced to complete ethnic and cultural genocide, then they would simply surrender the nation. America was not just an idea. Instead, it was their home, their heritage, and their legacy. There was a cultural and philosophical identity inherent to Americans. One could not simply become an American by being granted a temporary work visa or by sneaking across the border. The Great Transformation may be well underway, but Axel was not about to surrender his nation to those that sought to repopulate and fundamentally transform America. He would live or die with America First. His destiny had arrived, and his fight would continue.

29

THE BEGINNING

Young Caleb Berg enjoyed growing up in Crystal Springs. There were plenty of wide-open spaces and lots of room in his grandfather's old farmhouse. Life in Crystal Springs was simple. They didn't have a lot, but Caleb and his mom had each other, and they were sheltered from the chaos of the outside world. The farmhouse was on the outskirts of town enabling them to remain relatively secluded. Caleb was able to experience life without the constant threat of raids by government agents.

After initially taking the job at the diner just to survive, Elise found the companionship of Betty and the flexibility of the work hours comforting, especially after the birth of her son. Betty adored little Caleb who would play in the office of the diner while Elise was working. The Crystal Springs Diner continued to struggle financially, but they made enough to get by and took comfort in their friendship. In these difficult times, it was more critical than ever that they stick together and look out for one another.

Caleb had just celebrated his sixth birthday, and Elise was optimistic for the year ahead. He was a smart kid who, like his father, was passionate and determined. She was homeschooling Caleb so that he would remain sheltered, and his true identity would be protected. With every passing month, it seemed that President Rao continued to round up more White Americans on suspicion of being involved in the America First Network. Caleb would become a prime target of the Civil Information Division if they discovered the identity of his father, so Elise kept a low profile and didn't get too close to anyone in Crystal Springs.

A few weeks later, two imposing men in suits that obviously were not from Crystal Springs showed up at the diner. "Excuse me," one of the men said to Betty. "Do you know a woman named Elise?"

Betty was rattled. She didn't want to expose her friend to any trouble, but she couldn't be caught lying to these men. If they were from the Civil Information Division, she could be sent to an internment camp for providing false information. "We have an Elise that works here from time to time," Betty replied cagily.

"When did you last see her?" the man probed.

"It has been a few days now," Betty responded. "Should I tell her you came by the next time I see her? Your name is?"

"Thank you for your help," the man replied before they abruptly left the diner.

When it was clear that they had left, Betty went to the office and called Elise to warn her. "Elise, there were two men in suits inquiring about you at the diner today. You should take Caleb and head out of town for a while. We can cover for you at the diner for the next week or two until the dust settles."

Elise was stricken with terror. She had always been afraid that the Civil Information Division would find her and Caleb, and now it appeared that her greatest fear had become a reality.

"Thank you, Betty," Elise nervously replied. "You are a great friend, and we appreciate everything you have done for us. We will never forget you. Hopefully, we will meet again."

She packed up the old pickup truck with food and camping gear in preparation for an extended stay in the mountains. Elise knew that they would never be able to return to Crystal Springs. The small farm town had provided anonymity and protection for years, but now the government had tracked them down. Elise's worst fears had been realized, and she was anxious to leave. Caleb could sense his mom's anxiety and tried to be helpful as they quickly gathered their belongings. He always tried to be strong and show no fear despite all of the uncertainty in the new American nation.

They climbed in the old pickup truck and drove down the long gravel driveway. When they reached the main road, a black sedan blocked the driveway preventing their exit. Elise was paralyzed with fear. She couldn't possibly attempt to run with her little son in the vehicle, but the alternative could be much worse. Just as she was considering her options, two men in suits exited the sedan and began to walk toward the pickup truck. She looked at Caleb, who was sitting calmly in the passenger seat, and considered whether they could evade these agents. If she was going to run, then the time was now.

Perhaps sensing her anxiety, the men walked slowly and motioned with both hands toward the ground as if to signal that she should be calm and not escalate the situation. She looked again at Caleb who was sitting next to her, watching the men approach. Fearing for her son, she put the transmission in park but left the car running. Rather than sit helplessly in the vehicle, she opened the driver's side door and stood on the running board half inside and half outside of the truck.

"What business do you have here?" she asked authoritatively. "This is private property, and we were just leaving."

"Elise, we just want to talk," one of the men said. "We were sent here on behalf of the Secretary of Defense and the President."

She didn't move from her position. "Please stay where you are. What do you want to talk about?"

They stopped about twenty feet short of her truck. The same man replied to her inquiry. "Axel Berg, your former fiancé, has been detained for more than six years due to his actions against the government of the United States. President Rao wants to find a solution to the ongoing discontent and perhaps work out a better solution for Axel as well. She asks that you speak to Axel and encourage him to cooperate with her for the good of the nation. We would like to escort you to the facility where Axel is being held and coordinate a visit with your fiancé. If it makes you more comfortable, you can drive your vehicle and follow us to the facility."

"How do I know that you won't just lock me up as well?" Elise asked defensively. "President Rao has a habit of making people disappear. Do you really think Axel is going to cooperate with her?"

"We can assure you that you and your son will be safe," the man replied. "The President has an attractive offer on the table and wants to put an end to this chapter of American history. She feels that you may be able to help negotiate a truce. Would you be willing to help?"

Elise paused to consider their offer. Axel doesn't even know that he has a son, and this may be the only chance that he has to meet Caleb. It would be a tragedy if Caleb never knew his father. "OK," she replied. "I will meet with Axel and convey your message, but after that, you will leave me and my son alone for good."

"Thanks for your cooperation," the man replied. "I think you can make a real difference for everyone involved. Are you ready to go?"

"We will follow you," Elise replied.

The men returned to their black sedan and led Elise and Caleb on the journey to the Yucca Mountain Facility. They traveled for hours on a route that passed through Central California and across Death Valley into Nevada. Darkness set upon the desert long before the caravan finally arrived at their destination. Elise followed the government agents and turned off the highway into a makeshift parking lot with neatly arranged modular living facilities. After they parked, Elise leaned over to wake her sleeping son. It was a cold night, and they eagerly followed the officers to a trailer that would serve as their temporary home.

"Breakfast is at eight, and then we will discuss the meeting," the officer said after showing them to their unit.

Elise thanked him and led Caleb into their trailer. She was sure that it was bugged and that they were being monitored, so she kept her cool and focused on the needs of her son. Elise was suspicious of the officers' motives and remained distrustful. She was excited that Axel may be able to meet his son, but Elise was quite aware that she was a helpless pawn in a much larger negotiation. Axel was a principled man, and her influence was much less than the government believed.

The next morning, they met the officers for breakfast. When they sat down to eat, the lead officer briefed Elise on the plan. "Elise, the President would like Axel to denounce the violence and pledge support to her administration. She wants him to acknowledge that America First was a fantasy and that the Historic American Nation is a relic of the past. President Rao hopes that you can convince him that by renouncing America First, he will be saving the lives of countless Americans and unifying the nation. She believes that you could be the key to securing peace."

Elise listened intently and quietly. They clearly didn't understand Axel or the America First movement. He would never bend a knee to the multicultural mob or surrender to those that seek to replace Americans with immigrants. "I would love to help in any way that I can," Elise replied. "I only request that I not be separated from my son at any time and that I may speak candidly in my own words to Axel."

"Absolutely," the officer replied. "You know Axel best and are perhaps the only person who can persuade him to accept the President's offer. We will head out to the Yucca Mountain Facility after breakfast."

When they finished breakfast, a military van arrived in the parking lot to escort them to Yucca Mountain. On the fifteen minute drive, Elise caught her first glimpse of the massive internment camp that bordered over a mile of roadway. She and Caleb saw, in plain view, millions of gaunt Americans laboring under the bright Nevada sun. These once-proud American citizens were now corralled like animals behind by a double fence topped with razor wire. She was shocked at the lack of humanity and compassion that led to such a circumstance. President Rao had conscripted millions of Americans into hard labor and sentenced them to indefinite detention because they loved their nation and believed that the rights of American citizens came before those of aspiring immigrants.

They arrived at the Yucca Mountain Facility, which seemed like a small building carved into the side of a mountain. When they entered, however, Elise got a sense of the scale and fortitude of the structure. It was designed to be impenetrable and capable of withstanding any attack. The main level alone was massive and heavily reinforced with steel and concrete. This wasn't a typical military facility but more like a doomsday bunker for senior officials and critical operational resources.

Guards escorted them to an elevator where they traveled to the top floor of the facility. Once they arrived, Elise and Caleb were ushered into an interrogation room to the left of the observation suite. The officers that had persuaded Elise to cooperate assured her that they would be nearby if she needed anything and then left her and Caleb alone in the room to await Axel's arrival.

About ten minutes later, the door opened and two guards escorted Axel into the room. Elise couldn't help but get emotional. It had been years since she had seen her fiancé, and all of their hopes and dreams came rushing back into focus. Axel had aged and was thinner, but it was still her beloved Axel standing there just steps away.

"Axel," she said, "I almost can't believe it's you and that we are together once again."

He stood silently before her as if he didn't recognize her. After a moment, he suddenly embraced her and emotion overwhelmed him. After years of solitary confinement, he had resigned himself to dying alone without knowledge of what had become of his beautiful fiancée.

"Elise, I never thought I would see you again," he replied. "Why are you here? Are you OK?"

"Yes, Axel, we are OK," she confirmed as she put her arm around little Caleb's shoulder. "Axel, I want to introduce you to your son, Caleb Berg." She nudged Caleb forward to encourage him to go toward his father.

Axel got down on a knee and looked at his son. He was a handsome little man, and Axel was so proud. He spread his arms wide, welcoming his son. Following a brief moment of hesitation, Caleb rushed into his father's arms and gave him the biggest hug of his lifetime. Axel put his arm around his son and escorted Caleb and Elise to the table in the center of the room.

"I can't believe I have a son!" Axel replied with excitement. "This is perhaps the most amazing day of my life."

Elise burst into tears. She had tried to hold it all together, but the thought of what they could have had together just became overwhelmingly devastating. "Axel, I miss you, and I wish we could be together as a family."

Axel looked dejectedly at the table. "That, unfortunately, will never be possible. As long as President Rao and her cronies are in power, they will never release me."

"But Axel," she pleaded, "they told me if you agreed to renounce America First and declare your support for President Rao and the new American nation then they would reintegrate the detainees and reunify the country."

"Elise, they will never release me. They already tried to get me to surrender a few weeks ago. When I refused, they executed almost five hundred American detainees right before my eyes. The transnational elite and the globalists want us dead. They will never stop until they have complete control."

"Axel, think of all those people that are imprisoned in the work camp. Isn't it time to concede and save them?"

"If I concede, I will betray the memory and sacrifice of all those who gave everything to fight for the Historic American Nation. I would have to abandon all that is important and meaningful to me. My father gave his life in his quest to restore the American Dream. I cannot disgrace his memory by relegating my people to a life of subservience and oppression in their own nation. None of the detainees will ever truly be free in the new American nation. I cannot betray them or the cause. America is our home. America is the legacy left to us by our forefathers. I will never surrender it to those that seek to replace us and destroy our nation."

Elise looked dejected. Seeing Axel again rekindled many suppressed emotions, and she couldn't stand to lose him again. "Axel, think of your son. What about his future?"

"I am," Axel said as he turned to face Caleb. "Caleb, I love you very much. No matter what happens to me, you should always remember that your grandfather and your father fought every day to restore American greatness and preserve the legacy of our great nation for future generations. Son, sometimes you need to take a stand. There are people throughout the world that want to take what is yours, destroy your legacy, and debase our culture. They are evil people that feel entitled to everything that generations of Americans have built and accomplished. Whenever that occurs, you need to stand tall and show no fear in the face of danger. You must fight for your family, your home, and your nation. If you choose instead to succumb to fear and cavort with the enemy, you will be used and discarded by the forces of evil that want to fundamentally transform America and steal your birthright."

Caleb looked back at his father blankly. Clearly, he didn't understand half of what Axel had just said.

"My son," Axel said in his second attempt. "You must always be brave. You must always be strong. Never back down, and always fight for what is right. Listen to your mother, and remember that I always will love you."

Axel paused to let his son absorb what he had said before continuing. "Caleb, you are an American. Never feel guilty for being White. Never be ashamed of your heritage. Americans are an exceptional people. We must never give in to those that want to replace us with people that do not share our culture, our values, or our history. We will always rise above. We will always win because America First is our destiny. Be proud, be strong, and be bold in everything you do. You are an American, and we never surrender."

When Axel finished speaking to Caleb, he hugged his son. Elise, still overwhelmed by sadness, joined in the family hug for one last moment of joy. As they finished, Axel kissed Caleb on the head and kissed Elise one last time.

He took a moment to look at his family, marveling at the legacy he had created. At that instant, he realized that his battle was over. "Tell them that I will do it," he said emotionlessly. "Tell the Defense Secretary that I agree to his televised press conference and to condemn America First."

Elise was in shock. She couldn't believe that he had come around to their position, but she was overwhelmed with joy. Elise hugged Axel one last time before saying, "We love you, Axel. We will always love you."

Axel turned and knocked on the door of the interrogation room. The guards escorted him out of the room and he never looked back. He had made his decision, and he didn't want anything to change his mind.

After Axel was led away by the guards, Elise grabbed Caleb's hand and left the room to meet with the officers. When she relayed Axel's message, they were elated and took her directly to the observation suite. The Defense Secretary was there overlooking the internment camp and monitoring operations at the Yucca Mountain Facility. The lead officer approached the Secretary and privately told him that Axel had accepted the President's terms.

The Defense Secretary turned to Elise and Caleb. "Your service on behalf of the nation is much appreciated. This will be the first step toward reuniting our nation. Please, be our guests at the broadcast this evening."

"Of course," Elise replied eagerly. "It will be a momentous event, and we would like to be there in support."

"Excellent," the Defense Secretary replied. "The officers will escort you to a lounge where you and your son can relax before the event. We will broadcast live from the large conference room on the main floor at five tonight."

After thanking the Defense Secretary, Elise and Caleb followed the officers to a large executive lounge with multiple televisions, snacks, and beverages. The officers brought them both lunch, and they were allowed some privacy for the four hours until the broadcast. Caleb was in good spirits and couldn't stop talking about his dad. After six years of living alone with his mom in relative seclusion, Caleb had finally met his father. In his mind, his father was the bravest and most fearless man in the entire world, and Caleb wanted nothing more than to be just like him.

The officers returned when it was almost time for the televised broadcast. They escorted Elise and Caleb into a large conference room on the main level of the Yucca Mountain Facility. There was a wooden desk positioned in front of rows of American flags at the other end of the room. A large black curtain covered the cement wall behind the desk creating a stark contrast with the colorful flags. The officers led Elise and Caleb to the front row of chairs facing the desk. The Secretary of Defense had reserved these seats for them so that they would be a visible reminder to Axel about the stakes involved.

Multiple professional television cameras were in place to broadcast the event. No outside press was allowed in the high-security facility so all of the equipment was operated by military technicians. They were testing the equipment, conducting sound checks, and preparing for the production as other senior officers at Yucca Mountain began to file into the room.

Meanwhile, the Secretary of Defense was in his office on the phone with President Rao. She planned to deliver an announcement from the Oval Office to set the stage for Axel's public repudiation of the America First movement. Before the broadcast went live, she wanted to confirm all the details of the arrangement with the Secretary of Defense and ensure that everyone was clear about the expectations.

"General, this press conference is critical to ending the acts of violent terrorism in our country and restoring some sense of unity. You understand the stakes, correct?"

"Absolutely, Madam President," the Secretary of Defense replied. "I will personally speak to Axel to reiterate what is expected and ensure his compliance."

"Just to be clear, you understand the consequences for failure," President Rao continued. "It would not only embolden the America First movement, but it would severely weaken this administration. You must make clear that the penalties for noncompliance will be dire and immediate."

"Understood," the Secretary replied. "I will personally deliver the message to Axel and convey the consequences of betraying your trust."

When the Defense Secretary ended his call with the President, he called for Axel to be brought to his office. Four guards escorted him into the office before stepping outside to enable the Defense Secretary to speak privately. Axel looked fresh in a new suit that he was given to wear during the broadcast. They didn't want to legitimize him, but they also didn't want the public to think this was a coerced repudiation by a distressed hostage. The President wanted Axel's statement to seem genuine, and she wanted him to appear like he had been treated humanely and benevolently by the government, despite their disagreements.

"Axel, it is about time for the press conference," the Defense Secretary said directly. "To reiterate the terms of our agreement, President Rao expects you to fully denounce the America First movement as a folly and proclaim that her administration is legitimate and righteous. You must repudiate any fantastical notion of a Historic American Nation and embrace modern America as the inevitable evolution of the American idea. In exchange for your cooperation, President Rao will release people from the internment centers beginning with those found to be least culpable. Future cooperation and good behavior may even result in your own release, but there will be no guarantees. However, you do understand the consequences for betraying the President, correct? They will be swift and merciless. Compliance is your only option."

"Understood," Axel replied.

"Alright, the guards will escort you to the conference room to finalize preparations for the broadcast. I will join you momentarily, and we will begin."

When the guards brought Axel into the conference room, Caleb stood up from his front-row seat and ran to his dad. He gave Axel a big hug, startling both his father and the guards. Before the guards could separate them, Axel bent down on his knee and whispered to Caleb.

"I love you, Caleb. Be strong. Be brave. Be proud of who you are. You are an American, and we never surrender."

As the guards separated them, Axel winked at Caleb who was retrieved from the stage by Elise. Axel was seated at the large desk and given a glass of water. Within moments, the Secretary of Defense arrived and told Axel that he would signal when the broadcast was live. The technicians in the control room began a countdown to the President's Oval Office address. Two large televisions in the conference room would broadcast her speech live for all to see.

"Good evening," President Rao said in a serious tone. "I come to you tonight to announce a major development in our fight against domestic terrorism and the racist nationalist movement known as America First. As you know, these individuals were behind the recent bombings, including the destruction of the Henry Hub natural gas facility in Louisiana that left millions without power, food, and heat. These cowardly acts sought to sow division and foster hate as we try to build a more diverse and inclusive America. The Great Transformation, as it has been called, is an unmitigated success. Our nation has grown stronger and wealthier as we embrace the exceptional skills, unique perspectives, and diverse cultures of the millions of immigrants that we have welcomed to America under my administration. Together we will modernize the American idea to reward diversity, reduce inequities, and foster a multicultural society that is open to all.

"We are a nation of immigrants that come together when times are tough. We have coalesced in a unified effort to propel America forward. Together we are stronger. United we are unstoppable. Tonight, the leader of the America First Network, Axel Berg, will join me in promoting the future of America. We will put our differences aside and unite for a better future. Today, the principles of diversity and inclusion have a special significance as we welcome all Americans to embrace the modern multicultural American nation. In the spirit of unity, I invite Axel Berg to say a few words."

As the President concluded her remarks, Axel sat patiently at the desk waiting for his cue. The Defense Secretary stood at the side of the stage watching Axel closely. After a brief conversation with the control center, the Defense Secretary gave the signal that Axel was live on national television.

"Good evening my fellow Americans. I would like to thank President Rao for the opportunity to address the nation, and I very much agree that now is the time to unite. The Great Transformation has dramatically changed our nation. In the first two hundred years since our nation's founding, America was an overwhelmingly White nation of predominantly European heritage. As recently as 1960, America was eighty-nine percent White and was united by a shared history, a deeply rooted patriotism, and a distinctly American culture. But the Immigration and Naturalization Act of 1965 changed everything, and America would never be the same. The dramatic demographic shift away from a predominantly White and historically European nation toward one repopulated by Latin American and Asian immigrants has had profound effects on social cohesion, economic opportunity, and national identity. The fundamental transformation of America accelerates with every passing year and very soon our nation won't be recognizable."

The Secretary of Defense was glaring at Axel and motioning for him to move along and get to the point. He clearly felt that Axel was drifting from the agreed-upon message and needed to get back on track. Axel was oblivious to his surroundings as he focused on his message and continued to stare directly at the camera.

"President Rao asked me to speak to all of the disaffected Americans that have seen their jobs taken, their opportunities diminished, and their prosperity threatened. As the founder of the America First Network, the President recognized that I am uniquely positioned to speak directly to Americans that have been accused of racism, xenophobia, and bigotry for being proud of their ethnic identity and for seeking to honor the history of this great nation. So tonight I speak to all those Americans who feel that the American Dream has been lost. I speak to those that believe the multicultural transformation of our nation has eviscerated American Exceptionalism. I say to you, simply and directly, that we must cast aside all hesitation and reservations. We must suppress our fears and unite behind a common purpose. We must believe in a brighter future."

Axel paused briefly before grabbing the desk with both hands. With a piercing gaze, he defiantly and vociferously proclaimed, "We must fight to restore the Historic American Nation!"

Axel suddenly rose from his chair and stood tall. He thrust his fist into the air and proudly exclaimed, "America First is our Destiny!"

From his center seat in the front row, Caleb Berg rose from his chair without fear or hesitation. A look of admiration swept over the young boy's face as he pumped his fist into the air in solidarity with his father. At that moment, he understood what his father had tried to convey. He too was strong. He too was brave. And just like his father, he would never surrender.

As Axel locked eyes with his son, a sense of pride and happiness overwhelmed him. He had won. Axel smiled lovingly at young Caleb while taking comfort in the knowledge that the fight would continue. Brave patriotic Americans around the country would never surrender. The resurgence of the Historic American Nation was inevitable.

From the corner of the room, the Secretary of Defense stepped on stage and took a few steps toward Axel before pulling his service pistol from his side holster. Sound waves reverberated off the concrete walls as he fired a single shot striking Axel in the head and killing him instantly on live television. Axel lay sprawling across the desk as thick red blood pooled and began to drip on the ground.

Chaos erupted in the room with soldiers barking orders and technicians scrambling to cut the live feed. Yet Caleb Berg stood defiantly, his fist still thrust in the air, without grief and exhibiting no fear. His father was a hero, and this was his final salute. Caleb would bravely march forward. America First was his destiny, and he would never surrender the fight!

PRAISE FOR THE AUTHOR

Marshall Anders' first book, Fateful Destiny, is a fictional story that explores the rise of globalism and the concurrent decline of the Historic American Nation. He skillfully constructs a narrative that examines how contemporary social and economic developments foreshadow a dark future for America. Fateful Destiny follows the struggles of a young American in his quest to find his place in a country that is rapidly changing. As the traditions and culture of the nation rapidly decay, he discovers his true identity and purpose. Fateful Destiny is both triumphant and tragic as it follows the protagonist's journey to defend and preserve the heritage of the country he loves.

- M.A. Campbell